WELCOME TO THE BORDERLANDS

Anyone less desperate would have turned left at the top of the Hills. Left led down into the valley, to the world Scooter knew and understood.

Right led down deeper into the Borderlands.

He stopped briefly at the intersection of the two roads. He glanced down at the city, though the view was not good from here, and let out a long breath. He looked right, where the way was steeper and more winding.

Someone had nailed three hand-painted signs to a telephone pole on his side of the street, near the concrete pole supporting the defunct traffic signal. In fluorescent red letters against white painted wood, they read:

**HAUNTED FOREST!
ENTER AT YOUR OWN RISK!
I'D GO BACK
IF I WERE YOU!**

"Very funny," said Scooter.
And turned right.

BORDERLAND

CREATED BY
TERRI WINDLING &
MARK ALAN ARNOLD

with

Steven R. Boyett
Bellamy Bach
Charles de Lint
Ellen Kushner

A SIGNET BOOK

NEW AMERICAN LIBRARY

Many thanks to Betty Ann
Crawford, Peter Roberts,
and George Cornell, for
all their help

NAL BOOKS ARE AVAILABLE AT QUANTITY DISCOUNTS WHEN
USED TO PROMOTE PRODUCTS OR SERVICES. FOR INFORMA-
TION PLEASE WRITE TO PREMIUM MARKETING DIVISION, NEW
AMERICAN LIBRARY, 1633 BROADWAY, NEW YORK, NEW YORK
10019.

Cover art by Phil Hale.

CONTENTS

Introduction

Blow bugle, blow, set the wild echoes flying.
Blow, bugle; answer, echoes, dying, dying, dying.

Alfred, Lord Tennyson
"The Horns of Elfland"

Once upon a time (isn't that the way humans always start a story?) there was magic in the world, or so your bards and storytellers of old have always claimed: elvin lords in dark forests and sumptuous halls beneath the hills, dragons curled in mountain caverns sleeping upon hoarded gold, Nereids in woodland streams, mermen in the cold, gray sea.

Then there was none.

The tales differ as to why this happened (and I am not at liberty to confirm or deny them). Some say it was industrialization and the use of iron that drove the elvin folk away, some say the spread of Christianity; some say they "flitted" to a more hospitable world; some say magic did not die but merely lay sleeping with

King Arthur in Avalon, waiting for a new age to begin. Whatever the cause, magic vanished—mysteriously and completely.

Then one day it came back again. *We* came back again.

And that's when the shit really hit the fan.

Now, as every schoolchild knows, Elfland has reappeared and lies just beyond the Border that separates it from the World. Between the two lands is the Borderlands, and at the edge of the Borderlands sits that infamous city Bordertown, where elves trade with humans and control passage through the single gate that leads from world to world.

Humans, of course, are not allowed into Elfland, just as we've not exactly been welcome with open arms into your world. Yet here on the Border, where our magic and your technology work equally sporadically and unpredictably, elves and humans mingle in an uneasy truce. You have to be crazy to live here, crazier still to travel in the open Borderlands, where magic runs amok. But if you're willing to chance it (and many do, seeking easy money or the artistic muse or magic or thrills or out of sheer perversity), then come along. Here is one story of the past—when everything Changed—and three stories of the present, now that Bordertown has grown out of and beyond the ruins of the old city, with a culture quite unlike anything else this side of the Border or beyond. And the future? Who can say? In a world where the horns of Elfland blow clearly, anything is possible. . . .

Farrel Din
Bordertown

PRODIGY

Steven R. Boyett

—Six years after the return

He sat perched atop the highest point on Monaghie Drive, playing his guitar and watching the sound form shapes in the air. When his music was light and airy, the shapes were coruscating spear points that darted playfully, sometimes meshing in groups to form brief grids that sparkled in the clear air above the valley. When his music was moody, the shapes were nebulous things that coalesced in angry-looking cloud patterns of dark browns and brick reds. Today his music was intricate and involved, a collection of disparate threads woven upon his six-string Martin to form a tapestry before him. The bright, prismatic spear points made interlocking, ever-shifting patterns that grew out of the air and melded back into it. The spear points continually leapt into being, grew more vibrant with his playing, dimmed, and disappeared. They reminded him of playful dolphins enacting geometrical games, leaping from *somewhere* into the air, then diving back into wherever it was they came from.

Usually he was alone up here. With the automobile

gone the way of the dinosaur, people tended not to venture up mountain roads as casually as they had in bygone days. And hardly anyone lived in the houses in the hills, because there were no grocery stores for them to raid up here, no drugstores to loot for medicinal supplies, no way to obtain trade goods. There were rabbits and deer, but an awful lot of people were ignorant of how to live off the land. Besides all that, things tended to get weird up here. The people who lived in the hills before had been rich, he reflected, watching his fingers play along the neck of the guitar as if they had a mind of their own—and rich people sure as hell didn't know anything about living off the land. When the fragile social structures that tenuously supported them had dissolved, the *nouveau riche* had been among the first to become extinct.

His music changed as he mused, and he noticed that the shapes in the air reflected the change. The spear points of light had darkened and grown fuzzier, out of focus. He pursed his lips. It did no good to reflect on the past; better to concentrate on the music. His callused fingers picked up the tempo, and the spear points danced brightly.

Behind him someone said, in a bending Georgian accent, "Hey, he's all right, man."

He smiled and struck a loud chord. The lightshafts swelled and dimmed. He added a single, bell-like harmonic for good measure and chuckled when a lone arc of rainbow light chased after the others like a bug on water, following them into . . . wherever.

He stood and brushed dirt off the seat of his faded and frayed blue jeans. Below, the valley looked like the world's largest housing development. Years ago someone had described it to him as a hundred towns connected by 7-Elevens. Behind him he heard:

"Richie! What are you doing up here?"

"Came to watch the sunset, man."

A horse-like blurt. "You never stopped to watch a sunset in your life."

He pulled a stiff-bristled hairbrush from his back pocket and slid a green elastic band from the handle. Three fingers and thumb spreading it wide, he brushed his hair with the other hand, gathered it into a fist, and twisted the band on. A ponytail was a lot more practical up here, where the wind from beyond the Borderlands spilled over the hilltops and whipped at you.

After a long pause the second voice—Richie's—said, "I came up here to hunt fuckin' rabbits. I got a sling-shot, you know? A good one." There was a quick snapping sound of taut surgical tubing released. " 'Cuz I'll throw up if I eat one more can of Spam."

"Did you find any?" asked the first voice.

"Rabbits? Shit, naw. I haven't seen so much as a dog 'round here." A snort. "Hell, I'd probably eat me a dog if I could find one. All them rich people's poodles running 'round here in the woods with their pink toe-nails, afraid of all them coyotes."

He smiled, still not looking back. Instead he returned the hairbrush to his pocket and glanced at the guitar case at his feet, edged with light brown dust along the nearer curve. Time to put it away, he decided. Too many people. He didn't like being watched, not up here. As he bent to open the case, he heard:

"How's the burn?"

"Shit. Fucker *itches*, man! I nearly scratched half my damn head off last night. I woke up with skin under my nails." And again, in a completely different tone: "Shit."

He put in the Martin and shut the case, then turned around.

There were four of them. Two boys watched from halfway up the knoll, standing near the thorny bushes. One wore jeans so new the stiffness hadn't worn out yet, and a faded old Van Halen T-shirt. Hair as long as his own, but it probably hadn't been near a pair of scissors in years. A Fritos bag lay blown against a bush by his left foot. He stood almost in front of the other boy, revealing only an impression of black hair and pale skin.

The other two stood at the bottom of the knoll, near the road. It was they who had been talking. The one on the left was a short, slim, gaunt-faced young man with a dirty bandage around the top of his head. Gauze covered the area around his right ear. Richie, then. The left leg of his faded orange cords was torn away at the knee; the right knee had a hole in it. The pants were held up by a belt with the graven image of Marilyn Monroe on the stainless-steel buckle. He also wore a pair of brand-new Adidas tennis shoes and no shirt.

The other was older, late twenties, early thirties, with closely cropped red hair. He wore a plain white T-shirt and black jogging shorts, from which emerged a long pair of copper-haired, well-muscled, lightly tanned legs ending in sandaled feet. A small, black nylon daypack rested by them.

"Hey," said Richie in his light Georgian accent, a hand going to his head to scratch at gauze. "I never seen nothing like that before. You're all right, man. I mean, this is the first time I've ever been up here, and. . . ." He shrugged.

"We enjoyed it very much," said the redhead.

"Yeah. Hey, you know any Lynyrd Skynyrd?" Richie asked hopefully.

He shook his head, and the young man looked disappointed. The scratching finger lowered to wipe against a corduroy-ribbed hip, then the thumb hooked above Marilyn Monroe's head.

The redhead nodded at him from below, turned to his friend, and said, "Hey, why don't we ... ?" He glanced at Scooter, frowned, looked away again. "It takes two hours to get to the bottom of the canyon. Why don't you walk on down with me? You don't want to be out after dark. I have some burn cream at home; we could put some on that. Give you a fresh bandage while we're at it."

Loose hair—too short to band into the ponytail, long enough to get in the way—blew across his eyes in a gust of wind.

Richie was scratching at his bandage again. "Yeah," he said. "Yeah, all right. I ain't gonna get no rabbits anyway."

The redhead picked up his pack and slid one lanky arm through the strap. He looked up at him again, nodded a farewell, and turned to lead Richie down into the valley.

Richie looked back before they left. "Hey, you take care, man," he called, and repeated: "I never seen nothing like that."

He smiled slightly and turned away. The sun was lowering and shadows were lengthening. Ringed by hills, the valley was blued below him. The horizon was banded with cinnamons and Halloween oranges, bright colors filtering the light so that the clouds were touched with golds and siennas. We need rain, he thought. Half the hills around the valley are burning.

Fire had become a major problem in the city as well; with the dry season, low humidity, and widespread vandalism, arson was rampant—and there was no fire department to put them out. The whole city was bound to pull a San Francisco Fire number one day. He didn't want to be there when it happened.

He sighed. Well, time to descend into the Valley of the Shadow before it got dark. Roxanne ought to be home by the time he got there.

He picked up his guitar case by the handle and straightened to find that the two boys who had also been watching him play had stepped closer.

He stared at the one he hadn't seen clearly before.

The boy—if he could be called a boy—was tall. His skin was pale as rice paper. He looked frail, but that look was probably misleading. His hands were slim, with long fingers matching the toes of his bare feet. His large eyes were black balls in a face smooth and white as porcelain. His hair was dyed crow black, cut to nubs on one side, gradually lengthening across his head until, on the other side, it touched his shoulder. He wore pale blue Guess jeans and a black leather vest.

He didn't look real.

The other boy said, " 'Scuse me," and Scooter looked away.

This close, the boy's hair was dirty, and he looked as if he had probably forgotten what a bath felt like.

He wondered if they were going to try and take his guitar. Maybe they thought it was magic. "What can I do for you?" he asked.

The kid glanced at his friend, then looked back almost shyly. "I heard you playing," he said. "You're Tony Frazier, ain'tcha? You used to play lead with Stormtrooper." He played imaginary riffs on an air guitar. "Man, I used to listen to you all the time. You guys were hot." His grin was broken-toothed. His teeth had a light patina of green, darker near the gums. "I had all your—"

"You're confusing me with someone else," he interrupted, conscious of the black stare of the boy's companion. "My name's Scooter."

The kid frowned. "Scooter?"

He nodded.

"You sure?"

He glanced at those black eyes, that nearly albino skin, and made himself look away. "Positive." He hefted his guitar case and began working his way down the rise toward his bicycle, picking his way carefully among the loose stones and dirt. They watched him pass. He didn't look back as he leaned his guitar case against the tree to which his bike had been secured and fished a key from his pocket. The lock was a titanium U-bolt; he unlocked it and picked up his guitar.

Behind and above him he heard the boy say: "He's lying. I got his picture on albums. I'll show it to you. He's even wearing the same earrings."

He set the guitar case atop the book rack and against the long sissy bar he'd attached to the Schwinn ten-speed. He secured it with the U-lock and swung his foot over the frame. The front of the banana seat pressed against his butt. He glanced up.

The one who had questioned him was sneering down in open contempt; he disregarded the look.

The black eyes of the other were intent on him, white face inscrutable. He felt something appraising in that look, though, that made him want to flinch away. He did not associate much with those who came from beyond the Border, few though they were. They gave him the creeps.

Scooter stood up on the pedals, eased himself onto the hard seat, and pedaled a few times. The winding road was steep, and heading down was never easy. He looked back once, but the two figures were no longer there.

*   *   *

The descent into the valley was rarely a picnic. The curves were tight and the road was steep; Scooter's bike could reach forty-five miles per hour without judicious application of the handbrakes. Making things worse was the fact that road maintenance was a thing of the past, and most of the hill roads were strewn with gravel, rocks, and branches. Braking too late could cause an accident; braking too soon might cause him to lose control of the bike entirely.

The guitar on the back was not exactly an asset.

Scooter rode the brake most of the way down, artfully dodging rubble and swerving to avoid the occasional eternally parked car rusting away on the side of the road.

Doing thirty-five per around a steep intersection, Monaghie and Crescent, he was startled almost to the point of laying it down when something large and white jumped from the brush and darted across the road, moving nearly too fast to follow. He glimpsed four long legs and a horselike head, large, wild, black eyes, and a long, streaming tail.

Scooter jerked the handlebars, felt the rear wheel skid, leaned to his left, straightened, righted the handlebars, and shot a frightened glance back.

Along Crescent the grade was steeper but the curves less tight—this side of the hill, anyway; he refused to venture over the other side. Scooter let go the brake, but did not straighten up and ride without holding the handlebars until he was on the final, sloping straightaway that ran for almost a mile to Derrida Boulevard. A vandalized, graffiti-laden (ARCO PUMPS ANYTHING) gas station stood next to the long-abandoned Tiny Naylors on his right. Scooter permitted himself a nostalgic sigh for the many bouts of late-night sobering up that had occurred here.

Riding on inertia, hunching forward again to reduce the wind drag, Scooter leaned into the left turn as he hurtled onto Derrida.

Few people were out at this time of day. It seemed to Scooter that the city only came awake after sunset, that it possessed by night a kind of life not present during the daytime. The whole feeling changed, somehow, after dark.

Scooter found himself thinking of vampires.

Yeah, there was something in that—something hungry, something edgy, about the city at night. Yet he liked it for its vitality.

City at night?

He pedaled west along Derrida watching the angry orange light fade, and sang a Doors song like a drunk redneck.

The empty streets filled out his voice like studio equipment he had once paid a lot of money for.

Near Coldwater he saw a man in a gray sweat suit. Jogging, the man held a heavy chain leading to the spiked collar of a Doberman.

Scooter stared at the jogging man as he neared. A Walkman, he thought mournfully, my kingdom for a Walkman! Oh, to listen to Adrien Belew wailing on his fretless Fender again.

Scooter wheeled by the man and his dog.

The Doberman barked and bolted for him. Scooter swerved reflexively and pedaled faster. The jogging man yanked on the chain as the slack ran out and the Doberman was restrained—barely.

"Pixie!" he said sharply. "No! Back off!"

Scooter waved and pedaled on.

Pixie?

*   *   *

Home was a renovated bookstore in an arcade of abandoned shops near the corner of Derrida and Woodland. It had once been a mystery-novel/teahouse called Scene of the Crime. It had large plate-glass windows, and Scooter and Roxanne had taken down the old white draperies and put up heavy black ones to block the inside light at night. The outside was painted a sun-faded gray. The building was cinder block, retained heat well at night, easy to lock up—it had been well burglar-proofed by the original owner—and had the advantage of having a large stockroom where Roxanne kept her printing press and the huge, wheeled safe they had liberated from the Ralph's grocery store four blocks away. The safe had got away from them on the downslope and they had run like hell to get ahead of it and slow it down before a bump in the sidewalk could send it over. It weighed half a ton, and Scooter had vowed that if it fell down, it stayed down.

Home also had the distinct advantage of being stocked with tens of thousands of mystery novels, all alphabetically arranged on shelves that lined the walls. Roxanne had insisted that all the books stay, so he had insisted she come up with a way to keep the "new" hardbacks— six years old now—that occupied tables in the middle of the store, out of the way. After all, he and Roxanne needed room to live in. He had come home next day to find new bookcases in the second room, the tearoom, and Roxanne busily stuffing them with hardbacks— alphabetically, of course. They used the main bookstore space, with its red-velvet, floral-print wallpaper, red plush carpeting, and varnished maple bar at the cashier's counter, as a living and working space. The light was good here during the day and Roxanne could do her printing. The other half of the store had been a

Victorian-style tearoom, with red wallpaper in a different, brighter floral pattern. Scooter and Roxanne had thrown out most of the dining tables—they were still stacked in the parking lot out back—and Scooter had stocked it with guitars. He used it as a studio, or just as a place to be alone and think.

What Scooter and Roxanne did in their spare time—aside from arguing and making love—was read. Currently Scooter was working his way through John D. MacDonald and Ngaio Marsh; Roxanne was reacquainting herself with Ed McBain and was giving Elmore Leonard a try.

It was only six months ago that Scooter and Roxanne had decided to fix up the place and move in. Thinking about it, he couldn't quite pin down a time when they had decided—silently, but mutually—that they liked each other well enough to set up house together. But here they were.

Scooter partially dismounted from his bike and coasted the last twenty yards toward the back entrance, standing with his left shoe—a black high-topped, canvas, basketball shoe with white laces—on one crenellated pedal. The right shoe—same as the left, but white with black laces—hung down, toes pointed low. The bike made a ratchety sound as it coasted. Scooter squeezed the right handbrake, leaned the Schwinn against the beige-painted rear wall, and removed the key ring from his back pocket. He glanced around to see if anyone was watching him—he never saw anyone, and probably never would, even if someone were looking to see if the place was occupied, but Scooter couldn't break himself of the habit. He'd been living too long now with a better-safe-than-sorry philosophy.

With one key he unlocked the Kryptonite lock that secured the wrought-iron framework of burglar bars caging the door. He removed the lock, hooked it back in the hole, and shoved open the bars. With another key he unlocked the door, then opened it.

It was dark inside.

He brought in the bike and leaned it against the dry-wall beside the handpress. He left the back door open. In the dim light he groped between two paper bins on the lower level of the L of shelves occupying one corner of the former stockroom, now mostly Roxanne's workroom. His fingers brushed a small box resting atop another small box; it toppled over at his touch. He grabbed the second box. The raggedly bitten nail of his index finger scraped across the narrow, flinted side; he flinched in one quick spasm as a shudder ran down his spine.

Scooter slid open the box and pulled out a match. Only two boxes left, he thought. Have to remember to get more matches. He scraped it against the side and it flared. The smoke of ignition blew toward him and he breathed in a sulfur-tinged lungful. He set the box atop the printer, cupped the now-free hand near the match, and coughed. The glass and brass hurricane lamp on the middle shelf of the L glinted as he approached. He removed the thick-waisted glass chimney and lit the wick hurriedly; he could feel the heat in the tip of index finger and thumb by the time it caught.

Matches were in short supply everywhere.

The lamp brightened the room; Scooter twisted the slim brass rod that lowered the wick and the guttering light steadied. He replaced the chimney and wrung his hand a few times.

He went to the back door and bolted it shut.

When he turned back to the lamp, he saw a note held to the shelving above it with a plastic magnetic holder shaped like a banana. Scooter picked up the lamp and read:

Gone to Galleria to trade for matches & stuff. Back sunset.

R.

Scooter snorted. She was always a move or two ahead of him.

He looked up at the magnetic memo holder and shut his eyes, trying to remember the taste. It had been . . . heavy, heavy, yet paradoxically elusive if you tried to pin it down. You ate them with peanut butter on white bread, and with ice cream. . . .

He opened his eyes and looked down at the lamp. Better not to think about shit like that.

He carried the lamp and the box of matches into the main room. The old Doors tune, forgotten miles ago, had returned. He hummed it as he went about lighting lamps.

It had been years since he had eaten a banana.

He had just settled down onto the air mattress—with its anachronestic television pillow, a scented-oil lamp turned up bright on the low table that was his nightstand, and a used copy of *Cinnamon Skin* for company—when Roxanne returned.

At her knock Scooter set the book facedown, got up, and went into her workroom. He unbolted the door and there she was, all long brown hair and large blue eyes of her.

With a triumphant look she held up a brown paper bag.

"Batteries for my amp?" he asked hopefully.

She shook her head. "Presents, though."

"Aren't I supposed to beware of Greeks bearing gifts?" He opened the door wider and she brushed past him. He removed the Kryptonite lock (which he had forgotten about and left dangling for anyone to shut or take) and glanced around. Nothing but the few cars and the wild hedge across the garbage-strewn street. He shut the door and bolted it again.

"I'm not Greek," countered Roxanne as he turned to her. "Besides, it's 'beware of Greeks giving bears.' "

He grinned and stepped forward. They hugged. He smelled the sweat at her neck, the soft aroma of her hair, faintly floral. "I was starting to get worried," he said into her ear. His chin brushed the quail-feather hanging at her earlobe. He kissed.

"I'm a big girl. I can take care of myself."

He moved back enough to look down at her face. "Doesn't stop me from worrying."

She smiled, lifted up, kissed him. The paper bag crumpled with her tightening grip. "It's nice that you worry." She turned and headed into the "living" room, where the books and their bed were. "Somebody did follow me for a while, though," she tossed over her shoulder as he followed her in.

"Roxanne!"

She sat at the foot of the air mattress, set the bag atop her crossed ankles. "Only a couple of blocks. I lost him. It." She shrugged. "Whatever."

"I wish you'd take the gun when you go out." He sat awkwardly on the air mattress. He'd never get used to it; it was like stepping into a canoe.

"I'm safer without it. Somebody'd hurt me just to take the gun, if they knew I had it." She opened the bag, peered in, and put in a hand. "Besides," she said, fumbling—the light was too dim for her to see inside the bag—"we've only got the six bullets."

"Five," he said.

She looked up sharply.

He shook his head. "No, no. We lost one somewhere."

She tossed her hair back and shrugged with one shoulder simultaneously. "I'll see if I can get more. Meantime . . ." Her hand emerged from the bag.

He leaned forward. "Matches?"

She nodded. "Lucifer matches."

"What, you trade with the devil for 'em?" He slid the nightstand closer, moving the lamp between them so he could see better.

"Old Victorian term," she said. "They also call them whiteheads. You can light them against just about anything; they don't need a flint."

"I—" he began, then grinned. His dark eyes caught the lamplight; the silver scimitar in his right ear caught the flame and reflected it as something other than gold. "Hey, can I light one against a boot? Or with my thumbnail?"

She laughed. "Here, macho man." She tossed him the box. "Two boxes." Her hand disappeared again into the sack, rustled within, and reappeared.

"Razors!" He grabbed them from her. Gillette Trac IIs. His old Schick had become about as effective as a butter knife.

"I still couldn't find a straight razor," she said. "I asked."

He waved away her apology. "What else?" he asked.

"Well." She opened the bag wider, upended it. Things spilled out onto the comforter atop the air mattress. She picked up two small boxes. "Typewriter ribbons for me." A bulky bundle in a twist-tied, white plastic bag: "Three ears of corn."

"Who's growing corn?"

She shrugged. There were other things, sundry items

they needed; she announced them as she held them up and set them aside, finishing with: "A loaf of Mrs. Hernandez's bread and—"

He dove for the final, foil-wrapped item before she could mention it. "Chocolate!" He started to unwrap it, stopped, looked at her watching him, and set it on the nightstand. "Dessert," he said. "Who the hell's making chocolate? How much you have to trade for all this?"

"Not a lot. Mrs. Hernandez's baby is sick, and I traded her a bottle of ampicillin for bread and corn. She doesn't trust the street drugs. Said she knew someone who was killed by bad morphine. She obviously got the corn from somewhere else."

He frowned. "Bread and corn?"

"She owes me a fresh loaf every day for the rest of the week. Couple more ears of corn, too. I trust her. She's a good woman."

He leaned back, eyeing the chunk of chocolate. "Shame about the baby," he said. "She know about the pills?"

Roxanne nodded.

During the panic following the Change, Roxanne, though she did not understand *why* things were going wrong, could still see that things might not change back for a while—if at all. The city was closed off from certain commodities; the airports were closed and shipping was now more hazardous than most people cared to try and overcome. The valley didn't grow crops well; the soil needed too much chemical aid. Roxanne knew that she would need trade goods before long, and that certain things then taken for granted would become valuable as their supply was depleted and not replaced.

One afternoon she took a wheelbarrow from a hardware store that a few other people were busily looting, and trekked from pharmacy to pharmacy. Nothing was open by now, not with the power out, the police forces dissolving into anarchy, and the evidence of impossible things in and beyond the hills—what came to be called the Borderlands. Roxanne had to break into the first drugstore, a Rexall pharmacy. She threw a brick through the front window, wincing as glass shattered, then stepped through after it settled, pulling her wheelbarrow behind her. She half expected someone to yell for her to stop, or to hear the wail of a siren, but there was nothing.

From the back of the Rexall she had taken birth-control pills of varying estrogen levels, penicillin and ampicillin in tablet form, insulin pills, vitamins, bottles of morphine, syringes with fresh needles in sterile packets, methedrine, Seconal, Valium, nitroglycerine tablets, first-aid kits, "D" batteries, and tampons. She filled her wheelbarrow, dumped the contents in the ground-floor apartment she was living in at the time, and set out again. She looted three more drugstores and kept her booty locked in three large trunks taken from Sears. She didn't start trading them until demand started to grow on the streets as supplies dwindled from the steadily depleted grocery and drugstores. When "basement brewers" began synthesizing their own heroin, morphine, penicillin, barbiturates, amphetamines, and tranquilizers, she grew worried, but the worry soon passed. Half the drugs now available on the streets were ineffective; another ten percent was toxic, and the remaining forty percent was still not a significant enough figure for Roxanne to worry about—times were violent, hospitals were now small clinics working with a bare minimum of equipment, and lots of people needed what she had to offer. The batteries had been the first thing she ran out of. Tampons were next, but she kept a large reserve for herself. Necessary drugs became her trade goods for the next four years.

Roxanne found her drugs becoming less valuable as they got further away from the expiration dates printed on their labels. She could always fudge that, of course, especially when selling pills piecemeal, but her conscience wouldn't allow it. All too often lives depended on her wares, and sometimes hers depended on them being effective. She knew that if a drug had a printed shelf life of two years, it had been tested at four years; the FDA had halved such figures as a safety margin, allowing for more rapid decay of some brand, or for less than ideal storage conditions. She got a pharmacopoeia from a pristine Crown Books and started telling her customers that X percent of the drugs they bought might be ineffective. It lowered the value slightly, though it caused people to buy in slightly greater quantity, yet she was respected for her honesty. People bought from her before they would buy from a stranger.

Word spread about Roxanne the Walking Pharmacy. Sometimes she was followed home.

She took to carrying a knife. Soon after, she traded a healthy batch of penicillin and Seconal for a snubnosed .38 and two boxes of bullets. Ammunition, easy enough to manufacture by anyone who cared to learn how, had begun to surface again.

She kicked herself for not having thought to hoard coffee.

Cigarettes she hadn't bothered with—she didn't smoke, didn't like to be around people who smoked, knew that tobacco would go stale within a few months anyway, doubted that anyone would be able to grow it in this climate, and was happy to see it gone.

Marijuana, of course, had largely taken its place.

Scooter was one of the few people Roxanne knew who didn't smoke pot. Ironic, considering Scooter's past.

They'd met a year ago, when he had been scouting the trader's heaven of the Galleria for painkillers. He had followed the grapevine to her, and he asked for her help. A friend of his, a middle-aged man named Dennis Feische, had ditched his bike on one of the mountain roads, and gravel had chewed up his thigh. They'd gotten rubbing alcohol and washed the leg thoroughly, but apparently bits of gravel had remained in the wound and the leg had become infected. Dennis was hurting, Scooter told her, and he just wanted a good painkiller and maybe an antibiotic.

Roxanne did not think of herself as a practicing physician, empowered to diagnose and prescribe. She was not Florence Nightingale. She supplied a product, a *necessary* product, and asked a fair price for it. But there was something in Scooter's face, something at once desperate and forlorn, that made her ask him to take her to his friend.

Scooter took her to the Holiday Inn lobby where he and twenty other ex-headbanger rock-and-rollers had crashed. In a dim room lit by a single wax candle Roxanne was confronted with a dying man half out of his head with fever. He ranted incoherently. He had no color. He wore a shirt and no pants. He had soiled the mattress on the floor beneath him. His right leg was mottled black and dark purple from knee to groin. The room smelled of rotten pork. She gagged and fought for control.

"Can you do anything for him?" Scooter asked.

She tried not to look at the gangrenous leg. "I—I'll try. Leave me alone with him, okay "

Scooter and his buddies had left her alone, and she sat up half the night in the stinking room with the man, whose raving grew weaker by the hour. She quickly determined that amputation was impossible even if she could get him to a clinic; the gangrene had spread past the upper thigh. There was nowhere to cut after that. She pressed her fingers into the flesh of the other leg. White prints remained behind when she took her hand away. The other leg was going.

Dennis Feische was going to die, and slowly.

Sometime after midnight—she guessed; there was no clock and her wind-up watch was at home—she made a decision. She opened her knapsack and took out an ampule of morphine, a syringe, and a sterile needle.

Scooter had cried for days. Dennis had been his friend. Roxanne comforted him, brought him back home, fed him, cleaned him up, cut his hair (trimmed it, rather; he wouldn't let her cut it shorter than shoulder length), got him new jeans, new T-shirts, and new underwear from the more-or-less intact Surprise Store on Derrida, held him at night when he missed his friend, made love to him, and eventually fell in love with him.

He didn't move in with her then, and she wasn't quite sure she wanted him to. These days it took a long time to win her trust. Scooter went back to the Holiday Inn with every intention of rejoining his buddies. One look around told him otherwise. They were all lying around the lobby, looking for all the world as if they hadn't moved since he'd left. Bare mattresses covered half the floor. Trash covered the other half. From the entranceway he could smell the bathroom around the corner. The toilet wouldn't flush anymore.

"Scooter, man," said someone from a threadbare couch along one wall. "How you doin'?"

Scooter looked away from a man in his midtwenties and a girl in her early teens having sex on a dirty mattress in the corner. The man grunted with his thrusts;

the girl made little hissing noises with her rapid inhalations.

Scooter shook his head. He started to ask what had been done with Dennis, then decided he didn't want to know. "Fuck this shit," he said, and next day he had squatted a place of his own.

Months later Scooter described to Roxanne how the place had changed after he left it. She frowned and looked at him curiously. "It doesn't sound," she had said, "like *it* changed at all."

And that was when Scooter realized that *he* was in love with *her*.

After Roxanne put away her day's finds, they blew out all the hurricane lamps but the one beside the air mattress and took off each other's clothes.

"Did you miss me today?" he asked as they embraced.

"Did you go somewhere?" she rejoined blithely.

They fell, laughing, onto the air mattress.

"Let's see," said Roxanne, "if we can pop this thing."

They didn't—again.

Roxanne lay next to him, curiously childlike, her head nestled in the hollow of his right shoulder, the soft of her hair falling across her face and onto his chest, tickling when he shifted. Her right hand rested on his ribs; her right leg, bent at the knee, crossed inner thigh atop his thighs, crossed calf over his shins.

She jerked once, falling into sleep.

Scooter lay awake. Roxanne almost always fell into a deep sleep soon after sex; Scooter either felt a warm, contented glow that eased into sleepiness, or else he became restless.

When her breathing became slow and regular, he eased himself from beneath the down comforter and got out of bed. They had already blown out the lights for the night; he felt his way to the standing hat rack near the now-unused front door and removed his floor-length robe. He slipped it on, belted it, went back to the bed, and retrieved the lamp and matches.

Walking quietly, barefoot on thick plush, Scooter entered the second half of their home and breathed deeply. The old tearoom still retained a faint scent of its former existence, a delicate aroma like the smell of a Victorian woman's sachet kept in a drawer of lover's letters.

He liked that smell.

He struck a match (Lucifer matches, she had called them, and sure as shit, you could light them against the wall—he felt like a cowboy) and lit the hurricane lamp.

The room grew bright enough to see. Three long-necked shapes, variously slim- or slight-waisted, rested upright on stands against one wall.

On the left was the Les Paul, long quiet in its case. He ignored it.

Beside it were the Martin he had taken to the top of Monaghie this afternoon (recently restrung with nylon strings) and a Yamaha twelve-string. He had liberated them from the Guitar Center near Kester Avenue. The store had been shut tight with what had once been expensive burglar bars, and it had taken Scooter half the day to break in. In the end he'd had to use a fire ax, taken from the pitch-black basement of the AT&T building down the block, to break in.

He went in looking for a classical guitar he had lusted for since he had learned how to play—a Goya.

Twenty minutes later he emerged from the shop, bleeding from his left forearm and face where glass had cut him and grinning like the bandit he was. Home was a mile away, with only one slight uphill grade, and

Scooter had pushed his borrowed grocery-store pro-
duce cart—laden with the three guitars in their cases,
three stands, a fishbowlful of picks, two amplifiers—a
Fender pig-snout and a big Peavey, a half-dozen key
sets, plugs, six straps, and a big box crammed with
nylon strings for the Martin, steel ones for the Yamaha,
and Gibsons for the Les Paul—all the way back.

He'd been disappointed about not finding a Goya.

In the dim and flickering light from the lone lamp
Scooter opened a case and picked up the Martin from
its stand, pulled a pick from the bowl on the floor, and
sat on the folding metal bridge chair in the middle of
the room.

Cold metal touched the backs of his thighs. The waist
of the guitar was cool on his upper right thigh, but
warmed quickly.

The safe containing Roxanne's drugs and other trading supplies was a dim gray form facing him across the
room.

Scooter put the pick in his mouth and clamped
down with his teeth. An old habit.

He strummed an open G-chord, adjusted the treble
E-string, strummed it again. He nodded to himself,
removed the pick from his mouth, and tuned the guitar on harmonics, listening to the pure sound fade with
his ear against the body. When he was satisfied, he
returned the pick to his mouth.

He used to be famous for that old habit.

It had taken some time for Scooter to get used to
playing gentle music. Scooter played at The Factory
every Thursday night. He could have played his Les
Paul—certainly the place was set up for it—and could
even have played with a band, if he wanted.

He didn't want.

His priorities, his perspective, had changed a lot since

the strangeness began years ago, and he had set about destroying his history. He immersed himself in what he seemed to have become, rather than riding the inertia of what he used to be. Since Roxanne came into his life Scooter had, to his great surprise, discovered a quietness deep within himself, a contentedness interrupted only by occasional fits of nostalgia. The acoustic guitar was a more gentle creature, and the music he played on it—and the images he conjured when he played in the Borderlands, on Monaghie—reflected what he felt inside.

Scooter played.

His callused fingers spun a web of intricate melodies, brooding counterpoints, simplistic tunes that sounded as if they were searching to become something more. Scooter felt melancholy, and though he would never have thought to use that word to describe his feelings, his music conveyed it for him.

He looked up at a sound.

Nude, lamplit skin dappled with shadow, Roxanne stood in the doorway between rooms.

He started to ask how long she had been watching him, looked back down at the Martin instead.

"Are you all right, Scooter?" she asked.

A quick triplet held the final note, then slid into a D-chord on the bottom three strings. "Can't sleep," he said, slurring the "s" around the pick in his mouth.

She shifted her weight to one leg. A hand went up to twirl a strand of hair by her ear. "Something's wrong." Her tone did not rise on the last word: a statement, then.

Scooter shrugged. He removed the pick from his mouth, wedged it under a thigh. "You know. I'm not . . . I mean, I get like this." He shrugged again. "You know," he finished.

She said nothing.

After a minute he looked up from his playing. His right hand stilled the strings. "Some kid today. Up on the hill. He recognized me."

She lifted her right foot, scratched her left shin with her toes. He watched her foot: instep straightened, arch pronounced, looking seamed and waxen in the soft light, toes pointed. Like a ballerina, he thought.

"It's happened before," she said.

"Yeah." He brushed long hair from in front of his eyes. "It bugged me this time. I don't know. Why, I mean."

She waited nearly a minute before asking: "You really miss it sometimes, don't you?"

"Nah. Well, sometimes, sure." He leaned back in the chair, turning the guitar faceup on his lap. "But not if I really think about what it was like." He snorted. "I mean, I was getting fucked up almost every night. I did some crazy shit, you know?"

"I know. I can imagine, I mean."

"Shit, I'd be dead now if I'd kept that up. Your body, your system, doesn't want to handle that. Everything was a blur all the time. We were moving around a lot. It was really fast, you know, really busy. I guess what I miss is how fast it all was, how much was happening to me all the time. But if I stop and think about *what* it was that was happening to me—" He shrugged. "It don't mean very much."

" 'Full of sound and fury,' " she said, " 'signifying nothing.' "

He grinned. "Yeah. Like that. Everything was loud— our drummer, Phil, was half deaf—and I was goddamn *angry* all the time." He laughed. "I don't even remember what I was angry at. Everything. Nothing. Shit, I don't know. But I was always mad, and when I played I just felt madder. I hated the crowds, man; they were like this ... this big, hungry animal, and I played as raw and angry as I could just to see how pissed I could make it."

"But they didn't get pissed," she suggested.

"Hell, no! They ate it up! They wanted to see us break some heads. And even with everything happening to me, and all, I think underneath I didn't feel like I was *doing* anything, you know? But my playing was always trying to tell me. I'd get up there and wail, and it was like the music was trying to show me how mad I was at everything, how much I hated everything. Only I was too fucking stupid to listen." He looked at the guitar on his lap and shrugged again. "People work things out in different ways. Some of 'em write, some of 'em talk; they see shrinks, or break plates, or take kung-fu, or something. I got my guitar. Only I'm not as mad as I used to be; I feel a lot better about myself. So I can't play like I used to. It's different now. That's all."

"It's slower now," she replied. "But it's not all that different. For you, I mean, Scooter."

He frowned. "Why do you say that?"

She had caught herself twirling the strand of hair by her ear and lowered her hand. "Well, I mean, you still play. You still do gigs at clubs. You still have a loyal following. A lot of them know who you are—"

"Who I was," he interrupted.

"Who you are. They just don't mention it because they know you don't like to talk about it much. But you still play half the day and night, and you go up on Monaghie once or twice a week, and you hardly do anything else except read mysteries."

Shadows shifted across her body as she moved. "Don't take this wrong or anything, Scooter, but your gigs don't bring in enough for you to live on. That stuff in the safe isn't going to last forever. And since we moved in together it's started to—"

"Look," he said. "I know all this. What do you want me to do?"

"Why don't you help me with the press?" she asked, and he sighed. She continued regardless: "The work isn't that hard. You could write the ad copy or—"

"You know I don't write so good," he said.

"—or solicit ads, or do the printing while I drum up business and post them down at the trading board in the Galleria. Henry Harris wants to start up that review magazine, *Nightlife,* because the clubs are doing so well and people are starting to put on plays and all. I met a writer this afternoon who's writing a book about his year in the Borderlands. I'd love to bring it out—when was the last time someone published a book? Scooter, there's a lot you could do to help me with this."

He sat up and readjusted the guitar on his thigh. He retrieved the pick—warm from his body heat—and held it between thumb and forefinger. He struck a discordant arpeggio. "We've got enough stuff to last a while. I'll help when we need me to."

"That isn't fair, Scooter."

He looked up at her. "Look, I just want to play my guitar right now. Okay?"

She said nothing, but her mouth went tight.

"We can talk about this tomorrow, or something," he continued. "I—I'm just not in the mood for it. I don't want to deal with it right now." He looked around the room, his gaze finally settling on the guitar. "I'll just play for a while longer and come to bed. All right? Tomorrow we'll talk some more. All this . . . I mean, right now. . . . " He put the pick back in his mouth. "Not tonight," he finished lamely.

She watched him for a while, then whispered, "You won't feel like it tomorrow, either."

But he was playing again and didn't hear.

Scooter woke up when Roxanne drew back the curtains. "What time is it?" he asked sleepily, squinting in the brightness.

She held up her watch, though of course he couldn't read it from the bed. "Twelve-thirty," she said.

Scooter rubbed his eyes and blinked. He sat up and drew the covers up to his stomach.

Roxanne was dressed in khaki shorts, tennis shoes, and an oversized white T-shirt with the collar torn out. The outline of her bra showed beneath. Funny, he thought, how few women wear bras anymore. "Where you going?" he asked.

"Galleria. Trading. There's half a loaf of bread in the bathroom." She paused. "What are you doing today?"

"I don't know." He yawned, stretching, and cracked his knuckles. "Gotta play at The Factory tonight. You coming?"

She made a sweeping hand gesture that could have meant anything.

He glanced around the room. Dust specks settled in the light near the curtains where they had been disturbed. "You know," Scooter said slowly, "I was thinking maybe we could fix this place up some. I mean, we got what we need to get by, but it'd be nice if we had *nice* things. You know? A good bed, a big one, and dressers and chairs and stuff. Maybe a little sofa or something. This place ought to be more than just good enough. We've been saying, like, it'll do for now ever since we moved in." He squinted at her. She was silhouetted in the large window.

"What do you think?" he asked.

"I think," she said, "you should do whatever you want."

It was still fairly early and the Factory was uncrowded. Scooter played unobtrusive music on the stage erected near the north wall, where the long counter had been when the Factory was a mod clothing store. In the chaos following the Change the store had been ransacked, but had remained relatively undamaged. It had been a trendy fashion store with its own sound system, light show, and deejay, and when the "new management" —squatters who had claimed ownership—decided to open it as a local watering hole with live music, they had a place already rigged for sound and lighting. Out with the clothes racks and tables, in with a huge oak bar moved from an abandoned bar and grill called P. Eye McFly's four blocks away, and they had an instant gathering spot for those who still felt the urge to gather.

There weren't as many of those as there used to be.

It was Scooter's habit to play lighter pieces earlier on in the evening—mostly his own compositions, sometimes the works of others he particularly admired. Right now he was playing a pleasant piece by Alex DeGrassi called "Turning." He glanced around the club to see who had arrived. Regulars lifted their mugs in salute when they caught his eye. Pick in mouth, he nodded back. One of the waitresses, Tammi, had remarkably long legs sheathed in black mesh; torn (deliberately) at the calf, the back of the knee and the back of the thigh, and Scooter tried, without much success, not to ogle her as she bent over a table, tray on forearm, to set down mugs of cold beer before four boys Scooter would have guessed ranged between thirteen and seventeen in age.

The boy closest to her, the youngest, leaned in his chair to look up her short skirt. Tammi caught him looking, picked up his beer, and walked away without changing expression.

Scooter broke into a chorus of "nyah-nyah nyah nyah *nyah* nyah" on the Martin and the kid glared at him. Scooter grinned and switched back to "Turning." The kid said something to his friends and got out of his chair, still glaring at Scooter. Near the club entrance Tommy Lee cleared his throat loudly. The kid looked over: Tommy Lee was tapping his heavy truncheon against his thick biceps.

The kid sat down, Scooter continued playing, Tommy Lee got into animated conversation with a woman at the door who wanted to bring her dog in with her. Just another night at The Factory, folks.

The power went out around ten o'clock. Lamps were hurriedly lit, and Scooter could hear Marti the mechanic swearing, "God*damn* piece of shit," as she made her way to the generator in the back room.

A dog began barking at the front door and there was a loud, "Fuck you, asshole!" yelled by a woman. Tommy Lee, scarred and grinning face looking evil as hell in the light from the lamp at his feet, just shrugged. The next person waiting in line to get in—a kid with bleached-blond hair streaked with black—handed Tommy Lee two jugs of home-brewed. Tommy Lee unscrewed the cap on one, lifted it to his mouth, drank, lowered it, looked thoughtful a second, then nodded and replaced the cap. The kid entered and made his way slowly in the darkness to the bar to give the bartender the jugs to put in the refrigerator—which he would do when the power came back on. One for the kid, one for the house, and the kid got admitted to the club and got his beer cooled in the bargain.

Though the mike was no longer live, Scooter continued playing. The nice thing about an acoustic guitar,
he thought, is that it still works when the power fails.

The hubbub of conversation seemed louder without
the lights on, and in pockets of lamplight Scooter saw
isolated, amber-hued faces, some propped on palms,
regarding him attentively.

Tammi brought a hurricane lantern to the stage. "Is
this okay?" she asked, setting it by his feet.

"Fine," he replied. "Thanks."

Marti came back in, a battery-operated Coleman camp
lantern held near her face. "Ten minutes, folks. Twenty,
tops."

Mixed cheers and boos.

Marti went away. "Piece of shit," Scoooter heard her
mutter.

In a minute the sound of her hammering came from
the generator room. Scooter let the Martin hang on its
shoulder strap and raised his hands above his head. He
began to clap in time with Marti's hammerings. The
audience—its size doubled in the last half hour—took it
up. When they were going along on their own, laughing, Scooter stood up from the stool, pulled the pick
from his mouth, and began to play.

The hammering had stopped, the clapping continued.

Scooter toyed with funky beats that wrapped around
the metronome of the audience, chords coming hard
and fast. He swayed with the rhythm, and framing his
face, his hair swung in and out of his vision with the
swaying.

Someone banged his table with his mug and shouted:
"*Hooooeee!*"

The audience laughed, Scooter laughed, and the
rhythmic clapping grew ragged and became applause

as he ended his musical dialogue with them. Grinning, he bowed, and returned to his stool.

"I've, uh," he began, then waited for them to quiet. "I've been working on something," he said. "Now's a good time to play it, I think."

He adjusted the Martin on his leg, brushed hair out of his way, looked up at them. They watched silently. "I've messed with it a lot," he said, "but maybe you'll recognize it."

He began to play.

After the intro, which was new, and his, there was applause and a few intaken breaths when he eased into the long-held opening chord and two short, pumping minor chords of "We Don't Get Fooled Again."

They were quiet while he played. His version, though different from Townshend's acoustic version, was as mild, and they listened raptly, remembering.

The lyrics contained a different sort of pertinence than they had once held.

Near the end he heard someone blow his nose.

There was no applause for several seconds after he finished. He wiped his eyes dry against his sleeve. "Thank—" he began.

The lights came back on.

A rash of cheers broke out and died as quickly as it had erupted. Chairs scraped, and someone said, "Holy shit" in a mild voice. Tommy Lee turned at the commotion and gave a surprised start.

He sat facing Scooter from one of the tables in the middle of the room. He was perched on the edge of his chair as though ready to bolt at any moment. His back was board straight and did not touch the back of the chair. His hands, clasped on the table before him, were gnarled, large-veined, liver-spotted, bony-knuckled. The fingers were long, with long, ragged nails with crescents of dirt under the cuticles.

His skin was white as milk.

His hair was long as Scooter's and looked coarse. It was the color of brushed aluminum. It covered his ears, but Scooter knew what they would look like if he could see them.

His eyes, staring unwaveringly at Scooter, were the eyes of a coyote caught in the beam of headlights.

His face . . .

He was incredibly old.

He leaned to whisper something to his companion, and so raptly had Scooter's attention been held on him that it was only now that Scooter realized the old . . . man . . . *had* a companion.

Scooter had been holding his breath. He released it.

The companion was human, broad-shouldered, red-faced, with big hands but stubby fingers, curly brown hair inexpertly cut short. He whispered something back, glanced at Scooter, added something, then looked up suddenly at a tap on his shoulder.

"How'd you get in here?" Tommy Lee asked him. "You and your friend, you—"

Scooter leaned into the mike. "It's okay, Tommy—I, uh, I invited 'em," he said, thinking: Now, why did I say that?

The companion eyed him and nodded slowly.

The old . . . man . . . still stared at him; he hadn't even glanced at Tommy Lee.

Tommy Lee frowned at Scooter. "You sure . . . ?" he began, then shrugged. "Your party, Scooter," he said, and went back to the door.

Everyone was watching him.

The companion slipped the knife no one had seen

appear in his hand back into the sleeve of his air-force flight jacket.

Scooter regarded them another moment, then looked down and eased the tension somewhat by launching into a mournful ode to the banana split, now gone the way of the dodo.

When it was over he announced a beer break, not because he was thirsty but because their staring unnerved him—his hands were sweating and he'd missed a couple of notes on the last number.

He was sure they were here for him.

When he set the Martin on the stand beside the stool and stepped off the stage, the companion said, "Tony Frazier?"

Scooter didn't look at him.

"Tony Frazier?" he said again. His accent was hard—Alabama granite or Carolina mountain, Scooter couldn't decide which.

Someone stage-whispered from a nearby table: "Hey, his name's Scooter, man."

So the companion tried again: "Scooter?" He said the name dubiously.

Scooter stopped and turned slowly to look at the big man, acutely conscious of the lupine stare of the other, of the eyes of his audience watching them.

"That's me," he said.

"My friend here'd like a word with you," said the man. He held his lips tight and drawn in as he spoke, as if to prevent dentures from falling out of his mouth.

Scooter hesitated.

The man pointed a short, thick index finger at a chair. "Siddown. He won't bite. An' I won't 'less I have to." He sounded completely serious.

Scooter went to the table, pulled out the chair, and sat down. "What do you want?" he asked.

The man hooked a thumb at his friend. "His name's Aune'wah."

The pale, ancient head bowed at the mention of his name.

"He don't speak English," the man continued, "so I translate. I'm Grim."

You sure as shit are, thought Scooter. But he said nothing.

"What does"—Scooter fumbled over the name—"Ah-oo-nuh—"

"Aune'wah."

"What does he want with me?"

Grim leaned forward. Both elbows went onto the table, right hand resting along the edge, left hand accentuating as he talked.

Blue eyes were tattoed on the large knuckles of his gesturing hand.

"Aune'wah has a kid," began Grim, and Scooter tried not to wince as he got a whiff of his breath. "A boy who hangs out on this side of the hill. The kid, he's up on Monaghie the other day with one of his buddies, and he hears someone playin' the guitar. Only, this fellah ain't just playing, he's making pictures in the air." Grim unsnapped a sleeve cuff and reached in. Blue eyes flexed on his knuckles as he scratched his inner arm. He removed his hand from the sleeve and snapped it shut again. His gaze drifted past Scooter and something ugly formed in his pale blue eyes.

Scooter turned to see Tammi standing behind him. "Nice set tonight, Scooter," she said. "You want a beer?"

"Yeah," he said. "Thanks." And he wondered if the thanks had been for the compliment or for the offered beer.

"You?" she asked Grim.

His refusal was little more than a grunt.

"How about—"

"He don't want nothing to drink either," interrupted Grim. There was a happy violence in his eyes that made Scooter wish Tommy Lee was nearer.

Tammi frowned at him. "I'll get your beer, Scooter," she said, and left.

"Where was I?" asked Grim, watching her go.

"This guy's music was making pictures in the air."

Grim's gaze followed her. Scooter looked down at the table and was fascinated by the man's deeply ridged right thumb rubbing slow circles across blue-eyed knuckles. The larger knuckle wrinkled, winked briefly, folded, stretched, wrinkled again.

He looked up from the hand to see Grim watching him stare.

"Go on," said Scooter, wondering if the sudden surge of his pulse showed in his voice.

Grim stopped rubbing and leaned forward. His hands clasped; blue eyes peered out from a cage of fingers. "The kid, next time he's home, he tells his old man about it. Aune'wah says he never heard of no human being who could make pictures in the air. His folk, yeah, and there ain't even a lot of them who'll do it. So he sent me looking for the guy who does it." Grim splayed his interlaced fingers, a kind of shrug. "You were pretty easy to find."

Scooter returned the shrug. "I'm not hiding from anything," he said.

Grim said something to the old man in a language that seemed to be mostly vowel sounds, with a few Ls and Ns. The old man laughed—it was too high-pitched and melodious to be called a cackle—and said something back. His voice was much more pleasant than Grim's.

"What did he say?" asked Scooter.

"I told him what you said, about not hiding from anything. He thought it was funny."

Scooter caught himself playing with his hair in a habit similar to Roxanne's. He stopped. "What's that supposed to—look, I got songs to play here. Why don't you just tell me what you want."

Grim said something to the old man. The old man leaned forward. He narrowed his eyes and pointed a very long index finger at Scooter's face. He began speaking.

"He says he's heard Aarka'an—that's his boy—and now he's heard you."

"I still don't—" began Scooter.

"Shut up," said Grim. "He says you have a gift. You . . ." His hands separated, one going to his chin as he sought a word. "He says there's something in your music that's yours and only yours. He wants to know if you can do the same thing here."

"Here?"

Grim folded a non-eyed index finger toward his large palm, set a thumb on top of it, and pressed. It popped loudly. "In the valley," he said, looking at his hands.

Tammi set a beer in front of Scooter, startling him. She walked away before he could thank her, and Scooter looked back at the strange pair sitting before him.

"Answer him," said Grim.

"No," said Scooter, wondering why he didn't tell them it was none of their business, then realizing that it was because Grim scared the hell out of him. "No, it doesn't work here. Only on Monaghie."

Grim translated Scooter's answer. The old man nodded and said something else.

"You ever play your guitar past there?" Grim asked. He pronounced it *git*-tar.

"Are you crazy? Hell, no." Scooter sipped from his mug. Light beer—blecch.

The old man nodded while Grim translated, then looked thoughtful for a moment.

"You know," said Scooter to Grim, "it's probably not very smart for him to come here. I mean, people don't—"

"He knows," said Grim. "But he heard about something he wouldn't believe till he saw it.

The old man spoke again. He looked at Scooter as he spoke, not at Grim, and Scooter felt he was being scrutinized for his reactions. He tried to keep his face impassive as Grim began translating. "He says that where he's from there's some who do the same thing you can do. There ain't many, and he thinks they're either crazy, or brave, or stupid, and maybe all three. Over there, when you make music, sometimes you make something else. It's real simple in his language, but it don't translate well. That's the best I can put it."

The old man spoke again.

"Things are hard to control in the Borderlands," translated Grim, "and what you're doing is wrong. He wants to know why you don't just stay down here to play."

Scooter sipped beer again, set down the mug. "I don't know," he said, wiping his hand dry against his denimed thigh. "I don't know why I like to play there so much. I don't know why I should tell you, either."

Grim sat back. "You'll tell me," he said, "because *he* wants to know." He glanced at the old man. When he looked back at Scooter, the expression of quiet violence with which he had regarded Tammi had returned. "And because if you don't, I'll cut your guts out right here."

Scooter nearly laughed. People didn't *really* say shit like that? But Grim had, and what kept the laugh from emerging was his certainty that not only did Grim mean it, he had done the same thing before—he *liked* it. He *wanted* Scooter to tell them to mind their own fucking business.

He thought of the knife he wore at his back, on his belt, and knew that he would never reach it in time. "All right," he said. "It scares me sometimes, yeah." He stopped as Grim translated, then continued when the man finished. "But it's like . . . like what I see there, what I make up there, is the way it looks inside me, the way I picture my music in my head. I can't really explain it; I just like to go up there and play. Anyone who's seen it likes it." He sipped beer. "Why's it wrong?"

Grim asked the question for him, listened to the reply, and turned again to Scooter. "He won't tell you," he said. "You do it up there, but you don't know how you do it, and telling you would just make it worse. He—"

Suddenly the old man rose from his chair as if he weighed almost nothing. A long index finger made a cutting motion across his chest as he spoke in what Scooter thought was an angry tone, then curled with the other fingers into a ragged-taloned claw.

"He came to tell you," said Grim, "that what you make belongs to you."

Scooter stared from one to the other of them. The old man stared back, wrinkled white lids blinking over silver-cataracted eyes, curiously birdlike. Scooter waited for the man to say more or for Grim to translate further, but neither did.

"That's it?" asked Scooter. "That's what he came across the Borderlands to tell me?"

Grim smiled. His teeth blackened near the gums, a few of them rotted in small hollows. "Guess so."

Scooter frowned. He didn't get it. The Borderlands,

those hills, this city, they were *dangerous*. Especially to
an old man, human or not. This—*Aune'wah*—had come
through that to tell him something he might have read
in a fortune cookie?

Prease to excuse, lound ears, he thought, *but what you
make berong to you.*

It didn't figure.

"I don't get it," he said. "I mean, there must be more
than that. I mean, maybe you didn't translate it right,
or there's more, or something. Is he bugged because it
belongs to me? Does he think it ought to be his? Or he
wants to hire me, is that it? To show me off to his—"

"Don't mock him, boy." Eyed hand moved almost
imperceptibly toward right sleeve.

"I'm not mocking him, man; I'm just trying to understand. It don't make sense to me."

"He thinks it's important. Maybe he thinks you ought
to think so too."

Scooter shook his head in confusion. He picked up
his beer again, drained it, thunked the empty mug back
onto the table, and watched whitewash slip toward the
bottom. "Well, look," he said, pushing back his chair
and standing, "you tell him thanks, all right? Tell him
I'll remember what he said, and that . . . that I'm flat-
tered he came all this way to . . . to share his wisdom.
Tell him that, okay?"

Grim looked Scooter up and down, and for a moment Scooter thought the man was going to go for him.
His fist clenched on the handle of his mug in anticipa-
tion, readying to swing it on him if need be, but Grim
only finished his cold appraisal and looked up at the
old man. He gestured toward Scooter and began
translating.

The old man looked at Scooter while Grim spoke.
When Grim was done, the old man shook his head and

laughed softly. He came around the table to Scooter and stood close to him, looking into his eyes. He was Scooter's height, and Scooter was no midget. After a moment the old man raised a hand and set it against Scooter's cheek. The hand was rough and callused and smelled of resin. He spoke briefly, then dropped his hand and turned away. Everyone watched him walk to the front door, but no one interfered and he stepped out into the night.

Scooter watched him go, then glanced at Grim. "What did he say?"

Grim looked away from the tall wooden doors. He shook his head and stared evenly into Scooter's eyes. "It's a saying they have. 'Old enough to light a fire, young enough to get burned doing it.' It's his way of saying he thinks you're a goddamn idiot."

He bicycled home after The Factory closed, his guitar case strapped to the bike's sissy bar. He stayed close to the double yellow line—dim in the moonlight, but still visible—and thought about the strange encounter.

What you make belongs to you. Wow, hey. I got it. Thanks for sharing that.

He watched the shadows of figures as they ran across the moon-washed front of the old Sav-on supermarket. They slipped around the corner and disappeared into an alley.

At Van Alden he automatically swerved to avoid the Mercedes stopped in the midst of turning off of Derrida. The chocolate-brown car was nearly invisible in the darkness, but he could have piloted around it—and the cars by the meters lining both curbs, the semi caught in the midst of pulling out of the Ralph's grocery store entrance, the huge spray of broken glass in front of the

Fidelity Bank, the dumpster wheeled into the road near Cafe Rive Gauche—in his sleep.

Scene of the Crime was dark and quiet; he wheeled once around the arcade of stores before pulling in around back. Those black curtains were sure a good idea, he thought, swinging off the bike to balance on one pedal; they keep the light from—

He braked suddenly; the front tire skidded on gravel.

The burglar bars at the back door were open.

They *never* left those bars open.

Especially not at night.

Heart quickening, Scooter got off the bike and lowered it to the parking lot. He pulled the knife from its sheath at his belt, the black knife that would not gleam in the darkness. He went to one wall and crept toward the door to examine the grillwork. The Kryptonite lock, unlocked, hung through the hole in the frame. The black iron bars stood open; the door was closed.

Scooter tried the knob. It shouldn't have, but it turned.

Quickly he opened the door inward, slipped inside, shut it softly, and crouched.

No lights burned.

He moved away from the door to one wall, still crouched, and waited for his eyes to adjust.

He straightened.

After a whole, long minute, it was still nearly impossible to see.

Knife in right hand, Scooter walked with left extended. The carpeting muffled the tread of his basketball shoes. He checked Roxanne's workroom. The handpress was missing.

For a moment he looked at the space on the low table where it had been, then he continued looking around.

The old bathroom: the loaf of Mrs. Hernandez's

bread stood alone on the rack. A box of Kotex tampons that had been on a lower shelf was gone.

The bedroom/book room: the furniture was undisturbed. The bed was made.

The studio/tearoom: nothing he could see. The guitars and amps were still there.

The kitchen was undisturbed.

Back in the workroom he lit a lamp with a Lucifer match, carried it in one hand with his knife still clutched in the other. He had half expected to find the place looted. It was not, but things were still not right.

The safe stood open in the studio. Roxanne's trade goods—her pills, syringes, needles, tampons, everything—were gone.

The gun was missing.

Scooter's clothes were still in the top three dresser drawers in the book room.

In the bottom three, about half of Roxanne's clothes were cleared out.

Back in the workroom, half the matches had been taken. The boxes of paper were still there. The missing handpress had been a cumbersome, heavy thing.

Scooter stared at the steady flame behind the clear chimney of the hurricane lamp.

She left—she went, she's gone, she moved *out*, she left me!

No! She would have left a note; Roxanne would have left a note!

He looked around wildly. The circle of his lamp's light did not reach very far, and he could not tell whether a note was pinned to one of the walls. He rushed to the shelves and held up the lamp. The magnetic banana adhered to the metal, nothing held beneath it.

The bed? He went into the bedroom. The comforter

was pulled up and tucked at the pillows; the television pillow sat on top of it, leaning against the wall. No note, no piece of paper on the sheet. He lifted the television pillow. Nothing there.

The safe?

No.

He looked all over their home—all over the Scene of the Crime—and found many traces of her presence, evidence that she lived (had lived?) here: here a smiling crescent-moon earring, here a pair of socks far too small to be his, here a large conch shell from Key West, souvenir from a trip taken long ago. He stared at its flesh-colored opening for what felt like a long time, then put it back on the dresser.

No note. And no sign of a struggle. Much of what looters would have taken was still here. Most looters wrecked the places they plundered, just because they now had the freedom to, but the place was largely undisturbed. And only Roxanne could open the safe; only she and he knew where the gun was kept.

Gone, then. And no note.

He felt afraid then, began to tremble in a way he never had when stalked on his way home at night, or when Dennis had died. He simply did not know what to do.

He stood there in the book room, lamp in hand, turning this way and that, looking for some sign, something on the wall, some message from inside himself. He remembered his bike with the guitar on the back and brought it in. He locked the door, leaned the bike against the wall, removed the guitar case, took out the Martin, and returned with it to the living room where the lone flame burned beside the air mattress. He stood looking down on it, holding the guitar by the neck like a throttled, fat-bodied bird, and wondered what to do.

He thought briefly about going out to look for her, but dismissed it. It had been hours—as many as seven; she could have gone anywhere. He didn't know where to start looking, anyway; not at night.

Finally he sat in bed with his arms folded across the guitar in his lap, and he waited for her to come home.

He awoke with puffy eyes and throbbing head and realized he had been crying in his sleep. The Martin lay beside him. There was something vaguely obscene about it being there, in bed next to him, and he turned away from it and stood stiffly.

He was still in his clothes.

He tramped, bleary-eyed, to the black curtains, and pulled them open. Sunlight stabbed his pupils; he clenched his lids and threw a hand across his brow, cowering vampirelike in the late-morning brightness.

His mouth tasted foul.

He tramped to the bathroom, groped in the dimness for the tube of Crest, squeezed a chalky blue inch onto his toothbrush, began brushing—and stopped.

Roxanne's toothbrush was gone.

"Gaw fu'ing dammit," he said, and Crest-tainted saliva ran down his chin. He wiped it away with a finger and continued brushing, staring at the empty place in the holder where Roxanne's brush—it had been a red brush, curved in a narrow S, he remembered, one of those Swedish, high-tech things some people used to order from expensive catalogs for their executive friends. And now it wasn't there, and Roxanne wasn't there, and she wouldn't be coming back and her god*damn* toothbrush wouldn't be coming back with her.

He watched his face in the mirror as he finished brushing, rinsed with water from a plastic jug, spat, rinsed again, spat again. He made hateful faces at himself, caught himself, and felt foolish.

He tossed his toothbrush into the sink and left the bathroom. Not bothering to unsnarl the tangled mass of his hair with a brush, he dried the lower half of his face against the sheet on the air mattress, pushed his bike outside, got on, and pedaled onto Woodman, turning west on Derrida.

He didn't lock the door behind him. He didn't give a fuck.

Some people now referred to the Galleria as trader's heaven. Certainly it was never called that before, back when it was a large indoor shopping mall in an area of town that had been fairly expensive to live in, and when cash and not barter had been its stock in trade.

Times change.

Most of the stores had been looted long ago; everything worth taking, taken; all worth breaking, broken; all better left behind, abandoned. Records littered the floor in the Musicland, bins overturned atop them. In the B. Dalton, books were heaped in scattered piles with appalling lack of concern as to genre. Both stores looked to be ready for some straight-thinking, right-minded, God-fearing American to torch them at any minute. Glass fronts had been smashed, though the glass was swept away now. Mannequins in display windows were piled atop each other in plastic orgies. Inside, the stores were dark even during the day.

Whoever had designed the three-level mall, however, had wanted a sunny, open-air feeling along the walkways promenading the storefronts, so the ceiling was many triangular glass panels framed by aluminum and the central sections of the mall—the midway, it might be called—were bright, yet cool on all but the hottest days. Traders arranged their bins, tables, sacks, and whatnot, along the midway in the early morning, and by ten o'clock, when most of the locals were up and about, the "shoppers"—the term the regular traders used—were at full strength with bags or boxes in hand, and the trading went hard and fast.

Scooter got there at ten-thirty. He carried his Schwinn up a long flight of steps beside a frozen escalator until he reached the long, pebble-set walkway lined with dead trees in granite holders. He biked along until he reached the entrance between a onetime restaurant called Kerwin's and a McDonald's, and he locked his bike beside the dozen-odd already in the rack.

The glass doors stood open, and Scooter went inside.

Most traders were on the bottom floor; the bulk of them were in the center of the mall, a small court with a platform stage. There had once been a lot of greenery here; now it was all brown. Scooter leaned over the rail at the edge of the walkway, looking down on the bartering crowd for some sign of Roxanne. He saw none.

As he walked down the escalator to the court his stomach let out a loud growl. He patted it self-consciously. Later, he thought.

He walked among stalls and seated people hawking their wares: rechargeable batteries, car batteries cleaned and filled with electrolyte (sulfuric acid solution in plastic-lined cartons), solar batteries, homemade candles, matches, butane, breads, vegetables, meats (not many of those: rabbit, venison, a little chicken, and something that Scooter suspected was dogmeat), drugs (some salvaged, some homemade; some medicinal, some recreational), home-brewed beer and wines (someone with whiskey was making a killing), generators and alternators (small bicycle generators, powerful car generators and alternators, and a popular generator meant for motorcycles, hooked up to a bicycle to pedal for power), pistols, bullets (mostly homemade), and a great deal more. Scooter threaded his way among them, looking for Roxanne, or someone he knew who might have seen her. But his search, as he had half expected, yielded nothing.

He turned around and began working his way toward the escalator when someone called, in thickly accented English, "Scooter? Yoohoo, Mister Scooter?"

He looked back. A heavy woman in a floral print dress, her long, graying hair tied back, beckoned to him. She stood by the marble facade decorating the elevator shaft that rose in the middle of the mall. She did not look familiar, but Scooter headed back to her anyhow.

"You Scooter, ah?" she asked.

"Yeah. I was—"

"Your girl, Roxanne, she tol' me about you."

"Roxanne—have you—?"

She tugged on her hair, jangling a gold teardrop hanging from one earlobe. "I recognized you from those. I didn't see her this morning, so I guess you came instead." She held out a white paper sack; Scooter took it and looked inside. Bread. Fresh bread.

His stomach growled loud enough for both of them to hear.

"Mrs. . . . Hernandez?" Scooter said.

She nodded. "I owe her one more loaf, tomorrow, for the medicine she give my baby."

"Your . . . ? How is your baby, Mrs. Hernandez? Roxanne said she was pretty sick."

"He." The woman smiled. "Better, Mr. Scooter. I'm still worried, but every day he get better. Those pills, they help. Your Roxanne, she a good lady. You tell her I said that."

Scooter hesitated. "Mrs. Hernandez . . . I'm sort of looking for Roxanne. We—we had a fight last night, and she ran out, and I'm trying to find out where she is. You haven't seen her?"

"She run out on you?" Scooter saw Mrs. Hernandez glance at the sack of bread he held, saw her think about taking it back. He found himself moving the sack slightly out of her reach and clutching it tighter. He nodded at her question. "Have you seen her?" he asked again.

She shook her head. "Not today. Most days, she's here. Today . . ." She shrugged.

"Well, if you do see her, would you tell her I'm looking for her? Tell her—tell her I just want to talk to her. Please?"

She said nothing.

"Thanks, Mrs. Hernandez," said Scooter, backing away a bit. "And thank you for the bread."

She frowned.

Scooter left the mall.

Outside was the community bulletin board, which functioned the same way bulletin boards always had and probably always would—people needing and offering services, people requiring and selling items, announcements that the Borderlands was a communist-backed experiment endorsed by the pope, a faded and weather-beaten prediction that The End is Near. The only noticeable difference was that almost all the notices, announcements, and signs were hand-lettered, and because of that Roxanne's printing jobs stood out—one of the major reasons she managed to barter for any work at all.

But the bulletin board told him nothing new, gave

him no evidence of Roxanne's whereabouts. He thought she might have posted a notice looking for work, or to share a squat, or even a note to him, but there was nothing but her usual advertisements for her own business and for others.

Scooter carred his bike down the long run of stairs and headed farther east on Derrida.

The Holiday Inn was pretty much the same. Scooter hadn't been here in almost a year.

He wasn't sure why he had come.

In the lobby he looked around. He didn't recognize anyone—most of them were still asleep on mattresses dragged from rooms into the foyer, or were sprawled on worn-out couches or chairs—but it still looked almost exactly the same. The smell still came from the bathroom down the hall. Empty cans, wrappers, dirty paper plates, and worse littered the floor.

Down the hall the bathroom door shut and footsteps approached.

Still buckling his torn, faded orange cords, he turned the corner. He zipped up his pants and stopped, eyes widening. "Hey," he drawled, a hand going up to scratch fresh gauze at his head. "What're you—hey!" And that was him recognizing Scooter. His arms waved as though finishing his sentence in semaphore.

Scooter said nothing.

"What brings you up here, huh?" asked Richie, stepping closer. His toe caught the corner of a mattress, brushed someone's elbow, elicited a sleepy "Fuck you." Richie glanced back, seemed about to utter an apology, looked back at Scooter instead. "This place," he said, "Shee-it. Hey, they told me you used to live here. That right?"

Scooter nodded. "If you can call this living," he said.

Richie laughed. "Yeah, it's pretty bad, ain't it. I seen worse, though. Heck, I *been* in worse." Richie looked around the room, and Scooter wondered how different the room looked to him. "It's all right, though," Richie said decisively. "I mean, this is a good bunch. It's people that make a place, you know?" His gaze returned to Scooter. "Still, I'd leave in a minute if I had somewhere else to go."

"What about your friend?" Scooter asked. "The red-headed guy."

Richie looked down at his feet and shrugged. He looked up. "Hey, you want something to eat?" he asked.

Scooter shook his head. "I got bread," he said, and held up the sack.

Richie wiped his peach-fuzzed chin. Scooter might have found it comical if it hadn't been so pathetic. "Oh, man. Hey, you think I could . . . ?"

Scooter opened the sack and tore off a hunk from the end of the loaf. He handed it to Richie, who grinned and ate it savagely, crumbs salting his fledgling beard. "That was pretty good," he said after wolfing down the last bite. "Man, I haven't had fresh bread in . . . shit." He shrugged, then got that hungry look again. "Uh, would it be all right if I . . . ?"

Scooter stayed another hour, asking if anyone had seen Roxanne. Half the people he asked said they had, but no two descriptions matched. Scooter took to giving out phony descriptions—"Hey, you seen my girlfriend? She's about five-even, a hundred-forty pounds, missing index finger on her right hand, patch over her right eye?"—and usually got a response like, "Naw, not today. But I think I seen someone looked like that yesterday, over by—"

When he left, as disgusted with himself as with them and their place, he took a half-full bottle of Jack Daniel's he'd found poking out from beneath a filthy paper plate under a chair.

Home again, home again, Scene of the Crime.

He went into the studio with the bottle of whiskey and every intention of getting shit-faced and playing until he passed out.

He found the typed note tucked through the strings at the head of the Yamaha.

Scooter—

I put this where I thought you'd find it soonest. I'm going away, because I just can't take it anymore. I love you, but I also have my pride, and you just aren't pulling your weight. I won't keep pulling it for you. The world doesn't exist for you to play your guitar, Scooter. It's selfish of you, and I'm tired of waiting around for you to get off your ass and be responsible for yourself.

So I won't be responsible for you anymore. You're on your own. I know that sounds harsh. Maybe you don't believe it when I say I still love you, but I do. I just can't live with you like this.

Please don't try to find me, because you won't. I'm sorry to hurt you, but you'll get over it, I know. We'll see each other again, but not for a long time, I think.

—Roxanne

He read it three times, then turned it over to see if there was more, but there wasn't.

The Factory wasn't open yet, but Tommy Lee answered his knock—his pounding, rather, since the place was big and the doors were huge.

"Scooter," he said in his pleasant baritone. "What can I do for you?"

"Hi, Tommy. Is Marti around?"

"She's in back, I think. You want me to go get her?"

"Yeah, if you would."

Tommy Lee narrowed his eyes. "Bit early in the day to be drunk, isn't it, Scooter?"

Scooter flushed. "Just drinking, man. Not drunk."

Tommy Lee looked thoughtful a moment, then asked Scooter to wait while he went to get Marti.

Scooter waited.

Jesus, two sips of Jack Daniel's and he tells me I'm drunk. Well, maybe a little more than two sips. But not enough to get *drunk!* Still, he hadn't had more than a beer or two on the same night in at least a year. No tolerance.

Marti opened the door. A smear of grease warpainted one cheek; matching smudges marred her jeans. Her face was sweaty and her thin brown hair tied back. She wiped her hands on a dirty rag she carried with her. "Yeah, Scooter?" she said. "What's up?"

"Roxanne left me," he muttered.

Her look softened a bit. "That's a tough break, kid," she said. She looked Scooter's age; she was ten years older.

"Yeah, well . . ." He shifted uncomfortably from one foot to the other, hands in the front pockets of his pants.

"You wanna talk about it?" she asked. "I'm kinda busy, but you can come in back with me, if you want. I can work and listen at the same time." She opened the tall wood door a bit wider.

"Naw, naw, Marti. That ain't why I came here. I mean, I'd like to talk to you, but I got something I got to do."

"Well, then, what do you need, Scooter?"

"It's—" One hand came out of a pocket, turned palm

up. "It's sort of hard to explain. See, Roxanne left me and I'm really bummed, you know? And I just want to take my ax—my guitar, you know, my electric—"

"I know," she said. "I used to play in a band."

He looked up in surprise. "Yeah?" He shook his head. "You're always full of surprises. But right now I just wanna play my ax, you know? Take my Les Paul up on the hill and just wail. That's how I work stuff out, you know? Like this—" He mimed playing guitar. "I got a pig-snout amp, and I thought maybe you could . . ."

She opened the door to let him in. "Follow me, Scooter. We'll fix you up."

She led him through the empty, dimly lighted club— during the day they used as little power as possible—to the back room. It had once been the stockroom for the former clothing store; it had been converted to a generator room when the new management had acquired a propane generator. The door—with a hand-lettered sign that read MARTI'S ROOM—KEEP OUT OR I'LL KILL YOU— was locked with a simple Yale lock. Marti unlocked it with a key from a crowded ring on a belt loop and opened it to let him in ahead of her.

The generator throbbed loudly at the back of the room. Near it stood a few dozen bottles of propane.

"Here," said Marti over the thrum of the generator. Scooter followed her farther into the room, wanting to shield his ears from the noise. He was starting to get a headache. Marti led him to the generator. She pointed to a cylindrical object attached to it, with cables leading from that to a car battery on the floor.

"You power this thing with a car battery?" Scooter asked incredulously.

Marti laughed. "Scooter, people like you are the

reason people like me own the world. At least this part of it." She pointed again at the object attached. "That's an alternator. Got it from an auto-parts store. It was originally meant to go on a truck engine. I use it to charge batteries off the generator. It's a sideline business I run myself: sell batteries, then charge to juice 'em up again when they run low." She indicated a dozen car batteries, tagged with the names of their owners, against the far wall. "What kinda amp you got?" she asked.

"Fender."

She pursed her lips, thinking, then went to a trunk against the wall beside the batteries. She produced a key from her ring and unlocked the trunk, opened it, and removed a small box from inside. She shut the trunk and locked it again.

"Motor-scooter battery," she told Scooter, returning to him and placing it in his hand. It was heavy for its size. "Used to power one of those Honda Elites. Perfect for you—a Scooter battery, huh?" She laughed. "Anyway, it's all charged up and ready to use. Just bring it back when you're done with it, okay? Don't lose it, don't sell it, and don't keep it too long."

"I don't—I don't have anything I can—"

She put up both palms and shook her hands. "Don't worry about it. It doesn't cost me anything unless you lose it." She smiled knowingly. "This here's a gravy business for me, Scooter. The power's a fringe benefit from the generator, and they let me use it free, which means it doesn't even cost me any fuel. My only overhead is electrolyte—I gotta trade with those shitheads who squatted that car-battery shop on Veda." She shrugged. "So you're all set. You can do me a favor when I need one."

Scooter looked at the scooter battery in his hand. "Well—*thanks*, Marti. Thanks a lot."

She waved it away. "C'mon, I got stuff to do here." She led him to the door and opened it for him. "I tell ya," she said as they left the noisy room, "this is a hell of a life, you know?" She locked the door and began leading him to the front of the Factory. "I ran a garage for ten years before I could get the hell away from it. I came here to make it big. I was gonna be a filmmaker, you know?" She shook her head. "Then all this. And now the best thing, the most important thing in the world I can be, is a goddamn mechanic." She nodded at Tommy Lee and opened one of the tall front doors to let Scooter out. "Ain't that a bitch?" Without waiting for an answer she said, "You take care now, Scooter," and shut the door again.

It only took a little fiddling to connect the battery to his amplifier. He drank Jack Daniel's from the bottle while he rigged it up. He removed the Les Paul from its dusty case and ran a hand along its glossy black surface, then set it aside and untangled a cord from a heap in one corner of the studio. He plugged one end into the Les Paul, plugged the other into the amp, and turned it on.

An electric hum, and then feedback assailed his ears.

Wincing, then grinning in satisfaction, Scooter moved the guitar away from the amp and turned down the gain.

He pulled the pick from his mouth and struck a bar chord. For the first time in years, notes sounded from the amplifier of Scooter's electric guitar.

It was out of tune.

Scooter sat on the card chair in the middle of the studio and tuned it. When he was ready, he took another sip of Jack Daniel's, turned up the volume, and played.

The studio filled with loud music.

He ran scales, then old riffs, then played with the amp until he got the sort of distortion he wanted. He cranked up the volume until his ears hurt, and played hard and fast—and still he wasn't satisfied. He needed something else, something more.

Monaghie.

It was still early afternoon; he could make it there well before sunset, be back before dark. Sure; that was a good idea. A *great* idea.

He opened the back door and wheeled his bicycle outside. He put the Les Paul back in its case, looped the plug on top of it, snapped the case shut, carried it outside, and tied it to the sissy bar with thick elastic cords that had a hook on either end.

The amp was going to be a pain in the ass. It was about two feet square, eight inches deep, and heavy. He rested it on the support bar beneath the seat, then lashed it to the handlebars with more elastic cords. Steering would be a little more restricted, but he'd manage.

He put on his black-and-white-checked cotton shirt, the one with the big pockets, left it unbuttoned, and put the Jack Daniel's bottle in a pocket.

He set out.

Scooter reached Crescent Canyon in fifteen minutes— the same amout of time it would have taken him in a car six years ago. He turned right onto Crescent, pedaled another half mile, then shifted to low gear when he reached the long, gradual rise. There weren't very many cars, and there was plenty of room to avoid them.

When the road began to curve and the route grew

steeper, he walked the bike up. At the top he turned right onto Monaghie.

Monaghie Drive wound along the top of a line of hills, the unofficial line separating *here* from *there*, a kind of thirty-eighth Parallel dividing the human city from what lay beyond. All roads sloped down past here, leading deeper into the Borderlands.

There weren't a whole lot of people who went farther than Monaghie. Scooter never did.

On Monaghie he found he had exercised hard enough to come perilously close to sobriety; he fished the bottle from his pocket, uncapped it, and drank. From here the route wound up and down as well as back and forth. Scooter coasted on the downslopes and walked the upgrades. The final stretch, just past the fringe of an abandoned planned community called Crescent Hills, was long and steep, rounding a tight corner banked by a rise that was the knoll where Scooter usually played. Scooter took the guitar and amp to the top of the rise, leaving the bike behind on its kickstand. He didn't lock it; he had forgotten to bring the lock. Once he nearly slipped trudging up the sandy rise, but he recovered and reached the top.

He set down the guitar and the amp and looked out over the valley. The wind whipped his hair across the left side of his face. It was clear up here; most of the smog had died away some time ago, though there was a thin haze of gray to the west, where the hills still burned. The bare dirt rise on which he stood was littered with wrappers, bags, cans, bottles, even a rotting chair, color bleached away by the sun. Scooter looked out over the urban grid in the valley and remembered how it used to be. A Friday night, maybe, driving along the twisting road, at points seeing the city below him, spread out and winking in the dark like looking out from inside a chandelier, and, sometimes, the moon rising, a gibbous orange impaled by a distant peak. Monaghie would buck left, surge right, hungry gravel chewing beneath his tires while, behind, the impatience of close headlights. And he would feel he catwalked a wall separating halves of the world, and he would wonder if anyone else saw it that way.

Now Monaghie separated two worlds in truth, but the fairyland was on the other side—a much less inviting sort of fairyland—while the winking lights that had once been a testament to technology were now limited to a few isolated pockets.

Scooter shook his head, looking out over the still city. Everything changes, he thought. He said it aloud, and felt his eyes sting. Goddamn you, Roxanne. How could you do this?

He bent, unsnapped the guitar case, and lifted out the Les Paul. Sunlight reflected along its glossy black length, reminding him of the eyes of the boy he had seen up here the other day. He set the amp on a concrete survey marker that had DEPT. OF PUBLIC WORKS stamped into it, plugged one end of the tightly coiled cord into the Les Paul, plugged the other end into the amp, and turned it on.

A slight hum grew in the afternoon air.

He sipped Jack Daniel's, then set the bottle down by his foot. The sun was an outstretched hand's length above the horizon.

Scooter slung the strap over his right shoulder, bent to the case again, and selected a pick—a Fender Bullet. He straightened and looked around, feeling the wind in his hair, the sun's warmth on his face. He took a deep breath and let it out.

With a middle finger he damped the strings and plucked a harmonic.

A dozen feet away, a bright point arced in the air above his head. It faded quickly, leaving an iridescent afterimage that dissipated quickly.

He plucked harmonics. Pairs of crescents floated in sequence, then faded in the gilded light. They were similar to those that formed when he brought the Martin up here, but brighter, more vibrant, more energetic.

More electric, he thought, and strummed a G-chord.

An arpeggio of light swept upward, each distinct bar its own color, graduating up the spectrum from red to orange, to yellow, to green, to blue, to indigo, to violet, fading to nothing but a shimmer in the air.

Scooter grunted. So much for the pretty stuff.

He drank again from the bottle, set it down, adjusted treble and bass on the map, added a touch of reverb to fill it out some, and turned up the volume. He turned to face the valley. "Let's give this a try," he said, and began hammering triplets, wailing in the narrow frets near the body. The notes were piercing, slightly distorted, raw-edged.

Violet points beat in a triple-descendant pattern like the measure of a triple heartbeat, dripped down bloodlike, faded where they dripped.

Scooter turned up the volume and jammed. Raw notes emerged staccato, flickered above him in corresponding machine-gun bursts. Angry bar chords sent murky walls of light sheeting across the space before him. Long, keening, vibrating notes appeared as trembling, diamond-bright points that left flashbulb arcs behind, the color that burns against the eyelids when a dentist's drill slips and grinds into unnumbed nerve. Playing rapid scratch on muted strings sent bars of chrome yellow racing one after the other, disappearing into the wherever.

And the music was like before, like in the old days

when he carried that anger around all the time, when he and the rest of Stormtrooper would get fucked up beyond all recall and go out there in front of thousands of the motherfuckers and just *do it*, just jam like nobody else could.

Scooter smashed a final chord, held it, watched the angry cloud of light dim slowly as the chord dwindled, watched it disappear as it died.

His back teeth had grown numb from the whiskey. He reached for the bottle, knocked it over with a foot, picked it up awkwardly, leaving behind a small puddle in the dirt. "Shit," he said, and wiped the mouth.

He drank.

"All right," he muttered, left hand on the neck of the bottle lowering to his side, right hand muting strings around the neck of the guitar. "All right, Roxanne."

The sun touched the hills at the horizon. An arc of light reflected from his guitar, quivered at the foot of the rise, swept scythe-like across it as Scooter heaved the bottle away. *"All right!"* he bellowed.

The bottle hit dirt with a hollow sound, but did not break.

Scooter adjusted the strap on his shoulder. He fingered the neck and struck a crashing chord. "Roxanne!" he yelled. "You hear me down there? This is for you! This is for *you*, Roxanne!"

And he began to torture music out of the guitar. It was ugly, jarring, violent, fast, discordant, raw, enraged, hungry, primal, seething, laced with pain.

Above him the air churned, the colors roiled.

They grew. From electric brightness the colors dimmed to a boiling palette of reds and browns like dried blood, of funereal grays the color of slug bellies, of dark, dull blue-greens like bread mold, of deep oranges like rust and decay.

They acquired a look of solidity, of tangibility. The look blurred with Scooter's tears.

Molded by anger and loss, shaped by pain and loss, the colors took on form. Immersed in the cathartic of his playing, Scooter did not notice as the form began to pulse with a dull, leaden kind of life while it seethed and turned about and lowered a smoky length of itself toward the hillside.

He stopped playing when he heard the coyote screaming. Not howling, not baying, not yiping, but *screaming*—open-throated, helpless, unable to escape pain beyond imagining.

Scooter stopped playing.

He looked at the *thing* dipping into the brush, the thing created by his rage, by his music, the thing that persisted well after the last notes had died away. It had hold of a wild coyote and was somehow draining it of life.

All around him, in the hills, coyotes and wild dogs began to howl.

Scooter watched, not knowing what to do, as the coyote leaped out of the brush, twisting, snapping, spasmodic. It was trying to get at something it could not combat, an opponent nowhere visible to it, and as Scooter watched the coyote grew weak and fell over, panting, head toward him, tongue flopping from the side of its mouth onto the dirt, eyes beseeching. Scooter gripped the guitar tighter, then let go.

Cacophony from the amplifier behind him.

The coyote was sinking in on itself. The thing above pulsed as it—as it *fed*. The coyote whimpered now as it grew gaunt, as its ribs grew cage-like, its neck arched and corded, its legs brittle, its head little more than a skull. Its eyes grew madly wide as the skin tautened. Scooter could not look away from them. The eyes rolled wildly as the graying tail flopped, as a gaunt hind leg kicked feebly, then fixed on Scooter, and he watched the light in them fade until it was gone.

What remained was coarse-furred parchment stretched over bone.

The howling continued in the hills.

Scooter looked up at the thing his music had made. He could *feel* it, was in some way attuned with it.

And what he felt was hunger. Hunger, rage, violence, pain, a need for satisfaction that was a primal scream of yearning.

His hunger, *his* rage, *his* pain, *his* need.

The smoky tendril lifted from the dessicated husk that, not a minute ago, had been a living animal.

Deep within the thing, a redness pulsed.

Scooter backed up a step as the thing rose in the air. His calf swept into the amp, knocked it over, sent out a grating screech of feedback. Scooter glanced at it, looked quickly back to the thing.

It drifted toward him.

He ducked out of the guitar strap, dropped the guitar (crash of open notes and howl of feedback, sustained cry of a banshee), fled down the slope, slipped on gravel, slid, tumbled forward, came up (pant leg torn, gravel scraping open the flesh at the side of the knee, just like Dennis, just like him), looked back over his shoulder—

It came over the rise, dark and wanting.

—looked away, ran for his bike, swung cut leg over banana seat, tried to pedal away but couldn't—

The kickstand, goddamn, the *kickstand!*

—reversed the pedals, nudged the kickstand up with his heel, and pedaled down the long incline as fast as he could.

He looked back over his shoulder. It was there, and

gaining, this impossible, frightening mass of dark light following him down Monaghie Drive. Scooter leaned forward and put his back into it. The wind flung back his hair, hurled dirt in his eyes. He was doing forty miles an hour by the time he stopped pedaling and leaned into the first curve. The back tire jolted on a pebble; Scooter nudged the bike to compensate, fought for control, won, and resumed pedaling down the slope.

The curves here were gentle, the slope less steep; there were no cars and few obstacles in the road. Scooter hurtled past abandoned Crescent Hills on his right, the Canyon Overlook on his left. He wanted to look over his shoulder to see if the thing was still there but was terrified to look away from the road at this speed. One branch, one patch of gravel, one section of crumbled asphalt, and he would go down and not get up.

His palms were slick on the upturned handlebars.

He was cold sober now. Fear had chased away the alcohol; instinct and epinephrine won out over Jack Daniel's.

He negotiated the gentle curves, still pedaling, still accelerating in his downhill flight, the city spread out below him. He was panting. His chest felt constricted, as if the muscles were reluctant to work. Red tinged the edges of his vision.

There were cars and tight curves coming up in a few hundred yards, and he knew he had to slow down. He squeezed the right handbrake, but at this speed it had little effect. He squeezed tighter, heard it hissing behind him, then gripped the left brake.

He slowed.

Rounding a sharp left bend, he glanced back.

It was ten feet away.

He gasped, turned back, put on a fresh burst of

speed—his thighs were tightening now—leaned as he rounded the corner—

—and hit gravel. He felt the back tire go out from under him and knew there was no way he could recover. He turned the handlebars a little to the left and "stood" on the pedals, riding the bike in a power slide. A rusting Porsche with smashed-in windows loomed ahead of him; he let go, straightened, and "walked" off—left foot coming off the pedal to brace him, right still firm, the sole of his left shoe skidding a few feet on the pavement, gaining purchase, and he let the bike slide away from him. He fell, rolled, hit his back against the rear tire of the Schwinn as it rammed into the Porsche, and felt his insides lock up as the wind was knocked out of him. Mouth working like a fish out of water, Scooter tried to force himself to take in a breath.

He tried to get up as the thing neared, but couldn't. He scrabbled back as he watched its approach, thinking to squeeze himself beneath the car.

It swept by him and continued down the road.

Even in his pain and fear Scooter could feel it—a brush of presence against his mind. It wanted, it hungered.

Something relaxed and Scooter took in a rasping breath. Wincing at the pain in his back, he forced himself to stand and stepped away from the bike. He looked down the road and caught a glimpse of the thing as it rounded a corner, moving slower now.

Feeling numb, he went back to the bike, pulled it away from the Porsche, and examined it. The left pedal was bent, the handlebars were slightly askew, and the tape was scraped away on the left side. He rolled it and looked at the wheels; they were unbent. He'd gotten off lucky.

Scooter began to tremble violently and felt his eyes brim with tears. He shook his head rapidly, fighting for control. It's gone, he told himself. Whatever it was, it's gone now.

But he had felt it brush his mind, its presence like a tumor, and he knew what it wanted.

It wanted Roxanne.

He thought of the coyote collapsing inward as it was drained of life, the light fading in its eyes, the pain in its scream.

And he had made this thing, had created it with the rage of his music.

Scooter's eyes widened and he felt another pang in his chest.

What you make belongs to you. That old man—he'd known. He had tried to warn him, but Scooter had been too ignorant to listen. And in his ignorance he had made this *thing,* the product of rage, of pain and loss, the embodiment of a need that wanted only to be filled.

He had to find Roxanne before it did, and he hadn't any idea where she might be. It would search for her; he had felt that. It would not be satisfied until it found her. Scooter had to find help, someone who knew about this kind of shit, someone who could tell him how to fight it.

What you make belongs to you. He thought he knew where that help might lie.

He mounted the bike, trying to ignore the pain in his lower back, his scraped leg, his thighs, and he began to pedal.

He had an hour of daylight left.

Anyone less desperate would have turned left at Crescent Canyon. Left led down into the valley, to the world Scooter knew and understood.

Right led down deeper into the Borderlands.

He stopped briefly at the intersection of the two roads. He glanced down at the city, though the view was not good from here, and let out a long breath. He looked right, where the way down was steeper and more winding.

Someone had nailed three hand-painted signs to a telephone pole on his side of the street, near the concrete pole supporting the defunct traffic signal. In fluorescent red letters against white-painted wood, they read:

HAUNTED FOREST!

ENTER AT YOUR OWN RISK!

I'D GO BACK
IF I WERE YOU!

"Very funny," said Scooter.
And turned right.

An organism does not require more than the most rudimentary awareness in order to need. Plants need sunlight, ants need chemical trails to form worker lines to food, infants are born with primal needs that will not abate until either they are satisfied or the infant is dead.

It needed, and to satisfy that need it retraced the path marked by its creator during the day. It coursed slowly down Crescent Canyon. On Derrida it picked up speed and headed west.

It came upon a man taking his evening jog with his Doberman pinscher. The dog sensed it well before it was on them and turned on its chain, snapping, growling guttural warnings, baring its fangs. The man turned, saw it gliding toward them, and froze in fear. His dog strained at the leash, but the man pulled it closer.

It sensed them, and sensed that they were not what it needed. It would need to feed soon, but not yet. It passed them by.

At Scene of the Crime it paused, circled the block of shops once, and stopped at the barred back door.

Home.

It went past the door and inside. The rooms were dimly lit with its dull glow of brooding browns and deep reds.

There was nothing here, and it left.

Tommy Lee headed toward the front doors of The Factory to open them for the evening. The crowd waited outside, louder than usual tonight.

Tommy Lee stopped at a scream from outside. He had once seen a man gut-shot, and the agonized bellow that had come from the man had been nothing next to this.

Something came through the door. It looked like a fucking *stormcloud*, squeezed into an amorphous shape that pulsed with an inner life, sometimes flaring deep inside. Tommy Lee had seen some weird shit in his life, especially in the last half-dozen years, but he'd never seen *anything* like this.

It hovered there for a few seconds, then came toward him. Tommy Lee raised his bludgeon, then found himself wondering what, exactly, he was going to hit. He kept the club raised and waved his other hand. "Get outta here!" he said, feeling foolish. "Go on, get outta here!"

The thing advanced on him.

He backed up. One of the waitresses—Sheila—screamed.

Not looking away from the thing, Tommy Lee told her to shut up.

Marti appeared from the generator room, wiping her hands on her ever-present rag. "Whoa," she said mildly.

Still walking backward, Tommy Lee glanced back at her. He looked back at the thing, still advancing.

He was beside Marti now, near the door to the generator room.

His back pressed against the wall.

They watched it approach the door to the generator room, which Marti had closed but not locked. It paused before the sign, as if reading it, then disappeared into the door without a sound.

Marti and Tommy Lee exchanged a look.

"Heat lightning," she suggested.

"Right."

She shrugged and gestured at the door handle.

"Shit," said Tommy Lee, and opened the door.

It hovered near the generator. Tommy Lee entered, followed by Marti, who ran forward. "Hey," she shouted. "Hey, you leave that alone!"

It settled over the generator.

They watched for another minute, until it rose from the generator and left the same way it had come in. Tommy Lee dashed ahead of it and opened both of the tall wooden doors. People were shouting outside; it got louder when the thing glided out among them.

A body lay by the front door. It hardly looked human: the sockets around the eyes were hollow, the hands were skeletal, the skin paper thin over bone. It was mummified, grotesque. Its mouth was frozen open in a scream.

A young woman—spiked hair, torn T-shirt, riding boot on left foot, right foot bare—crouched next to her dirty Malamute. She stood quickly and grabbed her dog by the spiked collar when it bolted, barking, and felt metal slice across her palm. "Jesus *fucking* Christ!"

People ran. It showed no indication that it was even aware the crowd existed, but continued west, stronger now.

Despite the coming of night, Scooter pressed on. The farther he went, the weirder it got. He nearly turned back, once, when something the size of a station wagon leaped across the road in front of him. But it had ignored him, disappearing into the brush and crashing away until he could no longer hear it, leaving no evidence that it had been there at all.

It was dark now, but the moon was up, half full, and he could still see, a bit. He had gotten down Crescent before dark and without further incident, which he had been worried about, since the twisting road was in bad repair—in no repair at all, in fact. There had been mud and rockslides, and there were many cars rusting away along the road. But he had managed to get by them all and was now well past Sunett. As far as he could tell, the place still looked the same, despite its abandonment. As he crossed the boulevard the silhouettes of giant billboards rose to his right; to the left he saw what might have been torchlight in the distance.

It was difficult to maintain any speed with the left pedal bent as it was, but he felt he was making perhaps fifteen miles an hour. From what few tales he'd heard of the Borderlands, his pace might get him across in three or four hours. But the bike was gradually growing harder to pedal, as if it were being steadily shifted into lower and lower gears.

Scooter's thigh muscles felt swollen, massive, and

leaden. His lower back throbbed; his right knee burned from the gravel scrape. His stomach growled, and he had to stop and get off to throw up on the road. All he'd put in his stomach today had been half a loaf of bread and close to half a bottle of Jack Daniel's. He was thirsty, and now the taste of vomit made it worse.

A cry cut the night, and on his hands and knees Scooter looked up from the puddle before him. Something dark, not lit by the moon, with wings that flapped with a deep sound of unfurling sails, something the size of a Cessna, spread talons and landed atop a billboard advertising a movie that was coming soon.

Scooter got on his bike and tried to make like a cat. But then again, maybe it liked cats.

He pedal onward.

Years from now Mrs. Hernandez would tell her grandchildren—a generation more familiar with miracles, who yawned at impossibilities—about the living cloud that demolished the trader's heaven. She would tell them, sitting in her ancient La-Z-Boy recliner, about how she had been rushing to leave the building, and how worried she was because it was nearly dark and she had stayed to gossip and gab much later than was smart. She was walking up the escalator to leave from the second floor, where it was brighter, and she saw it gliding through the glass doors like an angry ghost, silently, seething with colors. Her grandchildren braided glowcotton into their hair as she described her fear and wonder. They glanced at one another as she told how it had enveloped the person closest to it, a man pushing a cart of goods who had stopped to watch when it entered the mall. She told them about the screams—screams of an adult turned into a baby by his terror, screams that came to her, sometimes, in her sleep. The man had fallen to his knees and began clawing at his face. The few people remaining in the mall came rushing up the escalator. Mrs. Hernandex watched the man—who had traded her an envelope of powdered milk for a loaf of bread only an hour ago—bat at the intangible lights surrounding him. She wanted to turn away, to cover her ears from the screams, but the man saw her and held out a hand to her for help. She had prayed to God every day since then, thinking herself surely damned—because she had not helped him. She had watched his flesh sink down to bone, watched the life fading from his eyes, watched the eyes drained of color as the ghost took his soul and left behind a husk. Slipping into and out of English (which her grandchildren were used to), she told how the windows had blown out, even from the skylights at the top of the huge building, and the way the floor had rumbled.

And then Gramma Hernandez would end as she always did, telling them to behave, to be good children who were always polite to elders like Gramma, or the ghost might come back after them.

And of course the children laughed and rolled their eyes at one another, liking their grandmother very much 'cuz she was such a weird old lady who told such great stories, and they'd go out to play Vanish the Rabbit, leaving Gramma to sit in her recliner and stare at the cracked and water-stained ceiling, wondering just how much her memories had become embroidered by time.

The bike had stopped working. The pedals wouldn't turn. Scooter coasted to a stop, swung off, and turned it upside down. He tried to turn the pedals, but they wouldn't budge.

"Okay," he said. He stood and looked around. On the right side of the road the sidewalk was broken into large chunks where tendril-like vines had forced their way past. One particularly long vine, thick as Scooter's arm, wound up a speed-limit sign.

There was something strange about the telephone poles. They extended horizontal spokes at irregular places along their tall lengths. Scooter looked back the way he had come and saw that on both sides of the road the telephone and light poles had these spokes, but that they diminished in length and frequency the farther back they went, until in the distance the spokes disappeared altogether and the poles looked like normal poles.

He looked back at the poles near him. Somehow, behind him, they had lost the wires that had once been strung atop them.

Cars were veined by some kind of crawling vine.

In the distance he saw an irregular shape the size of a building.

Scooter sighed. Shit—now he would have to walk through the night. He preferred to spend as little time as possible on his little odyssey; the deeper into the Borderlands he ventured, the more alien it became. He couldn't imagine what might lie on the other side.

But he wouldn't find out unless he got moving. Scooter began to walk, regretfully leaving his bicycle behind.

It paused at the entrance to the lobby of the Holiday Inn. Sensing the route of Scooter's day had brought it here. These were the places Scooter had searched for what he desired; these were the places it sought out.

There was life inside. The last place had had life inside, and it had fed, storing energy for what might be a long search. It was patient—at least, it was incapable of impatience—and as long as there was sustenance, it could seek.

It went through the glass.

Around it were voices. It knew voices because they were sound, and sound was part of its composition.

"Freddy, god*damn*—you see that?"

"See what?"

"Oh, Freddy, don't fuck with me, man. Really, don't you—"

And someone screamed, a white sound tinged with violet, colors it recognized, colors that had been elements of its genesis.

It stayed for over an hour. They threw things at it, things that went through it, things it was oblivious to. One of the things was a bottle that smashed against the window and cracked the plate glass, leaving behind diamond-white pinpoints of sound that left behind slowly fading afterimages of bright red.

"Hey, don't make it mad, asshole," and that was a tight sine-wave of deep blue.

"Shee-it," said a new voice. "I'm leavin'." And that was a rumble of green.

Finally it left, heading back the way it had come.

The telephone poles had grown limbs. As he had walked on, the limbs had forked, the forks had lengthened, the lengths had sprouted branches, the branches sprouted twigs, the twigs sprouted leaves, the number of leaves had grown.

The telephone poles had become a row of trees.

The asphalt had grown crumbly, and grass had begun to grow through it. The grass grew longer and more abundant, the road grew harder to distinguish beneath it, the asphalt had been broken up into dark pebbles in the vitalic grass.

The path had become pebbles in a tree-lined, grassy road.

The vines veining automobiles had thickened. They had grown into webbing encasing the cars, with only a few glimmerings of moonlight on glass or metal to prove that anything was still under there, had grown mottled and faintly luminous like some carpet-thick fungus, had grown thicker still.

What had been cars lining a street were now amorphous hedges near tall trees on a grassy path.

The night had grown brighter with silver light. The moon had thickened, waxed, grown full, become blemished rather than pockmarked, smudged rather than blemished, smooth rather than smudged, and had raised from near the horizon to directly overhead.

What had been a low half-moon with a cratered face was now a high, silver disk in the night sky.

Scooter looked for Orion, Cassiopeia, and the Big Dipper—the only three constellations he knew. He couldn't find them.

When he finally reached the building-sized, irregular shape, it startled him so much that he stood staring at it for ten minutes.

It had been a Bank of America building of steel and glass. It still was, after a fashion—but a tree had grown around it. Huge, many-limbed, gnarled, fringed with thick, ugly, spade-shaped leaves, the tree encased the building like an hallucinogenic vision of an octopus hugging a dollhouse.

Moonlight glinted from glass shards between tree limbs thick as most tree trunks, and Scooter thought it was hard to tell whether it was a tree that had grown around a building or a building that had been constructed within a gargantuan, hydralike tree.

Miles later Scooter sat in the fragrant grass at the side of the road and massaged his legs. He tried to ignore the sounds from . . . from the *woods* around him—screams like tortured cats, like starving babies, hissings of things slithering through long grasses, loud crunchings of heavy things with long strides, and, once, a faint murmur like children chanting.

Scooter was getting tired. He needed water, would need food soon, and was terrified that he might have to lie down to sleep for a few hours. He lay back in the grass, let out a long breath, and shut his eyes.

Roxanne stepped out from behind a tree. In her hand she held his Les Paul. Color darted about her head, formed a halo, dispersed, coalesced into a crown. He threw a whiskey bottle at her and she looked sad. The colors vanished and she turned away and headed back into the woods.

"Roxanne! Roxanne, wait!"

His shout woke him up. He sat up, heart pounding in his ears.

Something the size of a dog, hairless and slick looking, with cat eyes and hands like a tree frog, was sniffing at his feet.

He shot to his feet and let out a sound: *"Hnnnn-aahhh!"*

The thing made a loud snoring noise at him, then turned and loped away.

Scooter swallowed the knotted sock in his throat.

No sleep. Not yet. Later. Big, fluffy pillows, soft feather bed, warm blanket, all waiting at the end of the road. Promise. Cross my heart, hope to die.

He walked on.

*   *   *

Home again.

At Scene of the Crime it hovered above the air mattress, operating at a low level of energy, patient, searching but not moving. Scooter had come back here, it sensed, had gone from room to room, had stayed in this one spot for several hours. Attuned to Scooter, sensitive to the traces of its maker, it drifted from room to room, pausing, hovering before the remaining two guitars, lighting the room with itself, now settling above the bed because this was where Scooter had settled. It had no sense of the order of events of Scooter's day, merely an ability to feel his former *presence* in a place, to—know—that he had been here, had moved from this spot to that, had stayed in this spot for *this* long.

At this lowered energy level the hunger, the need, was not so strong. But it would move again, and the need would be there.

It would also need to feed.

Scooter's body won the fight with his mind; it was either find a place to sleep or drop where he was.

He climbed a tree, one of those that had evolved from telephone poles during the course of his long walk.

Arm muscles and lower back fairly screamed as he jumped up, grabbed a thick, low limb, and hoisted himself up. He swung a leg across and sat in the crotch, back against the rough bole, legs dangling on either side of the limb.

Something toad-sized squawked beside him; he brushed it away without bothering to look at it, then wiped the blade of his hand dry against his now-filthy jeans.

He shut his eyes and slept.

*   *   *

*He stood atop Monaghie with his guitar across his belly.
The valley was a sea of people—sell-out crowd, SRO. He held
the guitar high and a cheer went up, a cheer that came from so
many throats it sounded like the roar of a hurricane, and he
jumped from the knoll with his guitar held out before him like
a shield, and their upturned faces rose before him as he fell.
He felt a deep happiness, knowing that they loved him, that
they would catch him, but as he neared their faces grew
clearer, and expressions he had thought were adoring resolved
into horrified, open-mouthed looks, and fingers pointed up—
"Look: he jumped! He jumped!" Happiness became terror as
he realized that they weren't going to catch him at all, that they
were fleeing from the spot where they saw he would land—*

Scooter woke up feeling awful. He had slept poorly.
His neck was stiff; his legs throbbed; his back felt
branded.

He got out of the tree by the simple expedient of
losing his grip and falling. He lay on the grass where
he landed, feeling and flexing to see if anything was
broken. He was almost disappointed to find that nothing was; it meant he could get up and walk.

He did, albeit slowly.

He remembered a line of Peter Gabriel's as his muscles gradually loosened into the task of walking again.
We get so strange across the border. Yeah, that fit—though
he didn't feel strange at all. What he felt was thirsty,
hungry, sore, dirty, smelly, and emotionally numb. The
only relief he got was when he emptied his bladder
beside a tree.

It was the Borderlands that got stranger as he went.
Stranger and then more normal, in a sense: by day he
saw that he was in woodlands, surrounded by high
conifers and hardwoods. His calves parted long strands
of yellow-green grass with faint hissing sounds as he

walked. A cloud of butterflies rose ahead of him, fluttering yellow and black-edged wings that looked like back-to-back capital Bs.

Scooter turned around, squinted, and raised a shielding hand to his forehead. All he could see of what had been city was a faint patch at the foot of the hills, a slim line of gray that graded toward him into green. He had covered a lot of ground last night.

Hell, he had walked to another world.

After a mile or so he smelled something—something unidentifiable yet fresh, a cool something. . . .

He realized it was moisture in the air—he smelled water.

After a little searching he found it—a narrow stream loosely paralleling the path, zigzagging like the medical chart of a recovering patient. He knelt at the bank and sniffed, reflected sunlight leaving electric afterimages that followed his gaze.

The water smelled all right—not that he would have the faintest notion what "bad" water smelled like—but had a reddish tinge. He thought about typhoid fever. Were there mosquitoes around here?

Rhythmic lapping caught his attention. A hundred yards ahead, a deer had lowered its head and was drinking. Its dark brown eye looked to be watching him, but he couldn't tell.

He put both hands in. The water was cool. He scrubbed left hand with right, right with left, brought them out, wrung them, cupped, lowered his head, and began ladling water into his mouth.

He had never known that water tasted so damn good.

At his splashings the doe had darted off. Scooter didn't even notice. He could feel the cool water tunneling its way into his stomach and cautioned himself not to drink so much or so fast that he got sick.

He splashed his face, and it felt so good he decided hell with it, he'd take a frigging *bath*. The water was clear and shallow; the stream wasn't very wide, and it didn't seem likely that there were any local versions of piranha waiting to turn him into shredded beef. He scrubbed himself with torn-off clumps of grass, hissing as he washed his scabbed knee. The wound did not look infected, and that was something, anyhow.

Feeling about seven hundred times better, Scooter emerged from the stream and squeegeed himself with the blade of his hand. He hung his clothes across his left shoulder, tied his shoelaces together, and draped his basketball shoes around his neck, then basked in the feel of sunlight drying his body, of soft grasses sliding beneath the soles of his feet.

A boy stood by a tree, watching him.

Scooter froze, realizing that the boy had been watching him for a while now. He was thin, with long hair the color of wet ashes. His eyes were large and arctic blue. He was barefoot and unclothed, young enough that pubic hair had not yet grown around his genitals. His penis was uncircumcised.

For all of that, Scooter could not really tell if he was human.

He made himself smile.

The boy blinked.

Scooter extended a hand, fingers spread.

The boy shifted his hip, weight on back leg, front foot poised, as though ready to spring away at any moment. Scooter was reminded of the doe.

"Hey," he said.

The boy darted away.

Scooter blinked rapidly. He didn't think a human being could move that fast.

Maybe they couldn't.

He waited, but the boy did not return. Finally he shrugged and continued his southward journey.

In the morning it lifted from the air mattress, went to the black curtains—Scooter had left them open and sunlight muted the thing's dim glow—drifted across the room and into the bathroom, and hovered there for a few minutes.

Seething browns and reds reflected in the bathroom mirror. It drifted into the book room, through the doorway into the studio (left and right portions of it passing through the wall itself), and finally through the front glass and out into daylight.

It glided slowly east on Derrida. This time no one saw it pass.

Along the way it fed on a dog and a wild cat.

At Crescent Canyon it turned right, heading up into the hills.

Scooter was aware of being shadowed. He couldn't have said how he knew this, for no untoward sounds came from the woods, and he had not glimpsed the boy or anything else other than insects, birds, and another deer. But he was being stalked, and he felt it.

He had debated following the stream, figuring there was a good chance that sooner or later he would come across a community built near it. But he had decided to follow the path, since it *was* a path—it probably led somewhere.

After a few miles he could stand it no longer. He stopped walking and turned to face the row of trees. The wind blew through them with a waterfall sound. "All right," he said. "Why don't you just come out?"

He waited.

"Look, I know you're following me. I ain't gonna hurt you."

He listened hard, scanning the trees for signs of movement.

"Fine," he said. "Have it your way." He turned to resume walking.

The boy stood on the path in front of him, ten feet away. Scooter hadn't heard a sound. The boy watched him warily, still looking as if he would bolt at any sudden or suspicious movement.

Scooter kept still. "I'm looking for your people," he said. "Do you understand me?"

The boy cocked his head to one side. On the path, in the direct light, his eyes were an amazing blue.

"Do you understand me?" Scooter repeated. "I'm looking for your people. I need help." He searched his memory for the old man's name. Noo-nee something? A "w" in it somewhere, near the end. . . . "Aune'wah!" he said suddenly. "Aune'wah—understand? I'm looking for the old one, Aune'wah. Grim. Do you understand Grim?"

The boy frowned.

Aune'wah's son, the boy he had seen the other day on Monaghie. What was his name? Grim had mentioned it. A lot of "a" sounds in it, and strange stops. A "k" . . . Arkin? No, no—and he said it as he remembered it: "Aarka'an." He stumbled over the glottal stop separating the last two syllables, then said it again more accurately: "Aarka'an. Aune'wah. Can you take me to them?"

"Aarka'an," said the boy.

"Yeah, yeah—Aarka'an! Can you take me to him? Can you help me?"

"Inee Aarka'an kevesh't omaay. Oomani Aarka'an?"

Scooter shook his head, a finger going to his ear. "I don't understand."

The boy pointed into the woods, toward where the stream ran. "Aarka'an," he said. He pointed at Scooter, then into the woods. "Aarka'an oomani."

Scooter nodded eagerly. He gestured for the boy to lead on, and the boy, skin so pale and milky in the sunlight, turned and walked into the woods. He moved much faster than Scooter could, and he didn't make a sound.

Scooter followed.

At the knoll on Monaghie it tasted the flavors of electric colors, felt the traces of the scathing sheets of sound and keening notes that had so recently been given form here. It brushed by the husk of the coyote it had fed on yesterday—so drained that not even flies buzzed around it—and tasted the traces of the rage that had created it. This was the birthing place, the place where rage and loss and need had formed music and given it shape.

It sped down the road, hurtled past the empty houses, and wound quickly along the curves.

It enveloped the smashed form of a Porsche by the side of the road, and there tasted the dark-shifting oranges that were the traces of pain. A few minutes later it lifted, continued to the intersection of Monaghie and Crescent Canyon, waited where Scooter had waited, as if reading the signs itself.

HAUNTED FOREST!

It turned right, heading deeper into the Borderlands. Forces were different in this place, and it drew energy from the fabric of reality around it now. The further into the Borderlands it went, the stronger it felt.

There was a trace here, too, of what it sought.

The need strenghtened, the hunger grew.

There were no buildings, no streets, no structures of any kind that he could see—but it was a community. It was populated by more of the boy's kind—a tall, thin, white-skinned people with long, tapering, sensitive ears and large, almond-shaped eyes.

The boy led Scooter past a group of adults sitting in a circle on the grass. They were chanting in low voices. To Scooter's ear it sounded arrhythmic and dissonant. The chant was disturbing, belied by the smiling faces of the chanters. Most of them were nude; some wore clothes; some of these were blue jeans and T-shirts.

They stopped chanting and stared as Scooter walked by.

Sitting with his back against the smooth gray bole of a tree the size of a sequoia was an old man faced by a semicircle of children. He seemed to be teaching them how to weave baskets out of some material that glittered in places. Scooter did a double take when he saw that the old man was using no fibers or strands or straws to make the basket; he merely weaved with his pale, thin, big-jointed hands, and the basket took shape from his fingers as though woven from the air itself.

He stopped his weaving and stared with bright, hooded eyes as Scooter passed by.

Human clothing seemed much more prevalent among the young.

Two girls with cotton-white hair stood high on the thick branch of a tree, stick fighting with the thigh bones of a large animal.

A woman wearing a loincloth pointed her finger at a

gray rabbit standing on its rear paws near a clump of thorny bushes. The rabbit stood still while she approached, knelt before it, and passed a hand over its head to put it to sleep. The woman turned the rabbit onto its back and began skinning it with a Gerber hunting knife.

Wider and deeper here, the stream cut through this part of the woods. Two men—one of them fat, one of them skeletal, one of them brilliantly whiteheaded, the other dull gray, both with hair reaching near their buttocks—reclined by the bank, conversing in their vowel-rich language. Two cane poles were thrust into the bank ahead of them. One of the lines began swinging slightly in the water, then was tugged sharply, curling the tip of the pole. The thin man glanced at it, made a casual, beckoning gesture, and the pole flung itself back to land a small bass on the bank beside them, flopping in mercurial flashes beside the still forms of other fish.

Despite his incredulousness, Scooter's stomach growled.

Near a huge tree Scooter's guide stopped and pointed. Ahead, a group of adolescents was clustered around the trunk. They held wood chisels against it and pounded them with Black and Decker hammers. They seemed to be carving a figure into the tree.

"Aarka'an," said Scooter's guide. And ran away like a gazelle.

Without the boy, Scooter felt awkward, panicky, alien. This was their world, not his, and he didn't understand half of what he saw.

He walked nearer to the young men and women shaping the tree trunk and cleared his throat. They stopped and turned to stare at him.

One of them was perhaps seventeen years old. The tips of her ears poked up past hair colored copper that fell to a waist almost thin enough to span with both hands, a waist that flared around hips to frame a white tuft at her genitals. She was milky-skinned, strong-jawed, pale eyed, and the most beautiful woman Scooter had ever seen. She stared back at him unblinkingly, frankly, and Scooter felt his face grow hot.

He looked away at a voice, and it was a moment before he realized that it had spoken English. "You are the guitar player."

Crow-colored hair, bristly on one side, lenghtening to touch the pronounced collarbone on the other, blue jeans, long-toed bare feet, hammer in slim, long-nailed hand, he regarded Scooter with eyes like balls of black glass.

"Yeah . . ."

For no reason he could account for, Scooter found the group frightening.

Over Aarka'an's shoulder Scooter glimpsed a carved patch of trunk. It looked like . . . a hand?

"You are looking for the woman, I think," said the boy. "Arrux'ayann? She got here yesterday."

"No, I came to find your—" He stopped. Arrux'ayann?

His pulse quickened. "Roxanne?" he asked. "Roxanne; she's here? She came here?"

(*Don't try to find me,* she had written. *Because you won't.*)

"Yesterday. You can't see her, though. She asked sanctuary."

"Why not?" asked Scooter. "I *have* to—"

"I told you. She asked sanctuary." Pale lids lowered on eyes so black that Scooter could not distinguish pupils. "She has many skills to offer us."

"Your—your father," said Scooter. "He came to me, he came across the Borderlands to find me. To warn me about something. I have to see him. Can I talk to him?"

"He told you about your music," said Aarka'an.

"Yeah, he—"

"I know what he said." There was no mistaking the contempt in his tone. "He is both right and wrong."

"Something's happened," said Scooter. "I—I played my guitar in the hills, where you saw me the other day. I . . . I made something, something I think is looking for Roxanne. I think it'll keep looking until it finds her. I think it will kill her when it does. It'll come here."

The black eyes regarded him. Scooter could not read the boy's expression.

"Please," he said. "I need help."

They were all looking at him blankly. Finally Aarka'an handed his hammer and chisel to the boy next to him. "I'll take you to him," he said.

Scooter felt something unknot in his chest. "Thank you," he said.

Aarka'an stepped away from the tree, and Scooter stared.

Carved into the bole was a face, a contorted face with open mouth and clenched eyes, with lines of agony drawn in at the cheeks and the corners of the eyes. Fingers curled outward; lines of palm seemed to be emerging. It looked like a man embedded in a tree, frozen in the midst of trying to claw his way out.

It was horrible.

"What . . . ?" asked Scooter, then stopped. He wasn't sure he wanted to know.

But Aarka'an had read the question, and he smiled. "That?" he asked. He looked at his friends, and they returned his smile. He looked back at Scooter. "A joke," he said. "A prank."

And they laughed.

It paused at the upturned bicycle in the road, enveloped it, tasted the magenta of frustration. The forces around it affected it the way fresh air affected a man emerging from a smoke-filled room. It drank it in, was sustained, invigorated, replenished.

It left the bike and continued along the road that turned to grass lined by telephone poles that turned to trees and cars that became clumps of bush, heading toward the fusion of bank building and Yggdrasill tree.

Aarka'an paused beside a huge, willowlike tree with fronds so dense that Scooter could not see the trunk within. He glanced at Scooter, clapped his hands once, and let out a high, wavering note, then held a section of willow frond aside and gestured for Scooter to enter.

The old man sat inside, coyote eyes and brushed-aluminum hair faintly luminous in the dimness. The dense, drooping fronds formed a dome about them, cool with shade.

The old man sat in a natural chair formed by a curve of root emerging from the earth near the trunk of the great tree. His hands were held ahead and to either side of his face, arched with tension. Something flickered between them, some thin strand of luminescence that his eyes reflected.

He looked up when Aarka'an entered behind Scooter and moved the section of frond back to curtain the sunlight. He brought his hands together, turned palm against palm, and made a casting-away motion. When he separated his hands again, there was nothing between them, nothing held in them.

He said something in a low voice. He did not seem surprised to see Scooter.

Scooter looked questioningly at Aarka'an. The boy nodded at his father—whom he looked nothing like, whom he looked, in fact, with his jet-black hair and eyes, the opposite of—and translated. " 'What you make belongs to you,' " he said. " 'What have you made?' "

"You know," said Scooter, ignoring Aarka'an as he translated. "Yeah, all right, I . . . I don't understand it, but I made something on Monaghie. It's dangerous. I think it wants to kill someone . . . someone I love. I just found out she's here, with you people." He brushed hair out of his eyes. "I want to know if I can fight this thing, how I can fight it."

He waited for Aarka'an to finish.

The old man nodded and rubbed his smooth chin— they didn't seem to grow facial hair—with a long-nailed, long-fingered hand. He spoke.

" 'When you made your music,' " translated Aarka'an, " 'what were you thinking? What did you feel?' "

Scooter took in a deep breath and held it, remembering, then let it out. "My girlfriend left me. I—I didn't know it was coming, you know? I was hurt, but I was mad." He shook his head. "No, that's not strong enough. I wanted to tear things up, to break things. Oh, man, I wanted to scream until my lungs ripped open. I wanted to hit her, but at the same time all I wanted was for her to come back. I wanted to understand why she left me." He shrugged. "There's lots more, but I don't know how to put it into words."

Aune'wah asked a question of his son and nodded at the lengthy reply. He leaned back in his root chair, staring at a space above Scooter's head. Scooter shot a questioning look at Aarka'an, but the boy put a warning finger to his lips and shook his head.

The old man began to speak. Sometimes he used his hands for emphasis, curling them before his face as though something invisible rested there, brushing one to the side as if declining an offer. Scooter waited for the boy to translate, but he did not. He listened, nodded, interrupted once to ask a question, fell silent again while his father continued. Finally the old man was done and the boy turned to Scooter. "It is very hard to translate," he said. "You don't have the words for a lot of what he said, and some of the things he takes for granted here don't work where you come from. But I'll try." He glanced at his father, said something brief, and the old man nodded. Aarka'an looked back at Scooter.

"You want to know what this thing is," he said, tone changing as he translated. "The answer is simple and complex. It is a part of you. It is the embodiment of your feelings. Around us"—the boy's tone changed—"this is one of those things that doesn't operate the same in your world"—and changed back—"around us is a world of forms, an invisible . . . *essence* of things. There are ways of giving them shape, of bringing them into the world our senses can perceive. Music is one of these ways. Among us, a musician is a brave and foolish person." The boy hesitated a moment, glanced at his father, and looked back. "I should add," he said, more conversationally, "that some of this is pointed at me, because the main reason I cross the Borderlands is to make music. On your side it's just music."

"You're a musician?" asked Scooter.

"Not in the way you understand. I'll explain later; let me translate first."

Scooter nodded for him to go on.

"The musician takes a feeling," he continued, voice somehow assuming the more authoritative air of his father, "or a thought that exists inside him, and gives it a form that exists in the ear of another. That is the music. But there is a form that exists apart from the music, that is given a life by the feeling that . . . that engenders it. Is that the right word?"

Scooter shrugged. "I guess so."

The boy pursed his lips. "The musician must be careful what he or she plays, because he or she"—he frowned—"we have a word that doesn't specify sex, but you don't—because he or she is responsible for what lives on after the music is complete. The forms music may take can blind, can kill, can lust, can feel anything the musician feels. You have created a thing that is a product of rage and desire. It is consumed with a need for satisfaction, for . . . for fulfillment, I guess is your word, that will never be contented. It is sent into the world to look for the woman you love, and to take from her. It will never be far behind her. There is no doubt that because she is here, it will soon be here as well." The boy hesitated. "He says that we cannot have this thing in our land, because it will stop at nothing to get what it needs. He—he repeats what he told you earlier: what you make is yours, musician. You must stop it."

"But that's why I'm here! I *want* to stop it; I came to ask his help. Tell me how; I'll do everything I can."

Aarka'an translated.

The old man leaned back in his chair of root, folded sharp-angled arms across thin, leather-vested chest, and looked thoughtful.

Scooter waited, full of questions, needing answers, and feeling impotent.

The old man got up slowly, stepped down from the root, and approached Scooter. He stopped in front of him and looked into his eyes. Scooter found himself wanting to look away, to say something to Aarka'an, to turn and run—anything but meet that gaze. But he didn't look away.

He had the goddamnedest eyes.

The irises were bright, the lines radiating from pupil dark. They looked like fractured ice under bright moonlight. The wrinkled lids narrowed, wrinkled forehead furrowed, a nail came up to scratch roughly under the vest.

He turned to Aarka'an, and they talked.

"Aarka'an, I have heard this Man play, but in his world, not here. You have heard him play in the Borderlands, where his music takes shape. You have seen his music—you say he cannot understand us?"

"He doesn't know our language, Father."

The old man nodded. "I have been reluctant to allow anyone to mingle with his kind. They are concerned only with objects, they know nothing of forms."

"They make very good objects, Father."

"The world is filled with the dust and ashes of good objects. I only allow you to cross the Borderlands because you insist on making your ugly kind of music—"

"It is a good kind of music for me," the boy interrupted.

Aune'wah glared at him for interrupting, but responded to his words instead of ignoring them. "It is an ugly music. It loves nothing."

"It is a phase of my youth."

The old man snorted. "This discussion never changes between us. We will repeat it another time. I allow you to cross the Borderlands because there your music affects only the ears, and I do not grow concerned for what else it creates."

The boy sighed.

The old man disregarded this and looked at Scooter. "This one is different," he said. "He gives form to a thing inside him. He is a musician like our musicians."

"He used to be famous among Men, father."

"Mmm. He is important to me because he is the first

indication I have seen that Men may have something more to them than what I have perceived." He waved away the boy's objections before they were voiced. "I know you count men among your friends. You are young, Aarka'an."

"You are old, Father."

He turned away from Scooter. "And you are impudent!"

The boy looked down at his feet. "I . . . ask your forgiveness, Father."

"Ehh." He turned back to Scooter, who had grown alarmed at the shout, but who remained silent and respectful, afraid to offend them because he needed their help. "We cannot really help this Man because what he fights is a part of him. Therefore what he creates to combat it must come from within him. I cannot give him an answer, a method, a trick. That is what he seeks, and such a thing does not exist. There are things we can do, though." He walked a circle around Scooter, who stood almost at attention. "If he can defeat his work, I will be surprised. But if he does, I will consider allowing more dealings with men."

"Grim is a Man, Father," the boy ventured.

"Grim is an insane Man. Take a lesson from this naive Man's problem, Aarka'an. With your music, you could easily be in his place."

"Yes, Father," said the boy, without much conviction in his voice.

The old man glanced at his son and frowned. A problem for later, he decided. "Send runners out to watch the road and the stream. Tell them to look out for the thing. There will be no mistaking it, I am certain."

"Do you want them to look through the eyes of birds?"

"Deer, I think. If not, birds will do."

The boy nodded.

"Do you have your instrument near?" the old man asked. "What do they call it?"

"A guitar, Father. I have several."

"An ugly word. Get the one that makes music itself, the one without the vines that make it loud. Bring it and the other Man to that beautiful tree you and your friends are defiling. Yes, I think that would be an appropriate place. Before you go, tell him this, and I will take him there to make his stand. . . ."

Scooter endured it as patiently as he could. The old man had a tone that he found hypnotic and authoritative, and he had those *eyes.* But there was something about him that commanded respect, and Scooter kept quiet. Aarka'an seemed determined to show his father that he was old enough to do as he pleased, but he was obviously terrified of him.

In their conversation Scooter recognized only a few words—"man," "guitar," "Grim," their own names. Once they seemed to be arguing openly—about what, Scooter could only guess.

After what seemed like an hour, toward the end of which Scooter had begun glancing nervously over his shoulder as if he could sense the *thing* nearing behind him, the old man concluded what he was saying and Aarka'an turned to Scooter.

"I am going now," he said. "I will see you again. Do what my father indicates, and follow him where he leads you."

"He'll help me?" Scooter couldn't help the eager note that crept into his voice.

But the boy shook his head. "He can't. I can't tell you

why not. There are things we can do, and we'll do them, but this is your battle and not ours."

Scooter felt on the verge of tears. He wanted to shout, to tell them what selfish, uncaring animals they were, but he said nothing. Despite the magnitude of his problem, it wasn't *their* problem, and he didn't have the right to ask for help and complain when it was refused.

The boy watched Scooter grow angry, watched him calm as quickly. "I am to tell you a thing," he said. "You must think about it. All right?"

"Is this gonna be another fortune cookie like before? Like, 'What you make belongs to you'?"

"If you had thought about that," the boy replied without rancor, "none of this would be necessary."

Scooter nodded. "I'm sorry. I'm just . . . I'm scared, you know." He bit his lip, looked at his sneakers, looked back at the boy. In the darkness beneath the canopy of drooping fronds, Aarka'an's eyes looked like holes cut in the white paper of his face. "What are you supposed to tell me?"

The boy glanced at his father, looked back at Scooter. " 'To create a thing,' " he said, " 'is to suggest its opposite.' "

Scooter waited, but the boy said nothing more.

"That's it?" he asked.

The boy smiled. He did not have a pleasant smile. "It doesn't have to be long to mean something."

Scooter frowned. "All right. I'll think about it."

The boy nodded and said something to his father. The father replied with something brief. "I'm going now," said Aarka'an. "Follow him. Do what he says."

"I'll try," Scooter said, and hesitated. "Aarka'an?"

Black brows rose above hollow eyes.

"Your father—is he, you know, some kind of a king? I mean, a ruler, a chief, something like that?"

Aarka'an looked at his father, who watched their exchange as though he understood it. "He's my father," he said. He pulled aside a section of frond, stooped, and stepped out into daylight.

Scooter turned to look at the old man with the coyote eyes. "All right," he said. "What now?"

The old man smiled, and that was the only way in which he resembled his son.

They were back at the horrible tree. The old man pointed to a spot a dozen feet in front of the hideous carving and indicated that Scooter was to wait.

Scooter waited.

A crowd gradually formed. They made a wide ring around Scooter, open-ended on the tree side, and whispered among themselves. The younger ones seemed to mix English often with their own language. Scooter got the feeling they knew what he was doing here, perhaps knew more than he did—it wouldn't be difficult—but he tried to ignore them.

To make a thing is to suggest its opposite.

It was simple and infuriating. Yes, he understood that, if he could make that thing, he could make something that might counteract it, neutralize it in some way. But he had no idea how to *control* the making of such a thing—thought, in fact, that the very act of control might prevent the creation of such a thing. And he had nothing to create it *with*.

He looked up at a commotion in the crowd. Those in front of him were turned around, looking away. They moved to let something by.

A deer entered the circle.

The old man smiled at it, lowered to one knee and beckoned. The deer approached and lowered its head.

The old man stroked it a few times, whispering. Then he stood quickly and looked at Scooter.

In the light his irises were silver.

The deer snorted, turned, looked uncertain, then dashed out of the ring the way it had come in. The old man turned and called out. The crowd to the right of the hamadryad tree parted to admit three women. The two on the outside had an inner hand on the upper arm of the one in-between. At first Scooter thought she was short and heavy; he had already become accustomed to the generally tall and thin body type of these people. With a shock he realized that she was neither short nor heavy, that she was human, that she was—

"Roxanne!" He started toward her.

The old man whipped around and spoke a word. Scooter felt his feet slide out from under him and only just managed to break his fall with his hands. He whuffed and looked up. The old man smiled unpleasantly and shook his head.

Roxanne was nude, as were the two who flanked her. Both were a head taller than she was, small-breasted, long-necked, white-haired identical twins. Their strong hands gripped firmly around her biceps.

Roxanne craned to see past the old man. "Scooter? Scooter, what are you doing here?" She tried to get away from her escort, but they only gripped tighter.

They stopped in front of the old man.

"You gave me sanctuary," Roxanne said to him. "Why am I—"

The old man spoke, pointing at the hamadryad tree. Scooter stood as they led her to it. She started to struggle in earnest, but the one to her right leaned and whispered something in her ear. Roxanne frowned, looked frightened, and stopped struggling. Instead she looked back behind her. "Scooter? Scooter, what's going on? They said—"

They turned her around and put her back against the tree. Her head pressed against the tortured face caught fighting to escape. Scooter imagined the open mouth gnawing wooden teeth on the base of her skull.

They raised her arms to the wooden fingers groping for freedom. Aune'wah stepped in front of Scooter and he couldn't see what was happening, but the old man made patterns in the air with his hands and stepped away.

Wooden fingers clasped Roxanne's wrists.

Roxanne looked away from one bound arm. "Scooter? Goddammit, they gave me sanctuary! How did you find me? They said . . ." She glanced at the old man. "Scooter, what did you do? They said you came here to save me." She looked at one gripped wrist, looked away. "Tell them to let me go."

And he felt suddenly ashamed. "It was my music," he said, not looking at her. "I got drunk and went up to the hills." He looked at her sharply. "How come you aren't wearing any clothes?" He felt stupid even as he asked it.

"It's what they do here. I like it."

He nodded irrelevantly and looked away again. "You left. I looked all over the goddamn place, and I couldn't find you, and I didn't know what to *do*—" His voice broke. "I got a battery, and I went up on Monaghie and I just cranked, like I used to, and I was so mad—I *missed* you." He wiped his eyes, feeling foolish in front of everybody, while a part of him wondered how many of them understood. "I made this thing. It came from my music, the way the other lights always have. But it lasted after I was done, and it killed a dog, a coyote,

I mean. It chased me down the road, and I could *feel* it, Roxanne—it wanted you, it wanted to take you and, and—" He sniffled, made himself stop. "I came here to find help so I could stop it. The old man, he—"

The crowd parted again and Aarka'an stepped through holding an acoustic guitar. He hurried up to Scooter, nodding at his father as he passed by. "Listen," he said, shrugging out of the strap and handing it to Scooter, who accepted it automatically. "You have to hurry. I play it all the time; it's in tune. Here." He handed Scooter a pick that looked as if it was made of bone.

"What—I don't—"

The boy fluttered his hands. "Listen. Put it on, warm up, play scales, do whatever you have to do."

Scooter lifted the strap over his head, settled it onto his shoulder. "But I don't—"

A gasp at the edge of the crowd. Scooter turned to see them scattering, to see a shimmer of light approaching between the trees in the distance, following the edge of the stream, a dark blur in the air that grew.

The old man spoke.

"Turn around," ordered the boy.

"But I—"

"Turn around! Turn your back to it."

Scooter turned. A tickle began between his shoulder blades.

The old man spoke.

"Don't look back," said the boy. He glanced where Scooter was forbidden to look, black eyes wide, catching a glint of afternoon sun. "Look at her."

Scooter looked at Roxanne. She was looking behind him. "Scooter . . . ?"

The old man barked a word at her and she said nothing further. Scooter watched her throat work as she swallowed. He looked at the guitar he wore. It was a Yamaha cheapie, an inferior model, a shitbox. Playing this after playing his Martin would sound like the difference between a compact-disk player and a sewing needle held against a phonograph record turned by hand. His hand clasped, felt strings, rough to thin, against his fingers.

Automatically his other hand went to his mouth and put the pick there. He clamped it between his teeth, pressed its edge with his tongue. He brushed right hand against denimed thigh.

The old man spoke again, quickly.

"Tell her you love her," the boy said rapidly, backing away.

Scooter opened his mouth to speak, but the boy shook his head. "Tell her with your music," he said.

There was a shout, and Scooter heard people running. He started to glance back.

"Don't look! Play!"

His neck prickled. The skin of his skull felt tight.

Roxanne struggled to remain calm. "Scooter," she said, only a slight quaver in her voice, "I don't understand why they have to hold me here." She spoke more rapidly: "Please, Scooter, it's getting—"

"Be quiet and let him play," said the boy.

"I can't!" Scooter shouted. "I can't, I can't!"

His fingers moved.

"Let her go!" he screamed.

His vision blurred; he couldn't see Roxanne. Vision brightened, shimmered, and he realized it was not from tears. He looked down at the guitar.

His hands were making music. They played, and the air took shape in front of him.

From his right, calmly, Aarka'an said, "It's very close now."

Scooter played. He thought of the thing behind him, the thing he had made, the thing that wanted Roxanne, and he hated it, wanted it dead, wanted it drained the way it had drained the coyote.

The air before him darkened and churned.

What you make belongs to you.

He was doing it wrong; the hate was how he had made the thing in the first place, from hatred and rage and loss.

To make a thing is to suggest its opposite.

Roxanne! Think of Roxanne, not of wanting her back, but of what it's like when she's there. She sleeps holding on to you all night, she understands things about your music that nobody else does, sees things in it that no one else sees; she—

He missed a note.

—she printed up funny headlines for him when he felt down, left them thrust between the strings of his guitars. She made him tell her his dreams when they woke and told him things about them he never would have thought of by himself. She had brought him out of it, a year ago, had untied that knot of anger inside him, had pulled him out of the water when he hadn't even known he was drowning.

Maybe you don't believe it when I say that I still love you, but I do.

It was true; he knew it was true. Roxanne loved him.

The air brightened, drew in on itself, began coalescing.

Scooter played.

She loved him, had left him because he wouldn't think of the two of them as a pair, because he had done nothing to help keep *them* going. He had been living for his music and not for her, as though either could take away from the other.

The shining was steady, not pulsing, but restrained, like a light in fog, turbulent like the sun seen from a dozen feet beneath the surface of the ocean. It floated in the air, a perfect sphere.

There was nothing of flash in Scooter's music, nothing intricate. It did not strut, scream, wail, parade, spread peacock feathers, or incite. It was the sound of a naive guitar sounding notes that were almost childishly simple—because what he felt for Roxanne was almost childishly simple. He loved her.

The world darkened around him.

Aarka'an's voice: "It's around you now."

Cold blossomed inside him; a chilled thread dragged through his chest. He could feel it surrounding him, could feel its need, like a malignant cancer removed from his body and held before him.

He held his thoughts to Roxanne and kept playing. He could no longer see what his music shaped in the air between himself and the woman held by the hamadryad tree.

She loved to lie in the sun, he thought, loved to spread her arms in the grass in the hot afternoon, and he would look at her and almost feel her feeling the warmth in her bones.

"Scooter?" Her voice, ahead of him, terrified. He faltered, recovered, played. "Scooter, I—"

Light detonated around him.

Afterimages pulsed, red-tinged at their edges. They faded, dwindled, left behind a redness that was somehow black as well.

He blinked. He couldn't tell the difference between lids open or shut.

Lilting voices spoke an alien language around him.

"Can you hear me?" Aarka'an's voice.

"Yeah. Yeah, I can—" He tried to sit up and was gently pushed back.

"Can you see?"

"I'm . . . not sùre."

"How many fingers do you see?"

He hesitated. "I don't even see a hand," he said.

"All right." Something behind his head shifted; he realized a hand had been cradling it, had been removed. "I'll be back. Someone will be here if you call out. Try to stay where you are; don't move around."

"Where are you going?"

"To get a healer."

"Roxanne—is . . . ?"

"Wait."

"Where's your father?"

"He has a lot of thinking he needs to do. Now, please, I *must* go." He felt the boy walk away rather than hearing him.

The waiting, in his private darkness, was bad. He played his last visions over and over in his mind, seeing Roxanne against the tree, his world becoming colored in murky browns and sluggish reds, the explosion of white light. And her voice, just before that, trying to tell him something.

He wondered what.

He tried, but failed, to shake an image that came to him: the thing he had created, breaking through, enveloping Roxanne, taking from her, lifting, and leaving behind nothing but that agonized face in the tree, but changed into Roxanne's trapped face.

A woman's voice near his ear: "Tell me what you see."

"Who . . . ?"

"I am a healer. What do you see?" Her voice was gentle.

"I don't see anything."

"Nothing? Completely black?"

"No; it's—it's like red mist, with black between the red. Does that make sense?"

"It makes a great deal of sense. You would say that it means the optic nerve is still firing."

"What would you say?"

She laughed. "Never mind. Hold still now."

He felt her long hand across his forehead, thumb pressing right temple, index finger pressing left. "Still," she repeated.

He cried out.

The red mist began to recede. Sunlight edged his vision, trickled in as blackness bled away, grew brighter as the world focused around him. Her hand lifted, and he could see.

He blinked rapidly. She was the one with the copper-colored hair he had stared at, the one with Aarka'an, carving the tree. "I can see." He sat up. "I can see! Hey, that's . . ." He stopped.

She was still looking at where he'd been.

"Hey," he said. "Hey."

A hand caught her and helped her to her feet. Scooter looked up at Aarka'an in confusion.

"She gave you her sight," he explained.

"You mean she—"

Aarka'an shook his head. "Only for a few days. It's like that, with us."

Scooter said, "Oh," as if he understood.

"I'll take her back to her family now," said the boy.

"No, wait. What about—"

"Wait here." He turned away, leading her by the arm.

Scooter muttered to himself. They had restored his sight and he was grateful—*now where was Roxanne?*

He got up and looked around. Things were as normal—if that meant anything here—as if nothing had happened.

The face in the tree was unchanged.

He saw nothing of the thing that had followed him here, nothing either of the gently glowing sphére. He saw children making worker ants march in circles and figure eights, adolescents throwing stones that skipped hundreds of times along the stream before sinking, and adults examining leaves as if reading them. He did not see Roxanne.

He went looking for her.

She lay in the sun by the stream, nude, arms outstretched, eyes closed, unmoving.

He couldn't tell if she was breathing.

He ran to her, certain she was dead, and she sat up and opened her eyes.

He halted. "I thought," he said, and stopped. He saw her searching his expression for some hint of what he felt, a clue that would prepare her for what he might say, and he knew that, even though she loved him, their future pivoted on what came next.

He lowered his hands and splayed his fingers. "All right," he said contritely. "I'll get a job!"

GRAY

Bellamy Bach

—Many years later

She wakes in an alley and can't remember how she got there. There is blood under her fingernails and scratches across her cheekbone; a chunk of flesh is missing from one earlobe. She rises and stretches, hears her bones pop. The alley smells of garbage and cat piss. The sun is just rising over the Old Wall of Bordertown.

The morning is cold enough to make her breath frost, crisp enough to carry the sounds from the docks beyond the wall—the cries of the fishmongers, the clatter of cartwheels on asphalt, the whine of machinery, the slap of water against the river locks. Behind her, Soho is quiet, its residents asleep behind broken windows and doors hung with blankets and old rugs against the cold. The graffiti that lights the walls at night with the glitter of fairy-dust laced in the paint looks garish by day, decorating deserted streets where the wind rolls trash like tumbleweeds.

Gray pulls a wool cap low over her ears, over her spiky silver and gray hair, and cracked leather gloves over her blood-encrusted fingers. In a boys' jacket and

114

without the scraps of motley cloth wrapped around knees and shins as is the fashion these days in Soho, she might pass as a Wharf Rat on the docks and perhaps earn a bit of breakfast. If not, there are less honest ways to come about a penny or two on the crowded Riverway in the morning traffic.

She hesitates at the Wall and feels for the knife in the lining of her jacket; but it is only Riff-Raff on duty, eyes glazed with fairy-dust he should have left to decorate buildings. He does not challenge her as she walks past him into the fetid tunnel and out again, exhaling a breath held against the stench.

Unlike the ruined streets of the old city, Riverside and the rest of Bordertown are awake and open for business. The foot traffic and wagons on the Riverway are headed for Traders' Heaven, the market place for which Bordertown is famed and tolerated. There are no bikes on the road connecting the city with the human world for the spells needed to fuel them cease to work too far away from the Border, and the gasoline-powered bikes of the World exploded this close to it. Alongside the highway, the fishwives are set up for the morning trade, frying fish and thumb-sized potatoes over fire pits hollowed out of the concrete. Two pennies will buy half a fish and a bit of salty bread or potatoes roasted on a skewer, half a penny a cup of the green tea that is precious out in the World and common here so close to the Elflands. The smells make Gray's stomach ache with hunger. The hunting was bad last night.

Wharf Rats are crowded around an unclaimed fire pit, warming their hands over a trash fire under the skeletal frame of some unimaginable ancient dockside building. There are too many of them standing around idle, and Gray's heart sinks. Not enough work today, or the Rats would be out on the docks, hauling in nets, stacking crates, mumbling incantations at the direction of some two-penny wizard to keep the machinery moving. And idle Rats will notice a stranger in their midst.

Gray pulls her cap down lower as if this will hide her from the Rats—though even without it she can pass for human. Two Rats turn hostile eyes her way as she passes. She keeps her pace deliberately slow and casual, as if she has every right to be there . . . a fisherman's son, no, not dressed as she is. A messenger, then, on her way to Heaven.

The fishwives ignore her, gossiping in the lilting patois of the river people. The touch of elvin blood shows in their pale eyes, the white skin that looks as though it has never seen the sun in spite of all the hours on the docks and the river. Yet they consider themselves human and venture no farther upriver than the Border that separates the Elflands from the World.

Gray finds them frightening, more frightening than true blood elves. Even elves, like sensible folk, shun the open hills of the Borderland, where magic gone awry has created were-beasts and dust-devils and other creatures best not spoken of, where the moonlight, they say, can drive a man insane. Yet the river people live without fear on the banks of the aptly named Mad River, netting fish that swim in the waters of Faery. Few other humans will drink the blood-red river water, or touch its fish—said to be poisonous or enchanted or both. But Gray, whatever her unknown parentage might be, is not inclined to be overly cautious. She has not eaten in two days. And that last meal—well, better not to think of that now.

An old fishwife with a face like the trout she is frying, all pop eyes and drooping jowls, lifts a skewered potato invitingly from the flames and peers at Gray with an expression that is probably meant to be a smile. Grease drips into the fire and makes it sputter. Gray's stomach rumbles, and she wishes she had the elvin ability to turn leaves or asphalt pebbles into silver. No, she needs the real thing. And soon.

She edges into the crowd on the highway: the well-guarded wagon trains coming in from the cities beyond the Borderlands, local traffic headed to town at the start of another business day, newspaper hawkers selling sheets barely dry from the presses. Looking for an open pocket or a loose purse, she eyes a farmer pacing beside her cartload of eggs, a fat bureaucrat headed for some office in Courthouse Square, a young woman with a pushcart of denim jeans manufactured out in the World. Some of the goods on their way to Traders' Heaven will soon depart again for other corners of the World; some will feed and clothe and amuse the population of Bordertown; and some will vanish into the mysterious land beyond the Border.

No one ever knows what the elves will take a fancy to next. One month it will be cheese, the next day clay pots and light bulbs, the next suede boots two years out of style ... following merchantile needs and fashion trends unfathomable to the rest of the World. Dealing with elves is a risky business at best; turning pebbles into fake silver is the least of their tricks. But those who do so successfully are the richer for it, and there will always be those who are willing to try. Bordertown's great fortunes were made on such bargaining—and perhaps more fortunes in the World than respectable folk like to admit.

Sammy says the old city had been a thriving trade center even in the days before the Border ... but who remembers the old city? Except perhaps the eldest elves. And who can trust what *they* have to say?

Gray's eye is caught by a pretty trader with hennaed hair and so much gold and silver on his wrists that surely he won't miss a copper penny or two, or even a full new moon. Gray sidles up to him, wishing now for her despised country-girl skirts and braids, for with them he might not think it so odd if she smiles into his eyes and puts a hand on his thigh ... looking for a pocket of change or a purse, as Sammy has taught her. She nibbles her lower lip speculatively and wonders what he thinks of young boys.

"Hey there, darlin'." The trader laughs, catching her by the shoulders as she stumbles up against him. His pale cheeks flush then, thinking he's mistaken her sex, and he sets her more roughly back on her feet—but not before she had a hand in and out of his trousers. Empty. Back pockets maybe? Or a purse-string beneath the rhinestone-studded jacket? "Sorry, kid," he says, pushing long red hair out of his eyes with an irritated gesture. "But watch where you're going, ey?"

Maybe he keeps his purse in the top of his boot. . . .

"You watch where *you're* going, fishface," she says in her best belligerent adolescent mumble, giving the man another shove and disappearing into the crowd.

"Hey!" he says, but he doesn't pursue her. She wonders how long it will take him to figure out he is one gold bracelet the lighter.

She threads her way against the current of the crowd back to the quayside, where two fishwives laugh together with a sound like the distant gulls. One is the old wife who had smiled at her.

"What'er it be now, boy?" she says in the queer river singsong. "Taters or fish now, say? Taters for just a penny, they be smallish today, say?"

"What can I get for this?" she asks, her mouth watering, knowing the bracelet is too good to trade for breakfast, too hungry to care.

The old wife clucks her tongue and beams at her, reaching greedily for the gold, then pales even whiter than the true elvin born. "Get you out of here, boy," she hisses, no singsong in her voice now. "Out! Out of my sight!"

"But—"

"Out! I say out!" the old woman shrieks. A Wharf Rat looks up at the commotion, and Gray decides to take the old woman's advice.

As she dives back into the crowd and pushes her way to the opposite side of the highway, sliding on horse dung and knocking the breath out of an already breathless old man, she can hear the sounds of pursuit behind her. "Oh god's slimy breath," she mutters, heading for the warehouses and the Old Wall. She has a good start on the Rats, but this is their turf, as far as the wall. No way she is going to lose them or outsmart them here. She has to make it back to the gate. With only Riff-Raff on duty, she can expect no help—but the Rats don't know that. They won't dare follow her into the old city. A Rat is no more welcome south of Ho Street than she had been down on the docks. What possessed her, oh gods, what *possessed her* to try her luck on the docks this morning? Her growling stomach answers the question.

The soft slap of her sneakers on the cobblestones is echoed by the clatter of boots as she threads a course through empty alleyways, between shattered gray buildings. At least two Rats, maybe more. What kind of sporting odds are those?

She digs the knife out of her jacket lining as she

runs, replacing it with the offending bracelet. The knife springs open at her touch.

The gate is too far away, the Rats too near.

She stumbles on the cobblestones, feels a harsh grip spin her around.

"This way, stupid."

Sammy dodges the kick intended for a Rat, the swipe of her knife that could have disemboweled him, and pulls her roughly through a jagged window. She lands on splintered glass, and curses.

"Shut up," he suggests affably, and pulls her blindly into a darkness smelling of rotted fish.

Wicker jangles as she runs; the silver bracelets on both wrists jangle, the string of silver bells tied around her left boot jangles, the copper discs braided into her long pink-and-silver-streaked hair jangle like some exotic wind chime as she runs down Ho Street as fast as high-heeled boots will allow. It doesn't matter. She's run all the way from Fare-you-well Park, and it doesn't even matter, she is still late . . . two hours late to be precise. When she opens the door of the Dancing Ferret, the music immediately stops and they all turn to glare at her. Oh shit. Not again.

She gives Lari a bright, false smile, the kind that melts the hearts of elvin groupies and has gotten her out of scrapes since she was three. Lari does not look impressed. She tosses back her hair so that the copper discs clatter, opens her mouth wondering what's going to come out of it, what excuse she's going to invent on the spot this time . . . something a little more lively than: *I overslept* . . . but "Don't even say it," Lari says. "I don't even want to hear it. I don't care if your mother had an epileptic seizure, your cat went on the bends, your horoscope told you to stay in bed all day, your boyfriend jumped off of Dragon's Claw Bridge. Don't even tell me, Wicker. This is the fourth rehearsal you've missed since the *last* time we slugged it out, and I've had it."

The Dancing Ferret looks pathetic by daylight. The sun is merciless in exposing every crack in the wall, every stain on the floor. Tonight the room will glitter with lights and music and fairy-dust as though enchanted by some elvin spell and she'll give the best performance of her life, wait and see, and Lari will calm down again. For now, she replaces the brilliant smile with her abashed yet charming hand-caught-in-the-cookie-tin look, and saunters over to the stage.

Raven has got the arrangements to a new song spread out on the synthesizer. He doesn't look at her as she picks up a sheet, he is suddenly very interested in studying the designs on his gem-studded boots. This must be the music she heard coming up the fire escape—a good hard bass beat, just her style. "So where's the lyrics?" she says. "Look, I'll stay late today and learn them."

Raven looks like he wishes he was invisible, thin shoulders hunched beneath his New Blood Review T-shirt. Sprite is busy fussing with the strings on his guitar. Even the decrepit old wizard Farrel Din kept around to keep the electricity running looks away, embarrassed, hiding behind his wine bottle. Only Lari will meet her eyes, and the look he gives her is not encouraging. He is fidgeting with the ruby stud in his right ear like he always does before a gig . . . or a blowup.

"There aren't any lyrics. Just music. Aren't going to be any lyrics either—until we get a new singer. We're doing an instrumental set tonight, just dance music. Farrel Din agrees." The portly elf who owns the Dancing Ferret looks up at the mention of his name, then turns his back and goes on polishing the bar. This is between Wicker and Lari then. Oh lordy.

"Aw, come on, Lar . . . cut it out, okay? Look, let's just get to work, cut the shit, you won't have any more trouble from me—"

"Until we get on stage and you happen to decide to change the play list, or turn one of my love songs into a comedy routine, or weave a spell into the lyrics that gets everybody dancing till they drop of exhaustion three days later—"

"I'm the best goddamn singer this crummy band has ever had and—"

"And you're *still* more trouble than you're worth. Forget it, Wicker. We all talked it over; we're all agreed. Do a solo act, start a new group, find some human band looking for elf bait to front for them . . . or go jump off of Dragon's Claw Bridge yourself. I don't care what you do. But you're out of the Review."

She glares at him, glares at all of them. They can't be serious! Are they serious? She's made them the hottest band in town; the old Review couldn't get beyond the elvin clubs, and now they share top billing at the Ferret with Magical Madness and the Guttertramps. They *can't* just kick her out.

"Now wait a minute, Lari. Raven. John Thomas . . ." The big halfie bassist gives her a sad smile and lumbers out of the club. Sprite is packing up his equipment; it is past noon and the rehearsal is over. She's missed the entire thing—up all night fighting with Eadric, then cleaning up the smashed crockery after he'd fled down the stairs, then pacing her flat until dawn thinking about what he had said and what she had said, what she *should* have said and he *could* have said . . . until she'd fallen asleep over a cup of tea at the kitchen table while trying to wake up enough to catch a cab to Soho. . . .

"Look, Lar," she begins again. But he's not even listening now. He's packing up and out the door. Raven glances back at her as he leaves, looking like he wants to say something, pausing uncertainly in the doorway.

"Thanks for sticking up for me," she says sarcastically, and immediately regrets it at the look on his face. Why pick on Raven when it's Lari she wants to slug?

She sits on the empty stage, wondering what she's going to do now, too tired to care. From the hottest band in Soho to nothing in five minutes flat, that had to be some kind of record even for her. Sometimes she thinks her parents are right about her. She sighs and lights up a cigarette, watches the gray smoke drift lazily in sunlight slanting through the filthy windows. In the back of the club, Farrel Din is studiously ignoring her. Even the little wizard is gone.

Behind the stage is the room where bands keep equipment and costumes. Two of the members of Magical Madness are there, hacking around on guitars, but not Eadric. She doesn't know whether to feel sorry or relieved. She opens the mouth of her knapsack up wide and sweeps her makeup off the countertop into it without bothering to check if the lids are screwed on tight. She hauls clothing off hangers and jams that in her bag, too—they aren't going to give her stuff to some new singer, some cute little girl from the Hills with a voice like an anemic chicken. That's what Lari wanted for his love songs—sweet and sentimental. No fire and no guts.

Underneath her makeup table, the bowl of milk and fish she'd left out the night before is still sitting there untouched, except for the roaches. The tabby kitten has disappeared again, back to wherever it came from, no doubt—and just when she'd decided to take it home before the poor thing starved to death. She could have used the company today, some cheering up. She checks the dark corners, behind the doors, to see if it's still around sleeping somewhere; it has been hanging around the club for the better part of the last month. But no luck. This is definitely not one of her better days.

She walks all the way back to Fare-you-well Park, mindful of the money she won't be earning tonight after all, or any night for a while. Ho Street is empty this early but for a couple of runaways hanging out on an abandoned stoop, a little girl who cannot be any older than nine or ten with snot running down her nose and a ragged sweater too thin for the cold, and an older boy who is probably her brother. The glamorous Bordertown life. She wonders what draws them here, from the farthest corners of the Elflands and the World; she wonders if they ever find what they are seeking. *She* never has.

The old city is like elvin silver by daylight, revealed for the cheap illusion that it is. When night comes, it will be transformed. The avenue will sparkle with lights, glitter with a bright crowd of flamboyantly dressed kids on parade: the elvin Bloods in red leather, the color of madness and poets; their human rivals, the Pack, cruising Ho Street on motorcycles that look like they are held together with chewing gum and chicken wire; the Slummers from Dragon's Tooth Hill, children of the Bordertown bourgeoisie come to be fashionable and rub shoulders with Soho low life . . . for it is fashionable in Bordertown to at least pretend to live life dangerously, even if you take your risks in measured doses and go home at night to Mummy and Da and the hired nanny. . . .

North of Ho Street the city begins to rebuild itself; the buildings are newer and in better repair, policed by the City Guards and serviced by City Cabs. Fare-you-well Park is in the northernmost corner of the city, in the Hills, and she must pass through Traders' Heaven, the Scandal District, and Courthouse Square to get there. It is not a distinguished neighborhood, a working-class elvin borough of the sort that is common at the edge of Bordertown and that humans tend to forget exist, thinking that all elves live in elegant state on Dragon's Tooth Hill. She did not grow up in Fare-you-well Park, but in a neighborhood just like it; she doesn't know whether it is perversity or familiarity or just laziness that keeps her from seeking out a better place to live, particularly with the kind of money she'd been pulling in at the Ferret.

Hers is an old building with a new one growing out of it, the straight lines and hard angles favored in the past topped by the fanciful turrets and towers preferred now. Although it is an elvin neighborhood, her landlady is human. All Wicker knows of her is the omnipresent smell of cabbage soup that hangs in the stairwell and her statue in the lobby, a white marble monstrosity called "Madonna and Fish." This she has decorated with blinking lights and dead tree branches. Humans, Wicker has decided, are deucedly weird.

She climbs the narrow stairs to her flat under the eaves, hoping Eadric is home for a change and in a good mood for a change. She wishes she had brought the kitten home; her flat seems suddenly dark and dreary as she opens the door. There is a letter waiting for her on the mat. From Eadric. Telling her in print what he would not admit in person last night, that he's moving in with the halfie girl who plays the electric dirge in his band. Lots of vague excuses and mumblings, but the message is clear: Get Lost.

Wicker sets her pack on the floor. Sits down on the floor beside it.

"Aw shit," she says.

Definitely not one of her better days.

The darkness stinks of fish and decay and there is something unpleasantly soft underfoot. Gray hangs on the back of Sammy's coat as he leads her down dusty corridors and up creaking stairways. A floorboard gives way under her step, a balustrade crumbles at her touch, and by the time she's through the building and out the other side, climbing through the gaping emergency exit onto the fire escape beyond, she is bleeding, bruised, limping, and sneezing from the dust. "Wait!" she gasps as Sam begins to climb the metal ladder. She sinks down onto the metal grating and cannot stop sneezing. There may be Rats waiting below, but she has to catch her breath before she goes on.

Sammy squats down beside her, turns one corner of his mouth up in a sour grin. His dark curly hair just about covers his eyes in the front, making it difficult to read his expression; no doubt he does this on purpose.

"One of these days you're going to have to learn to take care of yourself, kid. What do you think I am, your guardian angel or what?"

"I can," she wheezes, "take care of myself."

"Yeah, right."

"You got anything to eat, Sammy?"

"Oh yeah, sure, kid; I always walk around with dinner in my pockets."

"I was just asking."

"Maybe if you came home nights once in a while . . ." But he can see the pinched and desperate look of hunger in Gray's expression and he relents. He pulls a flask from the hip pocket of his jeans. "Drink some of this; it'll warm you up. But not too much on an empty stomach, mind."

It is a dark red wine, not sweet enough for her taste—which means it is probably decent and not the stuff he calls swill that she prefers. She often wonders how a boy raised on the streets of Bordertown came to be such a snob about what he eats and drinks. She raises the flask for another gulp, but Sammy reaches for it, "Hey, not too much now," and the flask slips from her hand, does a little dance in the air, and smashes three stories below, leaving a stain like blood on the pavement.

"Oops," she says quietly, looking up at him with wide eyes.

He'd been about to say something vicious, but that look stops him; and he can't help it, he begins to laugh. She looks so damn pathetic, covered with soot and fish offal, her jacket cut to ribbons, her knees bloody, a bruise shadowing her left eye and cheek, scratches across the other cheek. She is sitting hugging her knees as if she doesn't know whether to laugh or cry, and his laughter tips the balance. She laughs so hard her slight body shakes with it and she can't stop sneezing, which sets them both off again.

The Rats are either gone, or deaf.

"C'mon now," Sammy says finally, rising and offering her his hand. "The sooner we get out of here the better; with the kind of luck you're having today, I ain't taking any chances." She feels limp as a rag as he pulls her to her feet. "Just remember you owe me one."

"A timely rescue?"

"No, a bottle of Brigot 37. That cost me a bloody elvin fortune."

She reaches into her jacket pocket, hands him the gleaming gold bracelet, soft as butter. "Are we even?"

she asks smugly. But his reaction is as unexpected as the fishwife's. He stares at it as if she's just put rat turds in his hand, his expression sour, and he makes a move as if to throw it out over the rooftops.

"What are you, nuts?" she protests, snatching it back from him.

"What are you doing with a thing like that?"

"Thing like what? What are *you* doing? It's mine. I swiped it fair and square off some guy this morning."

Sammy shakes his head. "That's faery gold, Gray. You don't want that stuff. It's magic—red magic. That ain't for people like you an' me, see." He curls his mouth with distaste. "That's your bad luck following you around. Only bloods can carry that crap, no human would touch it. Let me get rid of it for you before any other disasters happen."

"Aw, c'mon," she says, "it's just a lousy bracelet. Bet I can get a lot for it, too."

"No way. No human'll buy it."

"I stole it off a human guy."

"Yeah? Well, look at the great luck he had—getting robbed by you. Then you run off with it and have half the Rats of Riverside on your sweet little tail, not to mention nearly gutting me with that fish scaler of yours, not to mention practically breaking a leg or two in there, not to mention—"

"I get the picture, Sammy."

"I'm telling you, Gray, you stay away from that elf crap, you hear?" He's practically yelling at her now. Every Rat in five miles will hear. "Give me that thing and I'll get rid of it."

"I'll get 'rid' of it myself. And get a good price for it too. If humans won't buy it, I'll sell it up in Elftown— gold is gold. And it's pretty."

"And it's pretty," he mimics, hands on his hips, glaring

at her, stubbornness matched against stubborness. "Oh, bloody hells, I tried. You get yourself in trouble again girl, I ain't gonna be there to get you out of it. You understand that?"

"Who asked you to?" she says, glaring back. Whoever asked him to?

They don't speak again all the way back to the old city. She'll be damned if she'll speak first, or ask for his help though she is limping badly; and he doesn't offer it. He is a bigot, a bully, and a jerk—even if he is practically her only friend in Bordertown. Even if he did practically save her life. He probably wouldn't even have bothered if he suspected what she's known all along.

That she may be half elvin herself.

They are still not speaking by the time they turn up Chrystoble Street toward the Lightworks; but they are walking inches rather than feet apart—some silent half truce has been reached. Gray feels she could practically weep with relief to see the huge Electra Lightworks Building looming at the end of the block, the ugly remnant of a more extravagant age. It is one of the few buildings in Soho more or less intact, except for a chunk of the upper-right-hand floor, which looks as though a giant rodent has nibbled at it. The building's name is carved in stone in letters six feet high above the door.

Like most salvageable Soho buildings, this one is inhabited by squatters, runaway kids mostly, or members of the gang Sammy belongs to—the Pack—whose territory extends from Chrystoble to the wall, and north as far as Ho Street. The City Council doesn't seem to care that children have taken over the old quarter of the city. Nobody wants these crumbling ruins anyway.

Gray gets herself up the stairs to Sammy's flat by

concentrating on her bed at the top of them; by now she is so tired she has forgotten her hunger. Only sleep matters. Sammy lives on the third floor up. She was on the fifth until a few weeks ago, in a small flat she had more or less to herself since the Devinish girls she shared it with were not connected enough to reality to count. But Bloods or vandals have stolen the tin off the roof to sell up at Traders' Heaven, and now the fifth floor leaks when it rains.

As she limps in the door behind Sammy, Big Will Hernandez is just putting a kettle on the Magic Fire for tea, and Devinish Girl #1—their names are Polly and Pijin but Gray still can't keep them straight—is sitting in the bathtub that doubles, with a board on top, for their kitchen table. She's got all her clothes on, and there is no water in the tub; she is just sitting there, staring at her fingers. If Gray had ever been tempted to try fairy-dust or the river water, the Devinish girls would have cured her of that notion. But drugs have never appealed to her anyway.

Big Will's cat, Little Will, hisses as they come in, bringing the cold air with them. Will laughs. "He really don't like you, Gray. Damnedest thing I ever saw. Tea, babe?"

She shakes her head, peels off her ruined gloves, and puts them in the trash pile. Her jacket belongs there, too—and probably her jeans as well. She sighs. Tea would be nice, but it will take too long to boil over the weak flame of the Magic Fire, the elvin gadget Sammy stole from some fancy house on Dragon's Tooth Hill. Funny that for all his prejudices he doesn't mind making use of their magic: the little lightbox he reads by, the spells that fuel his beloved bike, now this. It is supposed to heat an entire room, but it doesn't seem to work very well. Elvin things rarely do, here on the Border, so close to the magicless World.

Gray runs her hands under ice cold tap water, wincing as the running water hits her scratches. She washes the grime off her face and, taking a deep breath, plunges her whole head under the tap and washes that, too. She dries herself on her shirttails, runs her fingers through her hair to make it stick up around her face in the way she likes. That's enough for now. She turns and finds Sam watching her from the doorway, with that same silent, unreadable expression he puts on when she stumbles home at dawn, unwilling to explain where she's been all night. She does not meet his eyes as she walks past him into the room she is sharing with the Devinish Girls.

The room gets no sun and is always cold. Ancient, moldy wallpaper of vine leaves and leaping goatmen is peeling off the walls, exposing cabbage roses beneath, reminding her of her family's overstuffed home back in Stratton-on-the-Pike. Devinish #2 is sitting before a cracked vanity mirror, dreamily combing her long black hair. Gray catches a glimpse of herself behind the older girl and grimaces. A purple bruise is swelling her eye, and she looks as though the Rats had gotten hold of her after all. Her clothes are definitely a dead loss. She puts her bloody shirt and her torn jeans in a pile to throw away, her slime-covered sneakers aside to clean, her knife and the elvin bracelet on top of the neat stack of meager belongings on the chair beside her mattress. She feels curiously better without the weight of the bracelet in her pocket; perhaps Sammy wasn't overreacting entirely . . . or perhaps he's simply spooked her with his story of curses and bad luck.

It doesn't matter. Only sleep matters . . . and a good meal, but she'll think about that later. She curls like a kitten in the nest of her blankets and falls asleep immediately. Little Will slips into the room, edges warily up to the mattress, sniffs, and then settles himself against the small of her back.

When they knocked on the door and I saw his face, I nearly gave it all away right then and there. Like a ghost, a piece of my past, standing on my doorstep looking just as he used to . . . well, not quite. He was in disguise, of course, passing for human with his hair dyed an unlikely red and lenses turning his pale eyes blue—but I would have recognized him anywhere. I've never understood why some people say they can't tell one elf from another.

Being fey, he'd barely aged in all that time, as though it had been ten days since our parting scene on Dragon's Claw Bridge and not ten years. Ten years. And I, being human, had aged, standing beside my respectable husband in the foyer of our respectable house, with gray in my hair and more than a few extra pounds on my hips, even then.

Our steward was fretting at the door, unaccustomed to unannounced midnight visitors who would not go away until a civilized hour, whose calling cards made his master blanch. Archer was with two other elves who were unfamiliar to me, an overly pretty young man who wore too many bracelets on his wrists and a cold-faced woman whose silvan features were not diminished by the false black curls she wore. Archer never let on, by glance or word, that he recognized me. I don't know what I would have done if he had.

My husband was not pleased to see them. It had been years since he'd set foot in Bordertown, and no one in this distant place knows the distinguished Warran Haugh fortune was built on elvin trade. I think he would have turned them out if he could have, if Archer had not been so insistent; and to this day I do not know if it was fear or, as I'd like to think, a fleeting moment of old loyalty that caused Warran to let them in, to send the steward to the cellars for one of the best bottles of Brigot and the upstairs maid to make up rooms for them.

They did not talk business that evening. Instead, we sat around the fire with the Brigot, while outside an ice storm raged with a severity I've become accustomed to in these climes but that was clearly a trial for our guests. Warran showed them every hospitality, as though they were the simple human travelers they appeared to be, delayed by the storm; yet he was clearly nervous. And think how much more nervous he would have been if he'd even guessed at the truth about Archer and me. . . . He'd forgotten I, too, had once lived in Bordertown. In ten years, he'd perhaps grown too accustomed to forgetting me; I was as necessary and as invisible as the steward or the upstairs maid.

I have always thought the steward a good man. He has been with Warran's family for so long. Yet it must have been he who betrayed us.

They stayed a week. Warran told Cook and the maidservants to stay at home during the inclement weather; the steward and I looked after the visitors ourselves. I don't know precisely what business they had with Warran; something involving cloth and trade routes and the movement of goods into and out of the Borderlands. Warran does not discuss these things with me, not since those long-ago days behind the stalls at Traders' Heaven. I shouldn't complain; in truth, he was the one I chose and I was making the best of it, had even convinced myself that I was almost happy . . . before Archer came.

I was not discreet, I must admit. I should have been more careful. All I know is that that week, so tense and fearful for my husband, was like a week of summer sunshine to me, for suddenly I remembered what it had been like to be sixteen, stealing kisses behind my father's stall and running off to the old town at night, where the elvin boys would buy me cheap wine and tell me pretty lies.

I was beautiful then. You won't believe me to look at me

now, a portly and proper Stratton-on-the-Pike matron. But I was beautiful enough as a girl that a true blood wanted me, headstrong enough that I almost said yes in spite of my father— and I felt beautiful again when Archer brought those memories to life. God forgive me, I have paid for that week every week I have lived since.

Yes, it must have been the steward who betrayed us. First me to my husband. Then my husband to the World.

Wicker had known it was a mistake to come. She had felt it in her gut as she stood in front of the mirror, decking herself out in metal and velvet, felt it again as the cab let her out three blocks above Ho Street, the farthest south the cabbie would go.

There is tension in the air tonight, a brittle sort of excitement and the sharp knife-edge of danger that so many kids thrive on, come to Soho looking for. Ho Street and Carnival are transformed with the glitter of fairy-dust and the sparkling crowd: elvin girls with painted faces and prisms hung from their silver hair; human girls with scarves and rags tied around ankles, knees, and wrists, aping the style of the lead singer for the Guttertramps, who in turn stole it from the members of the Pack. The Pack is out in force, cruising the avenues on stripped-down bikes, ignoring the Bloods gathered in the parking lot of the Dancing Ferret— though clearly each gang is just waiting for the other to make a single wrong move. Slummers from the hill are out in numbers, too, dressed in expensive imitations of old city styles, trying so very hard to fit in that in another mood it would have made Wicker laugh. There is an unusually long line waiting to get into Farrel Din's club—mostly Slummers, looking excited, like they are expecting something to happen. If it weren't for Lari, that line would be waiting to see *her*.

Maybe she should just go to another club—the Wheat Sheaf over by the Old Wall, or the old Factory, where she'd have to hide her silver hair. But no—the Dancing Ferret is *the* place to be tonight, where Lari and Eadric and Farrel Din are at any rate ... and if it isn't for them that she's dressed like quicksilver, to prove to them that nothing can keep her down for long, then why has she bothered?

She needn't have bothered. No one notices her anyway; no one looks at her twice at the Ferret because moments after she enters the room she is followed by the most extraordinary elvin woman she's ever seen, a beautiful lordling leaning on the woman's arm, the pair of them looking like they've stepped straight out of the Elflands. Nobility from the Hill, perhaps, come to observe the Soho scene like it's some quaint tourist show put on for their benefit. It makes her want to puke.

At least it gives the gossips something to talk about besides the fact that the New Blood Review is minus a lead singer, and that the old lead singer can be observed sitting in a dark corner getting herself royally smashed on a lethal combination of Chimera Milk and gin.

She does not stay to hear the Review play, or Raven's new song; watching Eadric perform with Magical Madness is bad enough ... she's not a complete masochist. There is some commotion on the dance floor as she leaves, with the elegant elvin pair in the center of it, but she's too drunk to figure out what. She's too drunk to walk straight. The last thing she remembers is climbing down the back fire escape, calling, "Here puss-puss, here puss," into the shadows, and the little tabby cat that's been hanging around the club trembling under her fingers, meowing pitifully for something to eat, its fur warm against her as she tucks it into the opening of her shirt and heads up Carnival to find a cab before she passes out. The Mock Avenue Bell Tower clock chimes one o'clock. The evening has barely begun.

She hums one of Eadric's songs to calm the kitten as she sways drunkenly up the dark avenue. Two elvin teenagers, from Dragon's Tooth Hill by the looks of them, pass her and giggle—because hers is a famous face and because she's wandering up the street talking to herself.

"I was that young once," Wicker whispers to the kitten, watching them turn onto Ho Street and disappear in the direction of the clubs.

In fact she is that young still, younger than either of the teenagers from the Hill.

She wakes in a strange place. That's the worst thing, never quite knowing where you're going to wake up, or quite remembering what happened the night before—except in foggy patches like a dream, trying to interpret reality from a cat's-eye view.

This time Gray's really done it. She's lying at the foot of someone's overly soft bed. That someone is a girl, judging from the outline of the body beneath the blankets, and an elf, judging from the cloud of silver hair across the pillow. An elf. My god. What has she gotten herself into now?

Gray rises carefully, feeling the ache of Changing in every bone of her small body. She has no clothes. Usually even the muddled feline portion of her brain can remember to stay in the general vicinity of wherever she left them at the time of the Change—but the last thing she remembers clearly is dancing at the Ferret, Magical Madness playing a riff that is hot and fast, sweat drenching her T-shirt, sliding down the back of her neck, and then the Change comes on so suddenly she's not even sure she made it safely out of the club before it happened. So where is she now? There are trees outside the window and a rose garden three floors below. Wherever she is, it sure isn't Soho.

She borrows a man's brocade robe of elvin red, lined in black satin, tied around the waist with a braided cord. She must find something more practical to wear and some shoes, or even slippers, and get out of here . . . but instead Gray finds herself wandering through the elvin rooms, fascinated, curious. So this is how *they* live, she is thinking.

There are soft rugs underfoot patterned with leaves, moss, and mulch like a forest floor. The walls glow with a sheen like the inside of a shell, and the sun pours thick and heavy through rose-colored window glass, lighting a bower of ferns and trailing vines, of dusty books and dirty clothes. In the largest room, the parlor, there is no furniture, just embroidered pillows scattered thick around the fireplace and books, yellowed with age, standing in precarious stacks. There are rocks and shells and a bleached animal skull on the mantel, beeswax candles and silver goblets on the windowsill, piles of laundry everywhere. Above the mantle is a very old, very faded print called *L'Embrace*—though it is not clear whether the man and woman locked eternally in the embrace are elvin or human. It hangs in a frame of heavy red gold worked with a pattern of leaves, like the bracelet Gray stole.

There is a small kitchen with tall wood cabinets, a bathroom much like any human bathroom, and the bedroom where the elvin girl sleeps looking like an enchanted princess from a fairy tale. One kiss . . . Bits of lace and glitter and satin are draped over the bedposts and litter the floor around the bed—a solid, human-looking four-poster with dragon's claws carved onto the feet. The girl on the bed has skin white as bridal satin and hair streaked a color like pink rose petals. Stains of makeup are smudged across and beneath her eyes. As Gray stands hesitantly in the doorway the eyes open.

"Whoever you are, be an angel and get me some head pills, will you? I've got the Border's own worse hangover. . . . They're in the bathroom."

Gray finds the bottle over the sink, brings it back to the elvin girl. The girl peers at Gray fuzzily, swallows the pill with red water from a fluted glass. "I must have been drunk last night," she says apologetically. "I don't even remember your name."

"Gray."

"A girl?" The elf girl's pale eyes widened. "Gods. I must have been *very* drunk."

Gray blushes. "I don't think—"

"Hey, where's my kitten?" the elf girl interrupts. She rises from the bed, naked and so beautiful in the rosy light that Gray's breath catches in her throat. "I meant to put some food out. Oh damn."

"It . . . um, it got out. This morning. I mean, I let it out. I'm sorry." Gray runs her fingers through her tabby-colored hair, a nervous habit. She has never been a good liar. What if the girl guesses the truth about the Changing? But the other girl just sighs.

"Damn. Poor starving little thing. Maybe it'll find some scraps in Missus B's garbage . . . Damn." She picks up a shirt from the floor and says, as she's pulling it over her head, "Well, look, I'm famished myself; you want some breakfast?"

Gray knows she should go, and quickly. All of Sammy's warnings about the true blood are running through her head. But she cannot resist the offer of food. She is always hungry. Last night she caught a mouse, but that is not enough to sustain her in her human body. And she is fascinated by the tall elvin girl, who is wandering around the small, bright kitchen looking elegant somehow in a torn New Blood Review T-shirt and elvin red panties, her white arms weighted down with dozens of silver bracelets. She fills a kettle with red water from the tap, lights the stove with a mumbled spell and a match. Gray recognizes her suddenly.

"You sing with the Review." Gray has seen her perform at the Ferret dozens of times.

The elf girl—Wicker Something-or-other, Gray remembers now—grimaces, and says, "I used to."

Wicker sets bread, hard cheese, honey, and a crock of butter on the table. She has to dig through the dirty dishes in the sink to find plates and mugs, rinses them off, and dries them with the hem of her shirt.

'Not anymore," she adds.

"How come?" Gray asks, sounding shy.

"I was bored," Wicker answers shortly. This isn't the whole truth, but it's at least part of the truth. If she hadn't grown so bored with the band she wouldn't have screwed around so much. They were hot when she joined up with Lari a year ago, but now the fans seem to want the same thing over and over ... and Lari seems willing to give it to them. Now the Guttertramps are taking over the Review's lead as old-city fashion setters. It galls her to be eclipsed by a *human* band.

The human kid is looking at the plate in front of her like she has never seen food before, doesn't know what to do with it. What the devils do humans eat, Wicker wonders, besides cabbage soup? "Look, you don't have to eat if you're not hungry. Have some tea."

But the kid, Gray, gives a funny laugh and claims to be starving. She attacks the food as if this is the literal truth—as perhaps it is, if she's some runaway, some elf-obsessed groupie living on handouts and petty theft down in Soho. Wicker sits down with a sigh. So she'll feed this odd, skinny, beaten-up-looking kid, clean her up, and send her on her way again—and maybe, as some sort of cosmic reciprocation, someone somewhere will do the same for her poor skinny, beaten-up-looking kitten. *Her* kitten. It makes Wicker smile to realize she is already thinking of it that way. Hell, a girl needs something to love, and guitar players have proven to be a bad risk.

The human kid keeps staring at her with big blue human eyes like she is having a holy vision. From the street below is the sound of the trash carts come to collect the garbage and elvin children chanting spells to make a jumping rope go round. A cold wind is blowing from the Border, rustling the vines around the window and chilling the room. Wicker rises to close the window, cutting the sounds of the street off abruptly. When she turns back, the kid is still staring at her. Gray looks as though she is about to say something, thinks better of it; then she blurts it out anyway:

"What's it like beyond the Border?"

The question takes Wicker by surprise. "Damned if I know."

"But you're—"

"A true blood, sure. But Bordertown born and bred. Hell, I've never been farther north than Dragon's Tooth Hill."

"Oh." Gray looks disappointed.

Wicker says defensively, "Have *you* ever left the Borderlands?"

"I grew up outside. I'm from Stratton-on-the-Pike— that's, um, pretty far out in the World."

"You ran away from home."

Gray nods.

"Because your parents didn't understand you," Wicker adds sarcastically.

Gray nods again, and grins around a mouthful of cheese. "I know," she says, swallowing, "I'm a walking cliché."

Wicker laughs and decides she might like this skinny human after all. "I don't know many—well, *any* humans," she admits. "The World seems as exotic to me as the Elflands."

"It's not. It sucks."

Wicker laughs again, pours tea into a mug with a hobgoblin's face. "Are there elves in . . . in wherever the hell it was you said you're from? I've heard that some of the fey live in the World, even though they can't use magic there . . . *I* would never do that."

"Not in Stratton-on-the-Pike you wouldn't. They don't go for elves there. They don't even like my mother—and she's human—because she's from the Borderlands. . . . And I think maybe because of me."

"Are you a halfie?" Wicker is surprised. Usually she can tell the blood.

"I . . . I think so. But my mother won't say."

"Aw, crap," Wicker states. "I bet every human girl with a streak of silver in her hair thinks she's the Lost Princess of Elvindom. You'll get over it. If you had the blood, you'd know it."

"How?"

"You'd just know. You'd be able to work magic, you'd feel it in your bones. Look, can you do this?" Wicker puts down her tea, extends her hand, stares intently at her palm. In a moment a tiny flare of light like a will-o-the-wisp dances above it. Gray's round eyes grow rounder, and Wicker is torn between pleasure and disgust at finding herself showing off with a school-yard trick in front of a human. "It's not good for anything," she says, blowing the flame out. "You can't even read by it. Any halfie kid can do it. Can you?"

Gray just shrugs. "I can't do anything like that. But maybe I could learn."

Wicker snorts. "You want to do magic, go hire a wizard."

"I don't want to buy a spell. I just want to find out what I *am*."

"So you came to Bordertown——"

"To find out, see. And to find out what elvin folk are *really* like."

"Oh?" The elf girl smiles, showing pearly, iridescent teeth. "And did you find out? What we're *really* like?"

"Well . . . no. You're the first I've ever talked to." She peers sideways at Wicker, sitting across the table in her T-shirt and panties. "You're not exactly like I'd imagined. . . ."

Wicker laughs, setting the copper disks in her hair clattering. "What did you imagine?"

"Um, you know. Well, you *know*. What they say about elves."

Wicker raises an eyebrow.

"Enchanting mortals, stealing babies, turning men into worms—that sort of thing." Gray runs her hand through her hair again, making all the chopped-off strands stand on end. She pulls the elvin robe tighter around her.

"What rot!" Wicker says. "Turning men into worms! Where did you hear this rubbish?"

Gray thinks about that. "My mom. She's from Bordertown, she should *know*. She used to sing me all these spooky songs, all this fairy-taley stuff about lords and ladies and turning people into monsters and stuff . . . you know." Gray is embarrassed. "She said she'd heard them growing up here, near the Border."

"Sing one," Wicker demands.

"Well, um, I don't—"

"I don't care what you sound like. Just sing one. Nobody's listening but me."

Yes, but that's bad enough, Gray thinks. Most of the songs her mother taught her make elves sound . . . bad. What if Wicker is offended? The elf girl is looking at her expectantly; Gray searches her memory and pulls up a song about a beautiful elvin queen. Her voice sounds strained and husky in the quiet of the elf girl's flat, and she stares at her toes as she sings.

> True Thomas lay on the grassy bank,
> And he beheld a lady gay,
> A lady that was brisk and bold
> Come riding over the fernie brae.

> Her skirt was of the grass-green silk,
> Her cloak made of velvet fine,
> And braided in her horse's mane
> Were fifty silver bells and nine.

> True Thomas he took off his hat
> And bowed him low down on one knee.
> "All hail the mighty Queen of Heaven,
> Your like on earth I've never seen."

> "O no, O no, Thomas," she said,
> "That name does not belong to me.
> I am the Queen of fair Elfland
> And I've come here to visit thee . . ."

Wicker sits still, with her cup of tea growing cold, forgotten in her hand. She is remembering a night long ago, when she was just a child, when a man—a cousin, an uncle, she can't remember—came out of the Elflands and visited her family. He sat by her bed one night telling fantastic stories—of knights and ladies, of creatures that lived in the seas and rivers and winged serpents that lived in the clouds—while she and her sisters shivered under the covers in delicious, fascinated fright . . . until her mother came to take the man away, scolding him for filling their heads with dreams and nonsense. His tales were like this song—magic, enchanting.

"You must come with me now, Thomas;
True Thomas, you must go with me.
And it will be seven years and a day
Till you win back to your own country."

She turned about her milk-white steed,
And took True Thomas up behind;
And when they crossed the Borderlands,
Her steed flew faster than the wind.

For forty days and forty nights,
They rode through red blood to the knee,
And they saw neither sun nor moon
But heard the roaring of the sea . . .

As Gray sings, she is also remembering. She remembers her mother, whom she prefers not to think of these days, for she is the only thing Gray misses about Stratton-on-the-Pike. Her mother's passion was her garden, filled with exotic plants brought from over the Border—though this was a thing whispered in Gray's ear, never spoken aloud where the servants could hear. Her mother would sing as she worked, as she dug in the rich black soil with strong, sun-browned hands.

Unless Gray's father came by. Then she grew silent.
And sad.

> They rode on and further on,
> Until they came to the Border green.
> "Light down, light down, you fair laddie,
> And I shall show you wonders three.
>
> "O see you not that narrow road,
> So thick beset with thorns and briars?
> That is the road to Righteousness,
> Though after it but few inquire.
>
> "And see you not that broad broad road
> That lies across the lily leven?
> That is the path of Wickedness,
> Though some call it the road to heaven.
>
> "And see you not that bonnny road
> Which winds about the fernie brae?
> That is the road to fair Elfland
> Where you and I this night shall go. . . ."

"A human in Elfland?" Wicker shakes her head derisively. She sips her tea and is startled to find it cold.

> "But Thomas, you must hold your tongue
> Whatever you may hear or see.
> Thomas, you must not speak a word,
> Or you'll ne'er win back to your own country.
>
> Thomas, you must hold your tongue
> Whatever you may hear or see.
> Or I'll tear out your bonny blue eyes
> And put in two of stone and tree. . . ."

"Oh gross," Wicker says.

Gray sings the song of Good King Henry, forced to wed a monster bride, who turns into a beautiful lady in his bed; and the story of the girl Jennet whose lover is stolen by the Fairy Queen.

"Tonight it is All Hallow's Eve
When the Fairy Folk ride;
Those who would their true love win
At Mile's Cross must hide.

"First let pass the horses black,
And then let pass the brown;
Quickly run to the milk-white steed
And pull that rider down.

"I'll be on the milk-white steed
Nearest to Bordertown,
For once I was a Worldly knight,
They give me that reknown.

"They will turn me in your arms, Jennet,
Into a newt or a snake;
Hold me tight, fear me not,
And do not me forsake.

"They will turn me in your arms, Jennet,
Into a lion bold;
Hold me tight, fear me not,
And we'll live to grow old.

"They will turn me in your arms, Jennet,
Into a naked knight;
You must cover me with your grass-green cloak
And keep me out of sight."

Now this is a tale Wicker has heard before—
but the way the stranger from over the Border told it,
it was an elvin girl who had to save her elvin lover from
a cruel queen of the World, not a human knight des-
tined to be sacrificed as a Tithe to Hell by the fairies.
As if the fey would do such a thing! Or would they?
Superstitiously, Wicker glances northward in the direction of the Border—though the northern view from
her window is the brick of the building next door—as
Gray sings of the wrath of the Fairy Queen after Jennet
steals her lover away.

> Up then spoke the Fairy Queen,
> And an angry queen was she!
> "Woe betide ye, ill-starred lass,
> And an ill death may you die!"

> "Had I known, good man," she said,
> "That this lass would claim thee,
> I'd have taken out your two gray eyes
> And put in two of tree!"

"Big on tearing folks eyes out, are we?" Wicker asks.
She is delighted. "What a lot of nonsense! No wonder
they don't like us out in the World if they believe all
that shit! Who made this stuff up? A tithe to hell for
the gods' sake."

"Nobody made it up. I mean, these songs are old,
real old, older than the Border, my mom always said
. . . though that might be a figure of speech."

"But Elfland isn't really like that, I'm sure."

"How do you know?"

"Well . . . I don't." Wicker looks thoughtful, tracing
the woodgrain in the table with a fingernail painted
with fairy-dust.

"Wicker?" Gray sounds shy again, using the elf girl's name. "Do you ever wonder what it's really like?" She is staring at Wicker from over her mug of tea, steam clouding her features.

Wicker pours herself another cup, attempts to sit cross-legged in her chair as Gray is doing, finds that her legs are too long for this. She leans over the table with her chin in her hand, pink hair framing her alabaster face, and sighs.

"Of course I do. How can you live on the edge of it and not wonder? No, scratch that. I grew up with people who have lived on the edge of it all their lives and never really wanted to know what was on the other side; I grew up thinking *I* was odd for asking. That there was something wrong with me for not being content in Elftown. I've thought about crossing the Border someday, but . . ." She laughs, shakes back her hair. "But I'd be terrified," she admits. "I've never been out of Bordertown."

"You wouldn't be scared," Gray says seriously, "or at least only at first. Then things get too . . . interesting . . . to remember to be scared all the time, or to want to run back home. At least that's how it was when I left the Pike. I would go if I were you. I'd have to. Just to find out."

"If you do turn out to be a halfie, you could cross the Border yourself. Hell, we could go together; that might not be so bad." She is startled to hear herself say this. She's only just met this kid, who may not even be of the blood. A human, gods! And Wicker has always been a loner, never gotten along with other girls very well . . . or for that matter—she makes a wry face, thinking of Eadric and Lari—with boys either.

"I really want to," Gray is saying, her round human eyes shining beneath the tangle of silvery gray hair.

"That's one of the reasons I have to find out. If I'm a halfie. Most people wouldn't want to be—I guess most elves, too, huh? But I think . . . I think I'd be glad."

"You need to talk to a wizard. A real one, not one of those spells-for-hire amateurs. Only an elf mage could tell you if you've *really* got the blood, even a drop of it."

"They cost a *fortune*."

"Ummm."

Sitting there in the elvin red brocade robe Eadric left behind, Gray could almost pass for true blood, and certainly looks as elvin as many halfies in spite of her small size. And there is something . . . odd about Gray, a lingering smoky resonance as of enchantment and spells, a kind of shimmering at the edge of sight, like when one tries to look straight at the Border. Yet Wicker cannot feel blood calling to blood. Odd.

"Wicker," Gray says, "have you ever seen bracelets of faery gold? They're about this thick around, and have a pattern of vine leaves and—"

Wicker is up and out of the room, rummages around in a drawer, dumps half its contents on the floor before producing a duplicate of the bracelet Gray stole the day before. "Like this?" she says as Gray follows her into the bedroom.

"Yes. Only maybe a little wider. I think."

"A man's bracelet then. This is a woman's. What about it?"

"I've got one."

Wicker sits down on the bed, plumps pillows behind her, lights a cigarette. "That doesn't prove you're an elf. And you know, Gray, it's not supposed to be good for those not of the true blood to wear faery gold. . . ."

"I know," Gray says ruefully, fingering the purple bruise on her cheek. "But do you think maybe I could trade it to a mage in exchange for—"

Wicker cuts her off with a snort of laughter. "You can buy them all over Elftown for a half-moon apiece."

"Oh."

Gray sits down on the edge of the bed looking deflated, looking like a woebegone child in the overlarge folds of Eadric's robe. Wicker grows thoughtful.

"Look, Gray, maybe there's a way you . . . we . . . could earn some money. I'm sort of out of a job myself . . . You interested?"

"Well, it depends on what it is. I don't sleep around and I'm not a very good thief."

"Oh gods, nothing like that. Wait here a minute."

Wicker disappears into a closet, reappears with a pair of star-covered trousers on and carrying a harp. She touches the strings lightly, and they make a soft, electric sound. "I've got to get the spell recharged on this," she mumbles as she tightens the strings. Slowly, she picks out the tune for Thomas the Rhymer and, once she's playing it confidently, begins to change it. She adds a beat that would have horrified Gray's mother but sounds familiar to the patrons of the Dancing Ferret. "What do you think?" she says to Gray.

Gray smiles at her but shakes her head. "I can't sing, or play, or anything."

"And you probably have all the stage presence of a rock. I don't want you to perform, kid, just teach me the songs. Okay? Teach me the words and tunes, and we'll work out new music together. I can get a band to back me up; I know some of the best unemployed elves in Soho. Maybe some humans, too . . . a mixed band, we can start a whole new fashion! We can magic up special effects, create a whole new look—something Elfland-y, like the silver gown that elvin lady was wearing at the Ferret last night, only wilder. . . ."

She is already picking up and discarding clothes from the floor, creating her new image as she talks.

"We'll be famous clear up to the hill!" she says, smiling conspiratorially at Gray, assuming Gray's compliance.

Gray smiles back at her, caught up by the elf girl's enthusiasm, but she is thinking:

God's slimy breath. What's Sammy going to say?

I have always wanted a child.

It was a great joy to me when the nurse explained that stomach cramps were neither a virus nor food poisoning nor one of those strange wasting illnesses that thrive in certain parts of the Borderlands, but merely a condition I had waited for so long and given up hoping of ever attaining so that I didn't even recognize it when it finally happened.

Warran, too, was glad—a child, perhaps a son, at last, to carry on the Haugh name and titles, inherit the Haugh fortune, which was sizable by now due to my husband's hard work and unspoken of connections north of the Border. For the first time since our early years in Bordertown he became a friend to me again, watching my belly grow round and delighting in the signs of life inside me. Suddenly I was once again more important than cloth or trade, and I confess that I forgot all about Archer.

What can I say, my dear? I have never pretended to be better than I am, only insisted that I am not as bad as they say. Archer became once again a teenage fancy, a middle-age foolishness; the little box that held the silver ring he gave me as he left Stratton-on-the-Pike, vowing to return when he could, grew dusty. I did not marry him back in the Bordertown days because he was an elf, beautiful and unpredictable, and I believed he would not be true to me as I aged in the quicker human fashion and lost my beauty. Yet it is I who have been fickle, who have been untrue. Not to Warran, as everyone believed, but to Archer.

*   *   *

Gray Changes back again in the back room of the Ferret. Thank the Gods there is no one there. The gray light of false dawn illuminates the single window; a cold wind blows through the crack in the pane. She wakes naked, curled on a pile of stage clothing. Her fingers are bunched tight like cats' claws, her flesh feels strange without the protection of fur. She has vague memories of alleys and moonlight and other cats and a contest over fishbones. . . . She has clearer memories of the evening before the Change, of watching Eldritch Steel rehearse, her mother's midnight lullabies transformed almost beyond recognition by power amps and a synthesized beat.

She was not impressed. Little Maggie Woodsdatter's skin drums sounded good with Wicker's harp but were drowned in the wailings of electric bass and fiddle. The penni-whistle player Wicker had found in a bar in Fare-you-well Park didn't seem to know what he was doing there at all, and the lead guitarist spent more time posturing than playing. Even Wicker was a disappointment. Raven, who'd been enticed away from the Review and perhaps now regretted it, had assured Gray that Wicker was never at her best without an audience to draw energy from, yet he seemed worried himself, particularly when Wicker announced that their first gig was already set up. Tomorrow night. At the Ferret.

As she'd sat watching them in the empty Ferret—a young elf pushing a broom around her to ready the place for the night's customers, Farrel Din lounging at his bar behind her—she'd felt the Change steal over her. Too suddenly, too soon. She'd barely had time to mumble excuses and leave.

Wicker will be worried about her. Or pissed off. Or both.

She searches among the piles and racks of clothes for something inconspicuous to wear. She comes up with tight black trousers, a black sweater that hangs almost to her knees, and elvin boots that pinch her toes. Her eyes in the mirror look large and smoky, her face pale, and there is a new scratch across one eyelid. Cat fights.

Farrel Din is smoking a pipe in the next room. Does he ever sleep? He is the only pudgy elf Gray has ever seen, yet he is known to be full blood, born in the Elf-lands. He smiles at her but it is an unfriendly smile. "Sleeping it off, my little one?" he says. Gray suspects he gave Wicker tonight's gig because it would amuse him to watch her fail.

She climbs down the fire escape to the alley, finds her clothes where she left them in a neat pile behind the dumpster. The morning air is heavy with rain, with the briny smell of the river. The sun rises weakly over the Old Wall as she turns down Ho Street toward Chrystoble.

The Lightworks is quiet as if the very concrete blocks of the building are as deep in slumber as everyone inside it—everyone except the person she hoped would be asleep. Like Farrel Din, he never sleeps. He is always there when she comes staggering home after these four-footed evenings, always gives her that same look, that flat stare that makes her feel like a child caught out by her parents. He runs the Pack and he thinks he can run her life as well. Just who does Sammy think he is—her mother?

"Good morning," she says as she comes in the door, with more belligerence than friendliness in her voice.

He pours her a cup of tea without a word. She puts her bundle down on the bathtub-table, her discarded clothing, and he gives her another one of those looks, noting the sweater she is wearing, made for someone much taller than she, and the elvin boots. She wishes he would say something, just once, so she could tell him it's none of his business where she spends the night. Better that he should think what he is thinking, anyway, than guess at the truth. But he doesn't say anything. He picks up the cracked old book he is reading and ignores her.

She hears a rush of water, the opening of the bathroom door, and Big Will emerges, Little Will at his heels muttering about breakfast. Big Will is yawning. "You just get back?" he says pleasantly.

"Doesn't anybody ever sleep around here?" She kicks on the Magic Fire. She is never warm enough these days.

"Meaning why can't you sneak home after a night carousing without anyone noticing, am I right?" Will is grinning. He doesn't care what she does. Little Will jumps into his lap, kneads his pants, and settles down, staring with unblinking eyes at Gray all the while. "Fancy boots, babe," he comments. "What elvin lord did you steal those off of?"

Sammy looks up at that, and she thinks he is going to say something at last. But he picks up his tea, goes into his room, and shuts the door.

"Said the wrong thing, didn't I? I oughta know better than to talk before my first cup of tea . . . pour me some, will you? Sorry 'bout that."

"Don't be. I don't care what he thinks."

"Oh don't you now? Since when?"

"Since he decided he could run my life! I'm not part of the Pack; he can't tell me what to do. He's just a goddamned townie bigot, he's worse than some of the folks out in the World."

"Look, babes—*I'm* not a 'townie bigot.' But even I know you gotta be careful around the blood. They're not bad, they're just not like you and me. They don't *think* like you and me. I seen plenty of babes go elf-struck, getting crushes on anything with two legs and silver hair . . . but I ain't seen many of them romances work out. Now me, I don't care how many nights you spend with your elf friend, I figure you can take care of yourself . . . but Sammy, he worries, even though he don't let on."

"He doesn't worry, he just can't stand the thought of a human being friends with an elf, pure and simple. And my *friend* happens to be just that, a friend. And a girl."

Will's eyebrows shoot up at that. "That's not what Sammy thinks."

"Well, I don't give a bucket of bloody river water what Sammy thinks," she says, loud enough for Sam to hear behind his closed door. Then she takes her own cup of tea into the room where the Devinish girls lie sleeping and shuts her own door behind her.

I did nothing. Absolutely nothing. When the police came to our door, I stood by, the meek little wife, and let them take Archer and the others away.

Warran denied it all—not that he knew them or had gone into partnership with them, but that he'd ever known they were from the Elflands or known the brocades and embroidered cloths that had become all the rage up and down the Pike were smuggled across the Border. His reputation was barely tarnished from the scandal, quickly hushed up. His elvin partners, of course, were ruined. The police confiscated everything they owned, the goods and gold that represented six months' worth of trading, six months' worth of stealth in a dangerous world.

I have had many years to brood on this, and I am certain it was the steward who did it, who found the association between a Haugh and the fey distasteful and put a stop to it, who blamed the wife brought back from the Borderlands for lead-ing innocent Warran astray. I'm certain he was the one who tipped off the police and who told Warran about Archer and me.

I am certain he thought the matter done with, successfully swept under the rug, and was as surprised as Warran that night two weeks later when the three of them stood at our door once again, looking silver and chillingly beautiful in the moonlight, no need of human disguise now. They'd been let out of the county holding cell with only the clothes on their backs, and given one-way train tickets to a town at the edge of the Borderlands. But before they left, they had a final visit to pay to Warran and me.

The steward did not want to let them in, but what is one elderly man against three elves and their rage? The woman swept past the steward and up to Warran, sparing a cold, contemptuous look for me, standing in Warran's shadow, my hands folded protectively over my large belly. I remember thinking, in spite of my fear, that she was beautiful to behold, like the angry Fairy Queen from one of the songs my people sing back in Bordertown. Warran was sputtering, trying first to smooth it all over with politeness, trying next, ineffectually, to insist they leave; she simply ignored him, pointed a slender, imperious finger at him. And cursed him.

"As you have taken all that is precious to us, so will we take what is precious to you," she said in the high elvin language that Warran could not understand but that I still remembered from the streets of my childhood. She made a sign with her hands and said some words I did not know. And then she left, like a chill wind blowing through the hallway. The pretty young man with the bracelets smiled a mocking smile, then turned and followed at her heels. I turned to Archer, expecting that same smile, the cold stare that I deserved . . . and found

only sorrow. There was a question in his eyes; I answered it by looking away.

It was Warran, seeing that look pass between us, believing then the rumors he had tried to deny, who adopted the mocking smile, the cold stare, which he reserves for me still.

He says a curse, like elvin magic, is meaningless in the human world. He proves this by pointing out that his business suffered not at all, his fortunes have taken no turn for the worse. Yet he has lost that which is precious beyond measure; his faith in his wife. And his only child.

The word has hit the streets. A new band at the Dancing Ferret. A band no one has ever heard before. A band with humans *and halfies and elves.* Crazy Wicker Leaf-and-Tree is at it again, as unpredictable as ever. At the Ferret, tonight.

The gangs are there, in force. The Pack is out on the avenue, and the parking lot is crowded with bikes. The Bloods are conspicuous in their river-red jackets, silver hair tied up with black bands. Even Dragon Fire—the gang from the Hill that no one can take quite seriously— is out tonight, looking uneasy as they lounge on the sidewalk in front of Farrel Din's club.

As Wicker waits backstage, she can feel the tension and excitement in the air. It is a drug, preparing her for the performance. Eadric is across the room putting on eyeliner, surrounded by the other members of his band and his pretty halfie girlfriend—but even that doesn't bother her now. Last night's rehearsal was terrible, so bad that poor Gray left halfway through. She doesn't care. That tension and excitement is enough for her. Tonight will be magic. She can feel it in her blood.

The kitten had turned up again, after last night's depressing rehearsal. She'd decided it was a good sign.

She'd left it in the back room with a dish of cream and some cheese, for clearly it preferred the Dancing Ferret to her comfortable flat in Fare-you-well Park. Now it is gone again, or hiding under some pile of costumes. No matter. It will come back. Everything will be okay if just please, gods, this gig goes right. She grins at Gray, who is painting a band of black across Raven's closed eyes. Then it's time to go on.

It happens every time: the bad rehearsals, the mediocre performances in front of an empty house, her voice strained and off pitch so that her band members begin to worry and even she begins to wonder if she hasn't lost it for good this time. But then, when the audience is there, a glittering crowd of kids all dressed up and hyped up and ready to hear whatever she has to give them, the magic happens.

They start slow and quiet, as traditional a tune as ever Gray's mother sang, with just the ripple of the harp and the skin drums marking the beat.

> I was but seven years old
> When my mother she did die;
> And my father he married the worst woman
> That e'er the Borderlands did see.
>
> For she has made me the laily worm
> That lies at the foot of the tree;
> And my sister Maggie she has made
> The mackerel of the sea. . . .

The electric guitars start soft and slow, the fiddle joins in and quickens the beat. Then in a rift straight out of the New Blood Review, Raven comes in with synthesized thunder, a bass roar echoing the quieter throbbing of the skin drums.

Seven knights have I here slain,
Seven lie beneath my tree,
And were you not my own true father
The eighth one you would be . . .

When the song ends, no one is dancing. No rowdy
kids are bickering at the bar, no action is going on in
the darkest corners. The club is eerily still as the kids
wait, quiet, enchanted, for the next song. Gray is right,
they are going to need dance music between the bal-
lads, and Wicker signals to the band to break into a
heavy metal jig, "The Road to the Border" performed
with an electric beat on a fiddle played as though possessed by demons and the synthesized harmony keeping up all the way. The kids aren't quite sure how to
dance to this, so Wicker shows them how, silver skirts
swaying, high-heeled boots stamping the floor, the gem-
stones woven in her hair catching the light and flashing
fire as she spins across the stage. Then she picks up her
electric harp and joins into the tune, keeping it going
as breaths become ragged and faces flushed and sweaty.
By the time the song ends, the kids are more than
ready to stand quiet, listening to another tale of magic.

As Wicker sings of a king who follows an enchanted
deer deep into a forest, there is the slightly smokey smell
of elvin magic in the room, and then the rustling of
leaves, the smell of a dark wood, the pounding of
hooves in flight.

The deer she ran,
The deer she flew,
The deer she trampled brambles through.
First she'd melt,
Then she'd shine,
Sometimes before and sometimes behind.

Oh what is this?
How can this be?
Such a deer as this he ne'er did see.
Such a deer as this
Was never born;
He feared she'd do him deadly harm.

All in a glade
The deer grew nigh;
The sun grew bright all in his eye.
He lighted down,
His sword he drew,
And she vanished ever from his view. . . .

The club is still, but for the rustle of shadowy leaves,
an illusory wind that lifts silver and dyed hair from
elvin shoulders, dries the sweat off human brows.

All around
The grass was green,
And in the wood a grave was seen.
He sat him down
Upon its stone,
And weariness it seized him on.

Great silence hung
From tree to sky;
The woods were still, the sun on fire,
As through the woods
A white dove came,
As through the woods it made a moan. . . .

They could see the shadow of wings among the stage
lights, hear the soft cooing of a dove.

The dove he sat
Upon the stone,
So sweet he looked, so soft he sang,
"Alas the day
My love became
A serving man unto the king."

The blood-red tears
They fell as rain,
And still he sat,
And still he sang,
"Alas the day
My love became
A serving man unto the king. . . ."

Crimson tears seem to fall from the stage lights, dissolving at the touch, as Wicker sings about the dove who was once a slain knight and his true love who had gone to court in man's clothing to serve the king . . . and the king who loves her. There is no applause at the end of the song, just a breathless silence, an enchanted wonder, and they plunge immediately into the next, about a girl who journeys to the Elvin Hall beneath the Hills to save her brother from the King of Faery. They finish the set with "Thomas the Rhymer."

"Oh see you not that bonny road
Which winds about the fernie brae?
That is the road to fair Elfland
Where you and I this night must go. . . ."

The song ends with a flourish of harping, an echoing drum, a shower of fairy-dust, and then they are gone and the stage is empty.

From the back room, limp with exhaustion, Wicker

can hear the thundering applause. Magical Madness is heading for the stage, looking sour at having to follow up such a set, and Eadric is looking at her over his shoulder with something of that old glint in his eye. She smiles back at him but she is thinking, delightedly, *Forget it, buster. You had your chance.*

"But where is Gray?" Raven says, and Wicker realizes suddenly that her friend is not there.

"She must be out front still," she says to Raven. "C'mon folks, let's go find her and get a bottle of something good off old Farrel and celebrate!"

She spots Gray's spikey hair as the human girl threads through the crowd toward the back exit. Where is she going? Wicker forces her way through a press of bodies, smiles at people who want to congratulate her but does not stop. Raven and Maggie are close at her heels, and it is Raven who reaches Gray first, puts a hand on her shoulder as she is about to slip out the door. She looks up with a strange, almost frightened look in her eye. Wicker pulls herself away from the Hill boy who wants to detain her and puts her arms around Gray.

"We did it, kid!" she says. "We did it! Come have some Brigot with us, we're going to celebrate."

Gray is making some protest that Wicker can't hear above Magical Madness; she is probably feeling shy, suddenly, with all the attention. Raven has a firm grip on her so that she won't slip away; Wicker slips her arm through Gray's and they propel her toward a table in the front of the bar.

"But I *have* to go," she hears Gray say clearly.

And suddenly there's a young punk in front of them, a member of the Pack judging by the grease-covered black T-shirt, the menacing stance. "Let her go," he says.

There are more gang members behind him, and

Bloods pushing through the crowd toward them, and Farrel Din saying agitatedly, "What's going on here? Wicker, what's going on?"

Damned if she knows.

The punk is taking Gray away from them, and Gray doesn't seem to want to go with him either, is shrinking back from him and glancing frantically back toward the exit door.

"Leave me alone, Sammy," she is saying. "Look, everybody, just leave me alone, I've got to get out of here."

"C'mon Gray," Wicker says, "we'll leave. Let's get you some air, okay?"

But Gray shrinks away from her touch as well, and someone from the Pack says, "Keep your bloody elvin hands off her," and that is enough to start it all. There are chairs flying and kids shrieking and she follows Gray to the exit door as fast as she can, the punk right behind her.

The punk is faster than she is; he reaches Gray in the rain-drenched alley, grabs her by a shoulder, and spins her around. "Look Gray, it's me, Sammy. It's okay now."

"It's *not* okay! You don't understand!"

"Yes I do. I do! It's some spell, some enchantment like they put in the music. You can't help it—"

"Now wait a minute—" Raven begins.

"You keep out of this, you elvin faggot," Sammy says, "and you, too," glaring at Wicker. "You just stay away from her from now on!"

Raven is cursing, but Wicker doesn't say anything. She is staring at Gray. The girl is trying to twist out from under the punk's arm, and as she twists there is a shimmer of magic, the smell like candles burning that means some spell is indeed being worked.

Gray grimaces as if in pain, tears leaking from eyes squeezed shut. Her fingers turn into claws against the punk's chest, tearing clothing and flesh. He lets her go suddenly, cursing, and she sinks to the ground. And is gone.

Gray's clothing lies in a puddle at the punk's feet. From beneath it scrambles the bony, tabby-colored kitten. With panic and something like the glitter of human tears in its eyes, it vanishes into the shadows and the rain.

"What have you done to her?" Sammy breathes, his voice choked.

Raven looks frightened. "*Did* the music do that, Wicker?"

Wicker bites her lower lip. "I don't think so," she says softly, and follows the kitten into the dark of the alley.

Warran never believed me. Whether it was magic or not, out here in the World, the curse worked. The elves stole Warran's child from him as effectively, as completely, as in the old songs where an elvin changeling is left in a human crib— for Warran never again believed the baby was his own, in spite of the somber blue eyes that were so much like his, the salt-and-pepper hair the color of his own.

That is why, my dear Gray he was never kind to you with more than a distant kindness, why he never acted as a father to you, why he watched you with that suspicious gaze as if waiting for you to sprout wings or breathe fire or otherwise manifest your supposedly magical ancestry. Perhaps it is because of this that you grew up so fey, in spite of having no drop of the true blood in you. Or perhaps it is because I am of the Borders, and it is true what they say, that Border blood is tainted with magic.

I should never have encouraged it. I shouldn't have sung you the songs my mother taught to me or talked to you so much about the elvin poets in Bordertown . . . but I was lonely.

Warran had turned from me again and—oh my fickle heart—I missed Archer. I didn't realize that the Border would call to you as it has always called to me.

Warran was not sorry when you ran away. I was not sorry either, though for different reasons. For too many years I have ignored the call—I am too old to dream of Elfland.

But I wish you well, my dear one. I hope you find the magic you seek; I hope you made it to the Borderlands. And when you find your magic, do not do as I have done. Do not turn your back and run.

She finds her on the docks. It is a simple spell that allows her to track Gray through the city, and Wicker is glad she has this advantage over the punk Sammy. She is glad she is the one sitting there, looking lazy in the early-morning light, leaning against a rotted pillar and chain-smoking cigarettes as Gray Changes.

"Here, put this shirt on," she says to the shivering girl. Gray looks bewildered and a little frightened, but she takes the Wheat Sheaf sweat shirt and spangled trousers and puts them on. Then she sits down on the dock beside Wicker and stares out over the red water.

"No wonder you thought maybe you had the blood," Wicker says at last.

"Or a curse," Gray mumbles, without looking at her.

"Is that why you didn't tell me?"

Gray nods. Wicker thinks of all the stories of cursed beasts wandering the Borderlands, were-wolves and were-panthers and demons and dust-devils, and is not surprised that her friend kept her Change a secret. The bigots of Elftown used to say that the cursed beasts of the Borders were the result of human and elvin coupling, that any halfie could turn into one.

Wicker is uncharacteristically quiet a long time. Then

she says, "You know, Gray, turning into a were-pussycat isn't exactly the most *horrible* thing I've ever heard of."

Gray turns to her and begins to laugh. There are worlds of relief in the human girl's eyes.

"So let's go find out what you *really* are," Wicker says. She rises and offers Gray her hand.

The elvin mage is not an impressive sight. She is blind in one eye and is allergic to cats. She sneezes and sneezes as she sits holding Gray's hand, studying her face with her good eye.

"No, you haven't got the blood," she says. She stands to dismiss them, drapes a garish polyester shawl about her shoulders.

"Wait a minute," Wicker says. "That's all? For all that money?"

"What do you want, a song-and-dance routine?" the old elf sniffs. "What more do you want to know?"

"Who her parents are. Why she turns into a *cat*. How do we make it *stop*?"

"You didn't pay me *that* much," the old woman grumbles. But she takes Gray's hand again. There is a burnt, magicky smell, and the old woman sighs.

"All rather boring really. She is the child of a human businessman and his wife. The business is cloth. The curse was placed by a true blood, of course; an enemy of the father's. Who, I cannot say." She sneezes again. "You haven't got the money for that kind of spell search. It wasn't a very competent spell, however. It is a spell for a Changeling; it doesn't specify Changing into what. It should have been more specific. A pussycat . . . Hmmpf. The spell became effective when the child came to the Borderlands; it will stop when she leaves again. It is that simple. Now go and leave an old woman in peace; this is really not very interesting at all."

Wicker opens her mouth again, but Gray stops her. "Wicker, let's go," she says quietly. The excitement, tension that had animated her as they'd approached the old mage's shop perched in the hillside above a narrow Elftown street, is gone. She sags like a tire that has lost all its air.

Elf children are playing a game with sticks and hoops and will-o-the-wisps on the street. The air is bright and crisp, clouds like fat sheep race across the sky, and Wicker feels her heart lighten with the beauty of the towers and spires of Bordertown laid out in the valley below them. Beside her Gray walks with her head bowed, her shoulders hunched, oblivious to the beautiful day. They take a long, winding road with many steps down to Trader's Heaven.

"I don't get it, kid," Wicker says. "You know the truth now. You're not a bastard, you have perfectly fine, respectable parents. Your mother didn't mess around like everyone said. You can go back to Stratton-on-whateveritwas and everything will be fine. You did what you came to the Borderlands to do."

"Ummm."

"And once you leave you don't have to be Were-Pussy anymore. You can have a normal life. Doesn't that make you happy?"

"Ummm."

"Stop saying 'ummm' and tell me what's wrong."

Gray stops in front of a trader's stall and fingers long, embroidered scarves of elvin-red silk.

"I thought maybe . . . I was magic. That I was different. I *am* different. I never fit in in Stratton-on-the-Pike before, I'm not going to fit in now. Only now I don't even have an *excuse*."

Wicker is looking at her like she almost understands, but not quite. "But you don't have to be different now.

You don't have to go through the Change anymore or be a cat ever again."

"But"—now Gray flushes with embarrassment—"but I kind of *liked* being a cat. . . . It's the only magic I've ever had. . . ."

Wicker is thoughtful. "I suppose . . . I suppose you could just stay in Bordertown then. Nothing would change."

"Except Sammy knows, and—"

"And Farrel Din is never going to let me play in his club ever again, I know. What a mess those punks make of it! Oh gods." She flushes, too, a bright red stain across her pale elvin skin. "Well, we were the hottest act in Bordertown, if only for a night, kid. That's something to be proud of."

"Yeah."

". . . .and how do we follow up *that* act?"

"Yeah."

They walk through the columned arcade of Heaven between exotic elvin goods and the more practical merchandise imported up from the World, ignoring sales pitches and come-ons from bored shopboys. The sun is warm outside the eastern door, and they sink down onto the steps, luxuriating in the unseasonable heat, passing a bag of fried potato skins back and forth with greasy fingers.

To the north, the green glitter of the Border shimmers in the Hills, beyond the gray suburbs and the pearly towers of Dragon's Tooth mansions. Wicker looks up at it thoughtfully; Gray stares at the Border wistfully.

"You can still go to the Elflands," she blurts out finally, bitterly. "You can still go."

"Not alone," Wicker says, surprised. "I wouldn't dare! Besides, that was just talk . . . we'd never really have gone . . . I didn't really mean to . . ." Her words die under Gray's withering gaze. Maybe Gray really *had* meant to. God.

She had dreamed of Elfland all her life, was proud of her blood, never dyed her hair human-colored like the other girls in the crummy section of Elftown where she'd grown up, "gave herself airs" perhaps, as her parents always said, "like an elvin princess." She loved living at the edge of the Border, so close to the promise of magic. Real magic. But to actually *go* there . . .

Who knew what lay behind the Border? Who knew what would become of a girl born and bred in Border-town? It had taken all her courage to leave her family's crowded house for the flat in Fare-you-well Park. Yet Gray had had the guts to come all the way from Stratton-on-whatsit. And she was such a skinny little thing, not an ounce of the true blood in her. . . .

Wicker makes up her mind in the sudden way she has, already planning what to take and what to discard, already moving herself mentally out of Fare-you-well Park for good.

"But you'll have to come too, of course," she says to her dumbfounded friend. "No way I'm doing this alone. I may be crazy, but I'm not *that* crazy." She'll have to get Gray some clothes, teach her some elvin manners. "On bother, such a lot to do. . . ."

"I can't go across the Border," Gray is saying irrita-bly, like she is talking to an idiot child. "You know that. I haven't got the blood. They won't let me through."

"Well of course *you* can't," Wicker says, distracted, thinking of the terrific farewell party they'll throw down in the old city—at the Wheat Sheaf, damn Farrel Din anyway—before they go. "We'll have to cross the Bor-der when you're a cat, of course."

Wicker is staring at her openmouthed.

"Now what's the matter? I thought you wanted to go?"

"I do! I do! I never thought of that! Do you think we really can? Do you think it will work? Do you really *want* to?"

By the gods, the girl is practically babbling. Now Wicker talks to Gray as if *she's* the idiot child, puts an arm around her shoulder, and steers her down the hill toward Soho.

"Well of course we can. We can do anything. We're the hottest team in Bordertown after all. Only . . ."

"Only what?"

"Only don't tell your boyfriend, okay?"

But of course she tells him. She can't just leave without saying good-bye to Sammy.

He is sitting on the roof of the Lightworks, looking down on the crumbling roofs of the old city. Gray sits beside him, the wind blowing through her short hair and chaffing her cheeks. He has a book in his hands, three knives in his pockets, a flask of Brigot beside him. She's going to miss him. Even if he is a bigot and a bully.

She doesn't know what to say. They are silent a long time.

They are facing north, looking out over the city. In the distance is the rise of Elftown to the west, Dragon's Tooth Hill across the Mad River to the east. Beyond them the Elflands shimmer in the morning sun.

He looks up at her as she stands. She still doesn't know what to say. She takes one of his cold hands in hers, turns it over, kisses the palm, and places it back on his lap again. His eyes are dark and wide.

"Take care of yourself, kid," he says as she turns to go—or at least she thinks he's said it. He's just sitting there, unmoving, staring off at the far hills over the Border.

STICK

Charles de Lint

Then to the Maypole hast away
For 'tis now our holiday.

—from "Staines Morris,"
English traditional

Stick paused by his vintage Harley at the sound of a scuffle. Squinting, he looked for its source. The crumbling blocks of Soho surrounded him. Half-gutted buildings and rubble-strewn lots bordered either side of the street. There could be a hundred pairs of eyes watching him—from the ruined buildings, from the rusted hulks of long abandoned cars—or there could be no one. There were those who claimed that ghosts haunted this part of Soho, and maybe they did, but it wasn't ghosts that Stick was hearing just now.

Some Bloods out Pack-bashing. Maybe some of the Pack out elf-bashing. But it was most likely some Rats—human or elfin, it didn't matter which—who'd snagged themselves a runaway and were having a bit of what they thought was fun.

Runaways gravitated to Bordertown from the outside world, particularly to Soho, and most particularly to this quarter, where there were no landlords and no rent. Just the scavengers. The Rats. But they could be the worst of all.

Putting his bike back on its kickstand, Stick pocketed the elfin spell-box that fueled it. Lubin growled softly from her basket strapped to the back of the bike—a quizzical sound.

"Come on," Stick told the ferret. He started across the street without looking to see if she followed.

Lubin slithered from the basket and crossed the road at Stick's heels. She was a cross between a polecat and a ferret, larger than either, with sharp pointed features and the lean build of the weasel family. When Stick paused in the doorway of the building from which the sounds of the scuffle were coming, she flowed over the toes of his boots and into its foyer, off to one side. Her hiss was the assailants' first hint that they were no longer alone.

They were three Bloods, beating up on a small unrecognizable figure that was curled up into a ball of tattered clothes at their feet. Their silver hair was dyed with streaks of orange and black; their elfin faces, when they looked up from their victim to see Stick standing in the doorway, were pale, skin stretched thin over high-boned features, silver eyes gleaming with malicious humor. They were dressed all of a kind—three assembly line Bloods in red leather jackets, frayed jeans, T-shirts and motorcycle boots.

"Take a walk, hero," one of them said.

Stick reached up over his left shoulder and pulled out a sectional staff from its sheath on his back. With a sharp flick of his wrist, the three two-foot sections snapped into a solid staff, six feet long.

"I don't think so," he said.

"He don't think so," the first of the Bloods mocked.

"This here's our meat," a second said, giving their victim another kick. He reached inside his jacket, his hand reappearing with a switchblade. Grinning, he thumbed the button to spring it open.

Knives appeared in the hands of the other two—one from a wrist sheath. Stick didn't bother to talk. While they postured with their blades, he became a sudden blur of motion. The staff spun in his hands, leaving broken wrists and airborne switchblades in its wake. A moment later, the Bloods were clutching mangled wrists to their chests. Stick wasn't even winded.

He made a short feint with the staff and all three Bloods jumped as though they'd been struck again. When he stepped toward their victim, they backed away.

"You're dead," one of them said flatly. "You hear me, you shit-faced—"

Stick took a quick step toward them and they fled. Shaking his head, he turned to look at where Lubin was snuffling around their prize.

It was a girl, and definitely a runaway, if the ragged clothes were anything to go by. Considering current Soho fashion, that wasn't exactly a telling point. But her being here . . . that was another story. She had fine pale features and spiked hair a mauve she was never born with.

Stick crouched down beside her, one hand grasping his staff and using it for balance. "You okay?" he asked.

Her eyelids flickered, then her silver eyes were looking into his.

"Aw, shit," Stick said.

No wonder those Bloods'd had a hard-on for her. If there was one thing they hated more than the Pack, it was a halfling. She wasn't really something he had time for either.

"Can you stand?" he asked.

A delicate hand reached out to touch his. Pale lashes fluttered ingenuously. She started to speak, but then her eyes winked shut and her head drooped against the pile of rags where she'd been cornered by the Bloods.

"Shit!" Stick muttered again. Breaking down his staff, he returned it to its sheath. Lubin growled and he gave her a baleful look. "Easy for you to side with her," he said as he gathered the frail halfie in his arms. "She's probably related to you as well as the Bloods."

Lubin made querulous noises in the back of her throat as she followed him back to the bike.

"Yeah, yeah, I'm taking her already."

As though relieved of a worry, the ferret made a swift ascent onto the Harley's seat and slipped into her basket. Stick reinserted his spell-box, balanced his prize on the defunct gas tank in front of him, and kicked the bike into life. He smiled. The bike's deep-throated roar always gave him a good feeling. Putting it into gear, he twisted the throttle and the bike lunged forward. The girl's body was only a vague weight cradled against his chest. The top of her head came to the level of his nose.

For some reason, he thought she smelled like apple blossoms.

She woke out of an unpleasant dream to a confused sense of dislocation. Dream shards were superimposed on unfamiliar surroundings. Grinning Blood faces, shattered like the pieces of a mirror, warred with a plainly furnished room and a long-haired woman who was sitting on the edge of the bed where she lay. She closed her eyes tightly, opened them again. This time only the room and the woman were there.

"Feeling a little rough around the edges?" the woman asked. "Try some of this."

Sitting up, she took the tea. "Where am I? The last thing I remember . . . there was this man. . . ."

"Stick."

"That's his name?"

The woman nodded.

"Is he . . ." Your man, she thought. "Is he around?"

"Stick's not much for company."

"Oh. I just wanted to thank him."

The woman smiled. "Stick's great for making enemies, but not too good at making friends. He sticks—" she smiled "—to himself mostly."

"But he helped me. . . ."

"I didn't say he wasn't a good man. I don't think anyone really knows what to make of him. But he's got a thing for runaways. He picks them up when they're in trouble—and usually dumps them off with me."

"I've heard his name. . . ."

"Anyone who lives long enough in Bordertown eventually runs into him. He's like Farrel Din—he's just always been around." The woman watched her drink her tea in silence for a few moments, then asked: "Have you got a name?"

"Manda. Amanda Woodsdatter."

"Any relation to Maggie?"

"I'm her little sister."

The woman smiled. "Well, my name's Mary and this place you've been dumped is the home of the Horn Dance."

"No kidding? Those guys that ride around with the antlers on their bikes?"

"That's one way of describing us, I suppose."

"Jeez, I . . ."

Looking at Mary, Manda's first thought had been that she'd ended up in some old hippie commune. There were still a few of them scattered here and there through Bordertown and in the Borderlands. Mary's long blonde hair—like one of the ancient folk singers Manda had seen pictures of—and her basic Whole Earth Mother wardrobe of a flowered ankle-length dress, feather earrings and the strands of multicolored beaded necklaces around her neck, didn't exactly jibe with what Manda knew of the Horn Dance.

In ragged punk clothing, festooned with patches and colored ribbons, their bikes sporting stag's antlers in front of their handlebars, the Horn Dance could be seen cruising anywhere from the banks of the Mad River to Fare-you-well Park. They were also a band, playing music along the lines of Eldritch Steel—a group that her sister had played with that had mixed traditional songs with the hard-edged sound of punk, and only lasted the one night. Unlike Eldritch Steel, though, the Horn Dance was entirely made up of humans. Which was probably the reason they were still around. Eldritch Steel's first and only gig had been in Farrel Din's Dancing Ferret and sparked a brawl between the Pack and the Blood that had left the club in shambles. Farrel Din, needless to say, hadn't been pleased. The band broke up, lead singer Wicker disappearing, while the rest of the group had gone their separate ways.

"What are you thinking of?" Mary asked.

Manda blinked, then grinned sheepishly. "Mostly that you don't look as punky as I thought you guys were."

"I'm the exception," Mary said. "Wait'll you meet Teaser, or Oss."

"Yeah, well . . ." Manda looked around the room

until she spotted her clothes on a chair by the door. She wasn't so sure that she'd be meeting anyone. There were things to do, places to go, people to meet. Yeah. Right.

"Do you need a place to stay?" Mary asked.

"No, I'm okay."

"Look, we don't mind if you hang out for a few days. But there's a couple of things I'd like to know."

"Like?"

"You're not from the Hill, are you?"

"Why?"

"Runaways from the Hill can be a problem. Up there, they've got ways of tracking people down and we don't need any trouble with elves."

"They're not like the Bloods up on the Hill," Manda said. "But like I told you, I'm Maggie's little sister. We grew up in Soho."

Mary smiled. "And so you know your way around."

"I lost my shades—that's all. Those Bloods were out to kick ass and when they caught a glam of my eyes, that was it."

"Stick told me—three to one are never good odds."

Manda shrugged. "I'm not a fighter, you know?"

"Sure. And what about your folks—are they going to come looking?"

"I'm on my own."

"Okay. We just like to know where we stand when irrate people come knocking on the door—that's all." She stood up from the bed, then fished in her pocket, coming up with a pair of sunglasses. "I thought you might like another pair—just to save you the hassle you had last night from being repeated."

"Thanks. Listen, I'll just get dressed and be on my way. I don't want to be a pain."

"It's no problem."

"Yeah, well . . ." She hesitated, then asked: "Where can I find Stick?"

"You don't want to mess with him, Manda. He's great to have around when there's trouble, but when things are going fine . . . he just gets antsy."

"I just want to thank him, that's all."

Mary sighed. "You know the old museum up by Fare-you-well Park?"

"Sure. That's his place? The whole thing?"

Mary nodded. "But I don't know if the whole place is his. I've never been there and I don't know anyone who has. Stick doesn't take to visitors."

"Well, maybe I'll wait and check him out on the street sometime."

"That would be better. I've porridge still warm, if you want something to eat before you go."

The idea of porridge first thing in the morning reminded Manda of too many mornings at home. She'd never even liked porridge—that was mom's idea of a treat. But her stomach rumbled and she found a smile.

"That'd be great."

Mary laughed. "Look, don't mind me, Manda. The Hood always says that I've got a bad case of the mothering instinct. Why do you think Stick drops off his strays with me?"

"Who's the Hood?"

"Toby Hood—our bowman."

Manda shook her head. "There's a lot about you folks I don't know."

"Well, if you shake your leg, you'll be able to find out some—we're just getting ready to ride. If you want, you can come along."

"No kidding?" Wouldn't that be something, riding around with the Horn Dance?

"Well . . . ?" Mary asked.

"I'm up, I'm up."

She threw aside the covers as Mary left the room and got out of the bed to put on her clothes. There was a mirror by the dresser. Looking in it, she studied her face. The bruises were already fading. She didn't feel so sore either. That was one good thing about having elf blood—you healed fast.

Riding with the Horn Dance, she thought. She gave her reflection a wink, put on her new shades, and headed out the door.

"This sucks, man." Fineagh Steel stared out the window onto Ho Street, his back to his companion. When he turned, the sunlight coming through the dirty windowpane haloed his spiked silver hair. He was a tall elf, with razor eyes and a quick sneer, wearing a torn Guttertramps T-shirt and black leather pants tucked into black boots.

Slouching on a beat-up sofa, Billy Buttons took a long swig of some homebrew, then set the brown glass bottle on the floor by his feet. Taking out a knife, he flicked it open and began to clean his nails.

"Hey, I'm talking to you, man," Fineagh said.

Billy eyed the current leader of the Blood, then shrugged. "I'm listening. What do you want me to say?"

Fineagh's lip curled and he turned to look out the window once more. "Stick's got to go."

That made Billy sit up. He ran his fingers through his black and orange mohawk, scratched at the stubble above his ears. "Hey," he said. "It was their own fault—bashing on his turf."

"*Our* turf," Fineagh said sharply. "And anyone that comes into it takes their chances. If you were to listen to Stick, you'd think the whole fucking city was his turf."

Maybe it is, Billy thought, but he didn't say the words aloud. There was something spooky about Stick—but Billy was in the room with Fineagh right now and he wasn't into messing with Fineagh either.

"So what do you want to do?" he asked.

Fineagh left the window and went to where his jacket lay on the floor by the door. From the inside pocket he took out a vintage Smith & Wesson .38. Billy's eyes went wide.

"Where the hell did you get that?" he asked.

"Lifted it—in Trader's Heaven."

"You got bullets?"

"What do you think?"

"Does it still work?"

Fineagh pointed it at Billy. "Bang!" he said softly.

Billy jumped as though he *had* been shot.

"Oh, yeah," Fineagh said. "It works all right."

Billy stared at the weapon with awe. The hand guard, the gleaming barrel, everything about the gun made him shiver. It was obviously in mint condition.

"Where are you going to do it?" he asked. "On the street?"

Fineagh shook his head. "We're going to beard the bastard in his den, my man. Maybe when we're done we'll turn that old place into a club—what do you think? We'll call it Fineagh's Place."

"How're we going to get in? That old museum is like a fortress."

"We're going to play a tune on Stick's heartstrings," Fineagh said with a tight-lipped smile. "There'll be this runaway, see, getting his fucking head bashed in right in front of old Stick's digs. . . ."

"Your sister's a drummer, right?" Big Will asked.

Manda nodded. "She plays skin drums."

Big Will was one of the Horn Dance's riders, a huge black man with a buzz of curly black hair and a weight-lifter's body. Manda had been introduced to them all, but the names slid by too quickly for her to put a face to every one and still remember it. A few stuck out. Oss, with his mohawk mane like a wild horse and wide-set eyes. Teaser, all gangly limbs, hair a bird's nest of streaked tangles and his jester's leathers—one leg black, the other red, the order reversed on his jacket. Mary, of course. Johnny Jack, another of the riders, a white man as big as Yoho and as hairy as a bear. And the Hood, dressed all in green like some old-fashioned huntsman, a tattoo of a crossed bow and arrow on his left cheek and his hair a ragged cornfield of stiff yellow spikes.

"What about you? Do you play an instrument?"

Manda turned to the girl who'd spoken. A moment's thought dredged up her name. Bramble. One of the band's musicians. A year or so older than Manda's sixteen, she was a tall willowy redhead, with short red stubble on the top of her head; the rest of her hair hung down in dozens of beaded braids.

"I used to play guitar—an electric," Manda said, "but someone lifted my spell-box and amp. I can't afford another, so I don't play much anymore."

Bramble nodded. "It's not much fun when the punch is gone. I know. I got ripped off a couple of years ago myself. Went crazy after a month, so I waitressed days in The Gold Crown and played nights on a borrowed acoustic until I could afford a new one."

Teaser rattled a jester's stick in Manda's face to get her attention. "So are you any good on yours?" he asked.

"Well, Maggie said we'd put a band together if I can get a new amp."

"We could use an axe player right now," Bramble

said. "The pay's the shits, but I've got a spare amp I could lend you."

"But you don't even know me—you don't know if I'm any good."

"Bramble's got a feel for that kind of thing," Mary said.

"And I've got a feel that we should be riding," Big Will broke in. "So are we going, or what?" He thrust a patched and ribbon-festooned jacket at Manda. "Here. You can wear this today. Consider yourself an honorary Horn Dancer."

"But—"

"You ride with us, you need the look," Will replied. "Now let's *go!*"

In a motley array of colors and tatters, they all crowded outside to where the bikes stood in a neat row behind their house.

"You can ride with me," Bramble said.

Manda smiled her thanks. "What's this all about?" she asked as they approached Bramble's bike. "What is it that you guys *do?*"

"Well, it's like this," Bramble said. "On one level we're like any other gang—the Pack, the Bloods, Dragon's Fire, you name it. We like each other. We like to hang around together. But—have you ever heard of Morris dancing?"

Manda nodded. "Sure." When Bramble gave her a considering look, she added: "I like to read—about old things and what goes on . . . anywhere, I guess. Across the Border. In the outside world."

"Well, what we are is like one of those old Morris teams—that's why we're set up the way we are—the six stags, three white and three black. Oss is the Hobby Horse. Teaser's the fool."

"And Mary?"

"She's like the mother in the wood—Maid Marion. Robin Hood's babe."

Manda smiled. "I've heard of him."

"Yeah. I guess he's been around long enough. Anyway, what we do is. . . ." She gave a little laugh. "This is going to sound weird, or crazy, but we're like Bordertown's luck—you know? The dance we do, winding through the city's streets, the music . . . it's all something that goes back to the stone-age—in Britain, anyway. It's really old, all tied up with fertility and luck and that kind of thing. We make our run through the city, at least every couple of days, and it makes things sparkle a bit.

"We get all kinds of good feedback—from the oldtime punks, as well as the kids. And it makes us feel good, too. Like we're doing something important. Is this making any sense?"

"I . . . guess."

"Are we riding or jawing?" Big Will called over to them.

Bramble laughed and gave him the finger. "Come on," she said to Manda. "You'll get a better idea of what I was talking about just by getting out and *doing* it with us."

"What would happen if you didn't make your ride?" Manda asked.

"I don't know. Maybe nothing. Maybe the sewers would back up. Maybe we'll all go crazy. Who knows? It just feels right doing it."

Manda climbed on the back of Bramble's bike. "I think I know what you mean," she said. "I always got a good feeling when I saw you guys going by. I never caught any of your gigs, but—"

"Yeah. There's a lot of bands in this city. It's hard to catch them all."

"But still," Manda said. "Ever since Mary asked me if

I wanted to come along—I've felt like I've just won a big door prize."

"*The Wheel of Fortune*," Bramble said.

"What?"

"It was an old game show."

"You mean like on television?"

"The entertainment of the masses—in the world outside, at least. Did you ever watch it?"

"No. Did you?"

"Yeah. A friend of mine had a machine that recorded the shows. It was great. We used to watch all kinds of weird stuff on these old tapes of his. But then someone ripped it off."

The bikes coughed into life, up and down the line, cutting off further conversation. Bramble kicked her own machine awake. The bike gave a deep-throated roar as she twisted the throttle.

"Hang on!" she cried.

Manda put her arms around the slim girl's waist and then suddenly they were off. Before they got to the end of the block, she found herself grinning like the fool's head on the end of Teaser's jester's stick.

Sitting in The Dancing Ferret, the two men made a study in contrasts. Farrel Din was short and portly, smoking a pipe and wearing his inevitable patched trousers and a quilted jacket. A full-blooded elf, born across the Border, he still gave the impression of a fat innkeeper from some medieval *chanson de geste*. Stick, on the other hand, was all lean lines in black jeans, boots and a leather jacket. With his deep coffee-brown skin and long dark dreadlocks, he tended to merge with shadows.

The men had the club to themselves except for Jenny Jingle, a small elvin penni-whistle player, who sat in a corner playing a monotonous five-note tune on her whistle while Stick's ferret danced by her feet. From time to time she gave the men a glance. She knew Stick by sight, though not to talk to. Trading off between waitressing, odd jobs and the occasional gig in the club, she saw him often enough, but tended to spend the times that he came into The Ferret amusing Lubin who had developed a firm interest in Breton dance tunes.

Stick wasn't one that you could cozy up to. Though he seemed to know just about everyone in Bordertown, the only person one could definitely call his friend was Farrel Din. The two seemed to go back a long way, which was odd, Jenny'd thought more than once. Not because Farrel Din was a full-blooded elf and Stick was definitely human—and not that old a human at that if appearances were anything to go by—but because Stick seemed to remember the times before Elfland returned to the world as though he'd been there when it had happened.

She finished the gavotte she was playing with a little flourish and Lubin collapsed across her feet to look hopefully up at her for more. Watching them, Farrel Din smiled.

"Seems like just yesterday when we put this place together," he said.

"It's been a lot of yesterdays," Stick replied.

He nodded as Farrel Din offered to refill his glass. Amber wine, aged in Bordertown, but originating in Elfland's vineyards, filled his glass. They clinked their glasses together in a toast, drank, then leaned back in their chairs. Farrel Din fiddled with his pipe. When he had the top ash removed from its bowl, he frowned for a moment, concentrating. A moment later, the tobacco was smoldering and he stuck it in his mouth.

"There's a Blood out on the streets with a gun," he said around the stem.

Stick gave him a sharp look.

"Oh, it's the real McCoy—no doubt about that, Stick. The sucker'd even work across the border. Mother Mandrake had it, only someone lifted it from her booth yesterday. She didn't see it happen, but she had a bunch of Bloods in that afternoon."

"Who told you this?" Stick asked.

"Got it from Sammy Tucker. He was in to see Magical Madness playing last night."

"Shit. Any idea who's got the gun now?"

Farrel Din shook his head. "But there's an edgy mood out on the street, Stick, and I think there's going to be some real trouble."

Stick stood up and finished his wine in one long gulp.

"That's no way to treat an elfish vintage," Farrel Din told him.

"I've got to find that gun," Stick said. "I don't mind the gangs bashing each other, but this could go way beyond that."

"Maybe they'll just use it for show," Farrel Din said hopefully. "You know how kids are."

"What do you think the chances of that are?"

Farrel Din sighed. "I wouldn't take odds on it."

"Right." Stick gave a quick sharp whistle and Lubin left her dancing to join him. "Thanks for amusing the brat, Jenny," he told the whistle player, then he left, the ferret at his heels.

Jenny blinked, surprised that he'd even known her name. At his own table, Farrel Din put down his pipe and poured himself some more wine, filling the glass to its brim. Aw, crap, he thought. He wished he hadn't had to tell Stick about the gun. But there was no one

else he could think of that could track it down as
quickly, and what they didn't need now was the trouble
that gun could cause. Not with tensions running as
high as they were. So why did he feel like the gun was
going to come to Stick anyway, whether he looked for it
or not?

Farrel Din frowned, downing his glass with the same
disregard for the vintage that Stick had shown earlier.
Maybe he could dull the sense of prescience that had
lodged in his head. Since leaving Elfland, the ability
had rarely made itself known. Why did it have to come
messing him up now?

He poured himself another glass.

Manda had a glorious time that day. The Horn Dancers took turns having her ride on the back of their bikes
and she wound up renewing a childhood love affair
with the big deep-throated machines. She'd always
wanted one. She'd even settle for a scooter if it came
down to that, but given her druthers, she'd take one
of these rebuilt machines—or better yet, a vintage Harley like Stick had.

Johnny Jack had given her a mask at their first stop
so that she could *really* feel a part of the Dancers. It was
like a fox's head, lightweight with tinted glass in the
eyeholes so that her silver eyes wouldn't give her away.
The mask had been collecting dust, he assured her
when she tried a half-hearted protest. Whether that
was true or not—and Manda was willing to lean toward
the former if he was—she accepted it greedily.

Masked and with her ribboned jacket, Morris bells
jingling on her calves, she happily joined in on an
impromptu dance at the corner of Ho Street and Brews,

hopping from one foot to the other along with the rest of them while Bramble played out a lively hornpipe on a beat-up old melodeon. Then it was back on the bikes and they were off again, a ragged line of gypsy riders leaving a sparkle as real as fairy dust behind in the eyes of those who watched them pass by.

That night the Horn Dance had a gig at The Factory, the oldest rock-and-roll club in the city. Manda was too shy to play, but she enjoyed standing near the stage in her new gear and watching the show. The audience was fun to watch, too, an even mix between pogoing young punks and an older crowd doing English country dances. By the time the second set was over, there were kids doing the country dances, and oldtimers pogoing. The main concern seemed to be to have fun.

By the middle of the third set, Manda was still feeling shy, but she was itching to play. That always happened when she saw a good band. Her fingers would start shaping chords down by her leg. It didn't take Bramble a whole lot of urging to get her up on the stage then to join in on some of the numbers she knew. "The Road to the Border," "Up Helly-O," "The Land of Apples," "Tommy's Going Down to Berks" . . . the tunes went by and Manda grinned behind her fox's mask, even joining in on the singing when the band launched into "Hal-an-Tow." Listening to the words, she realized that the song pretty well said what the band was all about.

> *Do not scorn to wear the horn*
> *It was the crest when you was born*
> *Your father's father wore it and*
> *Your father wore it, too*

Hal-an-tow, jolly rumble-o
We were up, long before the day-o
To welcome in the summer
To welcome in the May-o
For summer is a-coming in
    and winter's gone away-o

It didn't matter what time of year it was, Manda thought, as she chorded along on the chorus. The song wasn't just about the change of the seasons, but about day following night, good times following the bad; that there was always a light waiting for you on the other side—you just had to go looking for it, instead of stewing in what had brought you down.

Bramble laid down a synthesized drone underneath a sharp rhythm of electronic drums. Big Will was playing bass. Teaser hopped around in front of the stage, waving his jester's stick, while the rest of the band crowded around a couple of microphones. The Hood sang lead. Manda smiled as he began the third verse.

Robin Hood and Little John
Have both gone to the fair-o
And we will to the merry green wood
To hunt the bonny hare-o

Hal-an-tow, jolly rumble-o. . . .

The music had a sharp raw edge to it that never quite overpowered the basic beauty of the melody. Voices rose and twisted in startling harmonies. Manda found herself jigging on the spot as she played her borrowed guitar. There was a certain rightness about the fact that it was the same canary yellow as her own Les Paul.

God bless the merry old man
And all the poor and might'-o
God bring peace to all you here
And bring it day and night-o

The final chorus rose in a crashing wave that threat-
ened to lift the roof off of the club. Kids and oldtimers were mixed in whirling dervish lines that made
patterns as intricate as the song's harmonies. When
the final note came down with a thunderous chord
on the synthesizer, there was a long moment of silence.
Then the crowd clapped and shouted their approval
with almost as much volume as the band's electric
instruments.

"I knew you'd be hot," Bramble said as she and
Manda left the stage. "Did you have fun?"

Manda nodded. She bumped into Teaser who thrust
his jester's stick up to her face. "Says Tom Fool—you're
pretty cool," he sang to her, then whirled off in a
flutter of ribbons and leather.

The two women made their way to the small room in
the back that the club had set aside for the band to
hang out in between sets. Manda slumped on a bench
and tried to stop grinning. She laid her foxhead mask
on the bench beside her, her silver eyes flashing.

"See, we don't have elf magic," Bramble said, plonk-
ing herself down beside Manda, "so we've got to make
our own."

"What you've got's magic all right."

"Want a beer?"

"Sure. Thanks."

"I've talked to the others," Bramble said. "They were
willing to go along just on my say-so, but now that
they've all heard you, it's official: you want to gig with
us for awhile?"

Manda sat up straighter. Absently chewing on her lower lip, she had to look at Bramble to see if it was a joke.

"For true," Bramble said.

"But I'm not. . . ." Human, she thought. "Like you. It could cause trouble."

"What do you mean?"

"Well, like—"

Manda never had a chance to continue. The club's owner poked his head in through the door. "Hey, have you seen Toby? There's a guy outside looking for him to—" He broke off when he saw Manda. "What're you doing in here?"

"She's with me," Bramble said.

"Uh-uh. No fucking halfies in my club. You. Get out of here."

Bramble frowned and stood up. "Lay off, George. I said she's okay."

"No. You listen to me. The Blood's got their own places to hang out and I don't want them in here. This is a clean club. She's out, or you're all out."

"You're acting like a fucking bigot," Bramble began, but Manda laid a hand on her arm.

"It's okay," she said. "I was just going anyway."

"Manda. We can work this—"

Manda shook her head. She should have known the day was going too well. Everything had just seemed perfect. Under the club owner's baleful eye, she stripped off the ribboned jacket and laid it on the bench beside her mask.

"I'll see you around," she told Bramble.

"At least let me get the Hood and—"

Manda shook her head again. Blinking back tears,

she put on her shades and shouldered her way by the club owner.

"Manda!"

When she was out on the dance floor, Manda broke into a run. By the time Bramble had gathered a few of the band to go outside to look for her, she was long gone.

"This is the shits," Bramble said. "I'm out."

"What do you mean you're out?" the Hood asked. "We've got another set to—"

"I'm not playing for these assholes."

"Bramble, he's got a right to run the kind of club he wants."

"Sure. Just like I've got the right to tell him to go fuck himself. We're supposed to be putting out good vibes, right? Be the 'luck of the city' and all that shit? Well, I liked that kid, Hood, and I *don't* like the idea of being around people who can't see beyond the silver in her eyes."

"But—"

"I'll pick up my gear at the house tomorrow."

"Where you going now?" Mary asked.

"To see if I can find her."

"I'll come with you," Johnny Jack said.

Bramble shook her head. "You guys go on and finish the gig, if that's what you want to do, okay? Me, I just want to think some things through."

"I've got an idea where she might have gone," Mary said.

"Where's that?"

"Stick's place."

"Oh, shit. That's all we need. To get him pissed off."

"Bramble, listen to me," the Hood tried again, catching hold of her arm.

Bramble shook off his hand. "No, you listen to me.

Didn't you see how that kid took to what's supposed to be going down with us? She fit right in. I have a feel for her, man. She could *be* something and I want to see her get that chance."

"Okay," the Hood said. "Go look for her. But don't turn your back on us. Let's at least talk things out tomorrow."

Bramble thought about that. "Okay. If I find her, I'll be by tomorrow."

"We've got a commitment to fulfill here," the Hood went on. "For tonight at least. We don't have to come back."

"We shouldn't be in a place like this at all," Bramble muttered under her breath as she headed for her bike. "Not if they're going to be assholes about this kind of thing."

Manda didn't think it could hurt so much. It wasn't like she'd spent her whole life with the Dance or anything. So what if it had seemed so perfect. It wasn't like she'd ever fit in anywhere. Not with the kids her own age, not with Maggie's friends, not with anyone. Some people just weren't meant to fit in. That's all it was. They got born with a frigging pair of silver eyes and everybody dumped on them, but who cared? That was just the way it goes sometimes, right? Yeah, sure. Right. Fuck the world and go your own way. That's what it came down to in the end. Be a loner. You could survive. No problem.

A brown face surrounded by dreadlocks came into her mind. It was good enough for Stick, wasn't it? Sure. But how come it had to hurt so much? Did it hurt him? Did he ever get lonely?

She was crying so hard now, she couldn't see where she was going. Dragging her shades from her eyes, she shoved them in her pocket and wiped away the flow of tears with her sleeve.

Maybe she'd just go ask Stick how he did it. She hadn't even had a chance to thank him yet, anyway.

Still sniffling, she headed for the museum by Fare-you-well Park.

As the Horn Dance was leaving the stage in The Factory, Stick pulled his Harley up in front of the museum. Cutting the engine, he stretched stiff neck muscles, then put the bike on its stand.

"End of the line," he said.

Lubin left her basket to perch on the seat. Wrinkling her nose, she made a small rumbly noise in the back of her throat.

"Yeah, I know. It's long past supper."

What a night, he thought. Pocketing his spell-box, he chained the bike to the iron grating by the museum's door and went up the broad steps. Lubin flowed up the steps ahead of him. By the time he reached the door, she'd already slid through her own private entrance to wait for him inside.

"Get the stew on!" he called through the door as he dug around in his jacket pocket for his keys.

He was just about to fit the key into the lock when he heard it. Oh, shit he thought. Not again. Turning, he tried to pinpoint the source of what he'd just heard—a young voice raised in a high cry of pain. Now who'd be stupid enough to mess around this close to his digs? It was bad enough that he'd spent the better part of the day and evening unsuccessfully trying to run down a lead on Farrel Din's rumor, without this kind of shit.

The sound of the fight came from an alleyway across the street. Stick took out his staff and snapped it into one solid length as he crossed the street. Packers or Bloods, somebody was getting their head busted because he was *not* in a mood to be gentle with bashers tonight.

He slowed down to a noiseless glide as he approached the mouth of the alley. Hugging the wall to the right, he slipped inside. Bloods. Bashing some kid. It was hard to make out if it was a boy or a girl; a runaway or one of the Pack. He didn't stop to think about it. His staff shot out in a whirling blur, hitting the closest Blood before any of them even seemed to be aware he was there. The one he hit went down hard. The rest scattered toward the back of the alley.

Stick smiled humorlessly. Seemed they didn't know the alley had a dead end.

He moved after them, sparing their victim a quick glance before going on. Looked like a Blood—a small one, but a Blood all the same. Now that didn't make much—

"Hey, Stick. How's it hanging?"

Stick's gaze went up. The Bloods were making a stand. Well, that was fine with him. There were seven— no, eight of them. He shifted his feet into a firmer stance, staff held out horizontally in front of him. As he began to cat-step toward them, the ones in front broke ranks. Stick had no trouble recognizing the figure that moved forward. Fineagh.

"Times hard?" Stick asked. "Haven't seen you getting your own hands dirty for a while. I thought you just let your goons handle shit like this."

"Well, this is personal," Fineagh replied.

Stick gave him a tight-lipped smile. "Pleasure's mine."

"I don't think so," Fineagh said. Taking his hand from his pocket, the Blood leader pointed the stolen .38 at Stick. "Bye-bye, black man."

Christ, he'd been set up like some dumbass kid who should know better. He started for Fineagh, staff whistling through the air, but he just wasn't fast enough.

The gunshot boomed loud in the alleyway. The bullet hit him high in the shoulder, the force of the impact slamming him back against the brick wall. His staff dropped from numbed fingers as he tried to stay on his feet. A second bullet hit him just above the knee, searing through muscle and tendon. His leg buckled under him and he sprawled to the ground.

"You always were just *too* damn good," Fineagh said conversationally. He kicked the staff just out of reach of Stick's clawing fingers, then hunched down, eyes glittering with malicious pleasure. "Never could deal with you like we could anybody else. So you had to come down, Stick—you see that, don't you? We got a rep to maintain." He grinned mockingly. "Nothing personal, you understand?"

Stick saved his breath, trying to muster the energy for a last go at Fineagh, but it just wasn't there. The wounds, the shock that was playing havoc with his nervous system, had drained all his strength. He kept his gaze steady on the Blood leader's eyes as Fineagh centered the .38, but that didn't stop him from seeing the elf's finger tightening on the trigger. He could see every pore of Fineagh's pale skin. The silver death's head stud in his ear. The spill of dark laughter in his eyes . . .

Though he tried not to, he still flinched when the gun went off again.

Manda hitched a ride with a friend of Maggie's that she ran into on Cutter Street, arriving at the museum just in time to see Stick enter the alleyway. She was at the far end of the street, though, and paused, not sure what to do. She could hear the fight. Stick wouldn't want her getting in the way. But when she heard the first gunshot, she took off for the alley at a run, speeding up when the sharp crack of gunfire was repeated.

Lubin reached it before her, streaking across the street from the museum to disappear into the mouth of the alley.

When Manda got there, she caught a momentary glimpse of Stick's sprawled form, the circle of Bloods around him, Fineagh with the gun. . . . Just as Fineagh squeezed off his third shot, Manda saw the ferret launch herself at the elf's arm. Her teeth bit through to the bone, throwing off his shot. The bullet spat against the wall, showering Stick with bits of brick. The gun tumbled from Fineagh's nerveless fingers to fly in a short arc toward Manda, hitting the pavement with a spit of sparks. Hardly realizing what she was doing, she ran forward and claimed the weapon.

Fineagh screamed, trying to shake the ferret from his wrist. It wasn't until one of his companions reached for her that Lubin dropped free to crouch protectively over Stick. Fineagh aimed a kick at her.

"D-don't do it!" Manda called nervously. The gun was a heavy cold weight in her fist as she aimed it down the alley.

The Bloods turned to face her. Fineagh's eyes narrowed. He clutched his wrist, blood dripping between his fingers, but gave no sign of the pain he had to be feeling.

"Hey, babe," he said. "Why don't you just give me that back—maybe we'll leave you in one piece."

Manda shook her head.

Fineagh shrugged. "Your funeral."

As he started toward her, Manda closed her eyes and pulled the trigger. The gun bucked in her hands,

almost flying from her grip, but her fingers had tight-
ened with surprise. That was the only thing that kept
her from losing it. Her shot went wild, but the Bloods
no longer seemed so eager to confront her.

"Hey, come on," one of them said to Fineagh. "Let's
get the fuck out of here."

Billy Buttons stepped up to the lean elf's side.
"Nabber's right. We got what we came for, Fineagh.
Let's blow."

Fineagh turned to him. "You want to leave her with
that piece?"

"I just want to get the hell out of here."

Biting at her lower lip, Manda listened to them ar-
gue. She didn't know what she'd do if they charged
her. How many bullets did this thing have left anyway?
Not that she was sure she could even hit anything, no
matter how many bullets there were.

Fineagh glared at Billy, at the ferret guarding Stick,
at Manda. "Sure," he said finally. "We're gone."

Manda backed away from the mouth of the alley as the
Bloods approached, standing well away from them as
they stepped out onto the street.

"I won't forget," Fineagh said, pointing a finger at
her. "I *never* forget."

"Come on," Billy said. "Let's get that wrist looked at."

"Fuck my wrist! You hear me, babe? Fineagh Steel's
got your number. You are *not* going to like what I'm
going to do to you next time we meet."

"You . . . you can just . . ." Manda was so scared, the
words stuck in her throat.

Fineagh took a step toward her. "I ought to rip
your—"

He stopped when she raised the gun. She hoped
desperately that they couldn't see how badly she was
shaking. Fineagh gave her an evil smile.

"Later, babe. You and me."

He turned abruptly and led the gang away.

Manda waited until they turned the corner, then ran back into the alley.

"Easy," she said soothingly to the ferret. "Good boy. Don't bite me now. I'm here to help."

Help. Right. She almost threw up when she looked at the mess the bullets had made. There was blood everywhere. Stick was so pale from shock and loss of blood that she didn't think he'd have any trouble passing himself off as a white man if he wanted to. The light in his eyes was dimming.

"F-funny . . . seeing you . . . here. . . ." he mumbled.

Manda swallowed thickly. "Don't try to talk," she said.

She laid the gun down on the ground and knelt down beside him. Lubin made a suspicious noise and sniffed at her, then backed slowly away, growling softly. Manda closed her eyes and took a deep steadying breath. Leaning over him, eyes still closed, she began to hum monotonously. The sound helped keep her head clear for what she meant to do.

She sustained the drone for a few moments, then laid her left hand gently on Stick's thigh, covering the wound, her right on his shoulder. Here was one thing that silver eyes were good for. Elf blood. For once she was glad she had it. She stopped humming as she concentrated fully on the task at hand. Something inside her, some part of her Elvin heritage, reached out and assessed the damage done to Stick's body, mended the broken bones, reconnected arteries and nerves, healed the flesh, all the while taking the pain into herself. Not until the least of his cells was healed, did she sit back and take her hands away.

Stick's pain, curdling inside her, rose up and hit her like a blow. She tumbled over on her side. Her body, drained of the energy she'd used to heal Stick, tried to deal with the pain, shutting down all but the most essential life systems when it couldn't. She curled into a fetal position as a black wave knifed through her, sucking away her consciousness.

Lubin crept up to Stick, sniffing at where his wounds had been, then put her nose up against Manda's cheek. She whined, but there was no response from either of them.

Bramble pulled up in front of the museum and parked her bike beside Stick's. She put it on its kickstand, disconnected her spell-box and walked up to the big front door. There she hammered on the broad wooden beams for what seemed like the longest time. There was no reply.

"Aw, shit," she said.

She knew Stick was here—or at least his bike was. But what were the chances he'd take Manda in even if she *had* come knocking on his door? Thinking of what Stick was like, Bramble realized that it wasn't bloody likely.

Okay, so where else might she have gone? Back to the Horn Dance's house? Even more unlikely. So what did that leave? The streets.

Bramble tried the door again, waited, then sighed. Heading back to her bike, she kicked it into life. It looked like she was in for a night of cruising the streets. But she wasn't going to leave the poor kid out there on her own—not feeling as messed up as she'd obviously been when she'd fled The Factory.

She revved the throttle a couple of times, then took off, heading for Soho's club district.

*   *   *

The sound of Bramble's engine as she drove off roused Stick from a dream of a warm soft place. He'd felt as though he'd been lying somewhere with a beautiful earth goddess, his whole body nestled between her generous breasts. When he opened his eyes to find himself lying in the alley, it took him a few moments to realize where he was and how he'd come to be here.

Bloods. Bashing a kid. Who'd turned out to be a Blood. Part of a trap. And he'd gone charging in, like an asshole, and got himself shot—

He lifted a hand to his shoulder. His jacket had a hole in it and it was sticky with blood, but there was no wound there. He peered down and looked at his thigh. Same story. Only there he could see the scar. How the . . . ?

Then he remembered. The kid he'd helped last night—the halfling. She'd been here. It was then that he saw her lying beside him, all curled up in a ball. Half elf—with an elf's healing ability. That's what it had to have been. He had a dim recollection of her facing down the Bloods. Somehow she'd got hold of Fineagh's gun and sent the whole crew packing.

"You're really something, kid," he said.

He saw the gun lying just beyond her. Reaching over, he hefted it thoughtfully, then pocketed it. Lubin nuzzled his hand.

"Yeah, yeah," he said, ruffling her fur. "I remember you going one-on-one with Fineagh. Got myself a regular pair of guardian angels, don't I?"

He got slowly to his feet, marvelling that he was still alive. Retrieving his staff, he broke it down and replaced it in its sheath. Then he picked up the girl and headed for home.

"This is getting to be a habit," he said, talking to himself more than to her, for she was still unconscious.

"Only this time I'm taking care of you myself—I figure I owe you that much."

Not to mention that Fineagh wasn't likely to forget this. Stick knew that both he and the girl were looking to be in some deep shit and it was going to be coming down all too soon.

Stick awoke, stiff from a night on the sofa. He groaned as he sat up and swung his legs to the floor. Hell, he told himself. Don't complain. It sure beats lying dead in an alleyway with a couple of bullets in the old bod.

Putting on his jeans, he padded across the room to the doorway of his bedroom. His guest was already up and gone. Finding a shirt, he went to see if she'd left the museum or was just exploring. He found her on the ground floor, gazing with awe at a full-size skeleton display of a brontosaurus.

"Jeez," she said as he approached her. "This place is really something."

"How're you feeling?"

"Okay. A good night's sleep is all I usually need to recover from something like last night."

"Yeah," Stick said. "About last night. Thanks."

Manda grinned. "Hey, I owed you one." She looked back at the display. "Do you really have this whole place to yourself?"

From the outside, the five-story museum looked like a castle. Inside, the first four floors held natural history displays, everything from dinosaurs to contemporary wildlife—contemporary to the world outside, at least, for there were no examples of the strange elfish creatures that now inhabited the borderlands. All the natural sciences were represented. Geology, zoology, anthropology. Manda had spent the morning wandering from floor to floor, captivated by everything she saw. Her favorites, so far, were the Native American displays and the dinosaurs.

The fifth floor was where Stick lived. It had originally contained the museum's offices and research labs. Now most of the rooms stored the vast library that Stick had accumulated—books, records, videotapes; a wealth of pre-Elfland knowledge unmatched this side of the Border. A few rooms served as his living quarters.

"Except for Lubin," Stick said, "I've pretty much got the place to myself."

"Well, now I know why you know so much about the old days," Manda said. "But it does seem kind of decadent."

"What do you mean?"

"Well, there's all this neat stuff in here. It doesn't seem right to just keep it all to yourself."

"So what do you think I should do—open it to the public?"

"Sure."

Stick shook his head. "It wouldn't work."

"I know *lots* of folks who'd die to see this stuff."

"Sure. And when they got bored? They'd probably trash the place."

Manda gave him a funny look, then thought about what was left of the various pre-Elfland galleries and the like that she'd seen. "I guess you're right." She ran a hand along a smooth phalanx of the brontosaurus. "It seems a shame, though."

"Oh, this place had a use," Stick said. "This is where the Bloods that wanted to go into the outside world used to come. It was a place where they could learn a thing or two about the way things work out there so that they could fit in smoothly—if they didn't want to be noticed."

"Really?"

"Um-hmm. That's why I've got power—there's a generator that runs off a big spell-box that they left—and a lot of technological stuff works in here where it wouldn't work out on the street."

"You mean those TV sets and stereos and things up on the top floor really work?"

Stick nodded.

"Wow. I'd love to check out some of that stuff. I've only read about them before."

"Come on," Stick said. "I'll show you how they work." He bent down and held out his arm so that Lubin could slip into its crook, then led the way upstairs.

"Jeez, look at this stuff!" Manda cried in the music room. She pulled records from the big bookshelf racks that lined the walls. "Jimi Hendrix. David Bowie. Stormtrooper. The Nazgul." She looked up. "Is this stuff really as good as it's supposed to be?"

"Better."

Manda's mouth formed a silent "Wow."

"Listen," Stick asked as he turned the stereo on. "Have you got a place you can stay—some place out of the way, I mean, like *away* from Bordertown?"

"I . . ."

Well what had she been thinking anyway, Manda asked herself. That she was just going to be able to move in here or something? Jeez, it was really time that she grew up.

Stick saw the disappointment cross her face. "I'm not throwing you out," he said. "You seem like an okay kid and I owe you."

"That's okay. I can go. But not away from Bordertown. . . . This is my home."

"You're taking this wrong. See, the thing is—Fineagh—you know Fineagh?"

Manda nodded. "Sure. At least I've heard of him. He's the Bloods' latest leader."

"He's also the guy you put down last night."

Manda blanched. "Oh, shit."

"Right. So the problem is, he's going to come looking for us, and this time he'll bring every frigging Blood he can lay his hands on. I've got a feeling that they're going to bust into this place, and that it's going to be today."

"Can . . . *can* they get in?" Manda asked. She thought of what the museum looked like from the outside—an impregnable fortress.

"Well, the place's got a certain amount of built in security, left behind by the elves who used it, but there's no way it could stand up to a concentrated assault."

"So what are we going to do?"

Stick smiled. "Well, I want to get *you* to someplace safe for starters."

"No way."

"Listen, you don't know what's going to be coming down when—"

"I did pretty good last night, didn't I?"

"Yeah, sure. But—"

"And besides," Manda added, "I really want to hear some of this stuff."

"Listen, kid, you—"

"Manda."

"What?"

"My name's Manda."

"Okay. Manda."

Before he could go on, Manda laid down the stack of records she'd pulled out and walked over to where he was standing. "I'm not a hero," she said, "but I can't just walk away from this."

"Sure you can. You just—"

"Then, why don't *you* just leave Bordertown?" Manda couldn't believe it. Here she was arguing with Stick, for God's sake, like were they old pals or something.

"That's different," Stick said. "I've got a responsibility."

"To what? To this place that no one ever gets to see? To the people out on the streets who let you help them, but that you never let help you?"

"You don't know what you're talking about," Stick said. But listening to her, hearing the conviction in her voice, he found himself wondering what had ever happened to that sense of rightness he'd felt when he was her age. There was nothing he didn't have an opinion on back then—and a damn strong opinion at that—but somehow the years had drained it away. Where once his head had been filled with a strong sense of where he was going and what his place in the world was—he was its center, of course—he'd fallen into living by habits. Still doing things, but no longer sure just exactly why he was doing them. Like patrolling the streets like some comic book superhero, for Christ's sake.

He was so still, his face squinted in a frown, that Manda figured she'd gone too far. "Listen," she said. "I didn't mean to mouth off like that. You can do whatever you want—shit, it's your place. If you want me to get out of your way, I'll go back to Soho."

Stick shook his head. "No," he said. "You're right. Sooner or later you're going to have to settle this thing between Fineagh and you—same as I do. It might as well be now. But I'll tell you, Manda, we don't have a hope in hell of getting out of this in one piece—not if he musters as many Bloods as I think he will."

"Do you want to split?" Manda asked.

"Can't."

She grinned. "Well then, let's listen to some rock and

roll." She held up a record jacket with a full-face photo of a handsome curly-haired man. She was attracted to the group's name as much as the photo—mostly because of the time she'd just spent downstairs in the dinosaur display. The group was called Tyrannosaurus Rex. "Are they any good?"

"Yeah. They're great. Do you want to hear it?"

Manda nodded. She rubbed her hair nervously, making the mauve spikes stand up at attention. Way down inside, she was scared shitless. What she really needed right now was something to take her mind off what was going to be coming down all too soon. A little time was all she needed. Sure. And then she'd just face down Fineagh and his gang all by herself.

Music blasted from the speakers then, a mix of electric and acoustic instruments that pushed the immediacy of her fears to the back of her mind. After a short intro, the lead singer's curiously timbred voice sounded across the instruments, singing about a "Woodlamp Bop". By the time the second chorus came, she was singing along, Lubin dancing at her feet.

Stick left them to it while he went to see to some weapons. His staff just wasn't going to cut it, not with what Fineagh was going to bring down on them.

Bramble spent a fruitless night, going from club to club, stopping on street corners, asking after Little Maggie Woodsdatter's younger sister Manda, with no luck. Dawn was just pinking the sky when she ran down a rumor that was just starting to make the rounds of the Soho streets. Hearing it, she headed for home.

Mary was the only one up when Bramble came into the kitchen.

"Any luck?" Mary asked.

Bramble shook her head.

Mary sighed. "About last night," she said. "You know what the Hood's like. He's just into fulfilling obligations."

"Yeah. I know. But—"

"Anyway," Mary broke in. "We won't be playing there again—not even if we wanted to."

"Why not?"

"After the gig, the Hood collected our bread, then he decked George. 'That's for the kid,' he said. Left him with a beautiful shiner."

Bramble smiled. "I wish I'd seen that."

"Oh, I'm sure he'll be more than happy to give you a complete moment-by-moment rundown if you ask." She eyed Bramble thoughtfully. "So now what are you going to do? Are you still planning to pack it in?"

"No. Just before I got here, I heard a story that's making the rounds. Something about Stick and some kid facing down Fineagh and some of the Bloods. Whatever happened, the Bloods are planning a full-scale assault on Stick's place this afternoon."

"What's that?"

The sound of their conversation had woken a few other members of the band. The Hood sat down at the table with them, while Teaser and Johnny Jack fought a mock battle for the tea pot. It was the Hood who'd spoken.

Bramble gave them what details she'd been able to pick up. By the time she finished, most of the band was up and had joined them.

"This kid with Stick," Johnny Jack asked. "You think it's Manda?"

Bramble nodded.

"It makes sense," Mary added. "She was asking about him yesterday morning."

The Hood looked around at the rest of them. "Anybody here *not* want to get involved?"

"She seemed like a nice kid," Oss volunteered.

"And she *is* an honorary member of the band still," Johnny Jack added.

Mary shook her head. "But what can *we* do?" she asked. "We're not fighters."

"Oh, I don't know about that," the Hood said. "I've been known to kick some ass."

"You know what I mean," Mary said. "How could we possibly stand up to the numbers Fineagh can put together?"

There was a long silence. One by one heads turned to look at the Hood.

"Hell," he said after a moment. "It's simple. We just dance 'em into surrender."

"Come on," Bramble. "This is serious."

"I *am* being serious," the Hood replied. "The only thing is, we're going to need a wizard."

It was shaping up even worse than Stick had imagined it would.

"Oh shit," Manda said, joining him at the window. "What are we going to do?"

Behind them, the needle lifted from the LP by Big Audio Dynamite and the turntable automatically shut off. Neither of them noticed. All their attention was focused on the street below that fronted the museum.

Bloods rounded the corner and came down the street like a slow wave. There were easily more than a hundred of them, bedecked in jeans and red leather, silver eyes glittering in the afternoon light. Their hair was a multi-colored forest, ranging from elfin silver through every color of the spectrum. They were armed with knives and cudgels, broken lengths of pipe and chains, traditional elfin bows and arrows. The front ranks had sledgehammers and crowbars. One way or another, they made it obvious that they were cracking the museum open.

The Bloods alone were bad enough. But word had spread and the various gangs were showing up in force to watch the show. The Pack, in black leather. Dragon's Fire, down from the Hill, looking soft beside the real street gangs. Scruffy headbangers and Soho Rats, runaways and burn-outs.

Looking down at the crowd, Stick had visions of the bloodbath that was just a few wrong words away from exploding. He checked the load of his pump shotgun. With a quick snapping motion, he pumped a shell into place. Inside the museum, he had no doubt as to its reliability. But outside, beyond the elfin spells that kept the building and its contents in working order, he knew he'd be lucky if one shot in three fired.

Manda swallowed hard.

"Scared?" Stick asked.

She nodded.

"Me, too." When she looked at him in surprise, he added: "It might not be too late to get out the back."

"And do what?"

There was that, Stick thought. No matter where they went, they were going to have to face Fineagh sooner or later. Taking off now just meant the museum was going to get trashed and they'd still have the Blood leader on their ass. Making a stand here—maybe it was just suicide. But there didn't seem to be any other option.

"Did you ever get lonely?" Manda asked suddenly. "You know, just being here by yourself all the time?"

"I went out a lot—and besides, Lubin's good company."

The ferret was crouched on the windowsill in front of them. Manda gave her soft fur a pat.

"Yeah, but you didn't exactly hang out a lot when you *did* go out," she said.

"How do you know?"

"Hey, you're famous, Stick."

He sighed. "That's the kind of shit that got me into this in the first place. Always being the do-gooder." He gave her a quick look. "So maybe I got a little lonely from time to time. I guess it just came with the territory."

"You've helped an awful lot of people—did you never find one of them you liked well enough to be your friend?"

"It's not that simple, Manda. See, I've got to keep some distance between myself and the street. Without it, I can't do my job properly."

Manda nodded. "After being in here with you today, I can tell you're not as scary as you make yourself out to be down there." She nodded to where the gangs were gathering. "But how'd this get to be your job?"

"Kinda fell into it, I guess. The kids didn't have anyone looking after them and the gangs just started getting too rough on them. Hell, I'm no shining knight—don't get me wrong. But someone had to look out for them. Only now . . . shit, I don't know how it got so out of control."

Manda looked down. She could make out Fineagh now, standing at the head of the Bloods. He seemed so small from this height that she felt she could just reach out and squeeze him between her fingers like she might a bug.

"I guess we should . . . get down there," she said.

Stick nodded grimly. "Maybe I can shame Fineagh into going one-on-one with me—winner take all."

"Do you think he'd . . ." Manda's voice trailed off. "Look!" she cried.

But she didn't have to point it out to Stick. Forcing a

way through the spectators came a familiar band of bikers. It was the Horn Dance. An open-backed pickup truck followed the path the bikes made. That was the portable stage and power generator that they needed for their amps and sound system.

The bikes pulled up at the front steps, forming a semicircle around the truck. The truck stopped, its cab facing the museum doors, its bed directly in front of Fineagh.

"What the hell are they trying to pull?" Stick muttered as the band members began to strap on instruments. The whine of feedback and the sound of guitars and synthesizers being tuned rose up to their window.

"I think they're trying to help," Manda said.

"We'd better get the hell down there," Stick said. He strode off, Lubin at his heels, going so fast that Manda had to trot to keep on with him.

"Did you get it yet?" the Hood asked Farrel Din.

The wizard sat frowning behind the amplifiers in the bed of the Horn Dance's pickup. He looked at an old bumper sticker that was stuck to one of the wooden slats that made up the sides of the bed. It read, "I'd rather be Dancing." Well, he'd rather be anywhere, doing anything, he thought, than be here.

"Farrel?" the Hood prompted him.

"I'm thinking. I always have trouble with the simple spells. They're so easy that they just go out of my mind."

"Well, if you know some big smash-up of a one, go for it, for Christ's sake!"

Farrel Din sighed. "I never could learn the big ones," he said.

"We should have gotten another wizard," Bramble said to the Hood.

"Nobody else seemed to have a better idea when we got Farrel."

"Sure, but—"

"Will you go away and let me think!" Farrel Din shouted at them. "Why don't you start playing or something and as soon as I get it, I'll let you know."

"If you get it," Bramble muttered.

Farrel Din sighed, and returned to his task. It was such a stupidly simple spell, surely even *he* could remember it—couldn't he? It had been such a favorite— long ago, before Elfland left the outside world in the first place. But there hadn't been much call for it in the last few centuries. And he never was much of a wizard anyway. Why else did he run The Ferret? He'd always been better serving up beers than serving up spells.

Up front, Johnny Jack was arguing with Fineagh. The Blood leader wasn't ready to just wipe out the Horn Dance—they were too popular for him to risk that—but he was rapidly approaching the point where he just wouldn't give a fuck. He hadn't expected so many of the other gangs to show up either—but screw them as well. The Bloods were ready to take on anyone.

"Listen, you jackass," he told Johnny Jack. "I'm giving you two minutes to get that shit out of my way, or we're just going through you—understand?"

"Everybody tuned?" the Hood asked from the bed of the pick-up. He'd been keeping a wary eye on the Bloods and knew that they couldn't hold off much longer. Farrel Din, he thought. Get it together and we'll play your club for a month—free of charge.

"We're rooting to toot," Teaser called to him.

"Then let's get this show on the road!" the Hood cried.

* * *

Stick and Manda stepped out of the museum's front door at the same moment as the Horn Dance kicked into the opening bars of a high-powered version of the "Morris Call". The sheer volume of sound stopped them in their tracks. The Bloods looked to Fineagh for direction, but the rest of the crowd immediately began to stamp their feet.

"All *right!*" someone shouted.

Shouts and whistles rose up from the crowd, but were drowned by the music. Bramble kept an eye on Fineagh, then turned to see how Farrel Din was doing, all the while playing her button accordion. The portly wizard was hunched over, muttering to himself. Great plan, Hood, Bramble thought. She turned back to face the crowd.

Most of the punkers and runaways were dancing—a combination of shuffled country dance steps and pogoing. The Rats eyed the Bloods, ready to rumble. Everyone else seemed to be trying to figure out if they'd come to a free concert or a street fight, with the crowd from the Hill hanging back as usual—wanting to be a part of things, but nervous of a free-for-all.

Stick started down the steps, Manda and Lubin trailing a few paces behind. Fineagh's eyes narrowed as he took in Stick's shotgun. The Horn Dance broke into a medley of "Barley Break" and "The Hare's Maggot".

"Come *on!*" the Hood shouted at Farrel Din.

"Easy for you to say," the wizard replied. He counted on his fingers, shaking his head. "No. That's shit into gold. Maybe . . . ?" He squeezed his eyes shut, trying to think, while the music thundered on.

Stick moved along the side of the truck, the shotgun held down by his side. With his finger in the trigger guard, he only needed to swing it up to fire.

Bramble tried to catch Manda's eye. If Stick and

Fineagh started at each other—it wouldn't make any difference if Farrel found the spell or not. But Manda's gaze was locked on the tall Blood leader who awaited their approach. The Bloods began to press closer to Fineagh. Those armed with bows, notched arrows.

Stick stopped when he was a few paces away from Fineagh.

"Kill that shit," Fineagh said, nodding at the band.

"Not my party," Stick said.

Fineagh turned to his followers, but before a command could leave his lips, Farrel Din sat up in the back of the truck.

"Got it!" he cried.

He jumped up and ran over to Bramble, tripped over a power cord, and fell against the willowy red-head. The two went down in a tumble. Bramble was carrying the tune. When she fell, her accordion made a discordant wheezing sound. The band faltered at the loss of the melody line.

Farrel Din grinned into Bramble's face. "Play 'Off She Goes'," he said as they disentangled themselves.

"But—"

"Trust me. Just play it."

Bramble nodded to the Hood. The band stopped, and she broke into the jig. She played the first few bars on her own, then the others recognized the tune and joined in. In the meantime, eyes closed in concentration, Farrel Din stood directly in front of Bramble. Hopping from one foot to the other, he waved his fingers around her accordion in a curious motion, all the while singing something in the old elfin tongue.

The effect was almost instantaneous. Anyone not already moving to the music, immediately began to dance, whether they wanted to or not. Rats and Bloods shuffled in time to the lilting rhythm. Those in the crowd already dancing seemed to move into high gear, happily swinging partners and generally having fun. In the back, the crowd from the Hill looked embarrassed as they flung themselves about, but seemed to be having a good time all the same.

The Bloods fought the glamour, but the spell, combined with the music, gave them no choice. They lifted one foot, then the other, keeping time with the beat, frowns on their faces. Only Fineagh, through the sheer stubbornness of his will, stood still. Fineagh and Stick.

Jigging on the spot, Manda couldn't believe that they weren't affected. Even Lubin was dancing—though the ferret loved to at any time, so perhaps that didn't count. But then Manda saw that even their feet were tapping slightly.

"This doesn't stop anything," Fineagh said. Fires flickered in his eyes.

Stick shrugged. "It doesn't have to be like this—you could just walk away."

"Can't."

"You mean, you won't."

The hate in the elf's silver eyes became a quicksilvering smolder. Stick knew they were both moments away from falling prey to the glamour in the music.

"Give it up," he said.

Even if he said yes, Manda wondered, how could they trust him? But the Blood leader had no intention of giving up. One minute his hand was empty, in the next a throwing knife had dropped into it from a wrist sheath. The blade left his hand, flying straight and true for Stick. He brought up the shotgun, knocked it from the air. Leveling the gun, he pulled the trigger. The shell was a dud.

A second knife appeared in Fineagh's hand at the same time as Stick pumped a new shell into place. The boom of the shotgun was lost in the thundering music, but Fineagh's chest exploded as the load hit him. He was lifted into the air and thrown back a half dozen feet, dead before he hit the ground.

The band's music stopped as suddenly as though someone had pulled the plug. Hundreds of eyes stared at the blood-splattered remains of the tall elf. The sound of Stick's pumping a new shell into place was loud in the abrupt silence. He leveled the shotgun at the ranks of Bloods.

"Anybody else what to play?" he asked.

Their leader was dead. Gone with him was the mania that had brought them all to this point. The Bloods were suddenly aware of just how out-numbered they were.

"Hell, no," Billy Buttons said finally. "We're cool."

Turning, he shouldered his way through the Bloods. Long tense moments passed, but slowly the Bloods followed him, leaving Fineagh's corpse where it lay.

"Th-that's it?" Manda asked softly.

Stick looked at her, then at the Horn Dance and the crowds still gathered.

"It's not enough?" he asked.

Manda swallowed. "Sure. I mean . . ."

Stick nodded. "I know."

With that, he turned and retraced his way back up the museum's steps, the shotgun hanging loosely in his hand. Lubin ran ahead, disappearing before him. Stick paused at the door to look back.

"Come visit sometime," he said. Then he too was gone.

The door closed with a loud thunk.

Manda stared at it, but all she could see was the pain she'd discovered in Stick's eyes. Damn him! Didn't he realize that it didn't have to be like this? He had friends.

The Horn Dance had turned out to help him. Farrel Din had. She was here. Tears welled up in her own eyes and she wasn't sure if they were from feeling hurt, or for him.

She started to move for the door, but Bramble appeared at her side. She caught Manda's arm.

"But I want . . . I should . . ."

"Not a good time," Bramble said.

"But . . ."

Bramble pulled a couple of notes from her button accordion, then softly sang.

> There was an old woman
>   tossed up in a blanket
> ninty-nine miles, beyond the moon
> And under one arm
>   she carried a basket
> and under t' other she carried a broom
> Old woman, old woman, old woman, cried I
> O wither, O wither, O wither, so high?
> I'm going to sweep cobwebs
>   beyond the sky
> but I'll be back again, by and by

She ended with a flourish on the accordion and gave Manda a lopsided smile.

"I don't understand," Manda said.

"Clean your own house, and let him clean his. You heard what he said. He *did* ask you to come visit him sometime."

"Sure, but—"

"But now's not 'by and by'," Bramble said. "Come on. Give the Horn Dance a chance. We've got a captive audience—what with Farrel's spell. We could use your licks, kiddo."

Manda looked up at the museum's fifth floor. Was there a movement at the window? But then she realized that Bramble was right. While Manda wasn't sure what she wanted from Stick, it had to come at its own pace. She'd give him a bit of a grace period, but if he didn't wise up soon, then he'd find her camped out on his front steps.

"Hey!" Big Will called from the back of the truck.

Manda looked up at him and saw he was holding out Bramble's canary-yellow Les Paul. She followed Bramble up onto the back of the truck and took the instrument with a smile of thanks. Someone had already removed Fineagh Steel's body. Bramble led the band in a rousing version of the "Staines Morris". Teaser and Mary moved amongst the crowd, showing the steps. Manda was about to join in, when Johnny Jack caught her by the arm.

"I think you're forgetting something," he said. He held out her foxhead and mask and the ribbon-festooned jacket.

Manda propped the Les Paul up against its amp and put them on. Then she slung the guitar on and joined the tune with a flashy spill of notes. Bramble gave her a grin.

Leaning into the tune's chords, Manda looked out at the sea of bobbing faces. The Rats had left soon after the Bloods. The crowd that remained didn't need Farrel Din's glamour to join in. And neither did she, Manda thought, jigging on the spot with Johnny Jack.

The music was good and the people were good. Maybe it was about time that she stopped backing away from things and took the plunge. If she couldn't do it herself, how could she ever expect to set an example for Stick?

She glanced up at the fifth floor again, and this time, while she didn't see Stick, she could see Lubin dancing on the windowsill. Smiling, she turned her attention back to the music.

CHARIS

Ellen Kushner

I.

I have this very blond hair, see, almost white. About the most thrilling thing I've ever done in my life was to go to this Elvin club called the Wheat Sheaf which is in Soho. It's not like the Border itself, I mean they can't actually keep you out if you're human, but it's understood you don't go there if you are. I put on a ton of makeup, made my face utterly white, painted on swirls which were the thing that year, covered my ears up, and left my hair just the way it is. I got in all right. The music was not bad, what I heard of it. And the lighting was truly weird, gorgeous colors swirling around in the air, almost *too* bright, too vivid for my eyes. And there were all these elves, dancing the way they do, as though they didn't have any joints in their bodies. Some of my friends spend hours after school trying to teach themselves to dance like that.

About the most thrilling thing I've ever done. That says it all. I stood against the wall and watched elves dance. I bought myself a drink, and drank half of it. Then I went home. Scullion trailed me all the way, to make sure I didn't get roughed up by any halfie kids.

Scullion never told on me, either. He knew my parents would skin me if they knew, but he told me once that wasn't his job: Lena and Randal hired him to protect me, not to spy on me.

Scullion's all right. He's half elf, half human, born and bred in B-town. He's very tall and very strong. What he doesn't know about the streets here isn't worth knowing. He has a Tree of Life tattooed all the way up his left arm. I loved looking at it when I was young. I don't know where he came from, but I suspect he was in some kind of trouble, and Lena got him out of it on the condition that he become my guard. Bordertown's a rough place, even if you live up with the other privileged folk on luxurious Dragon's Tooth Hill, like we do. And important High Council members are an easy target for unrest. You'd figure, in a city made up of poets, wizards, halfies, runaways, and folk trying to strike it rich, there'd be plenty of unrest. In the middle of this chaos, anything that needs ruling gets ruled on by the Council, or some branch of it, from regulating currency prices to deciding what crimes are punishable by banishment to the open Borderlands.

So now we're getting ready for the M-Bassy Ball, *the* social event of the year for little old B-town. I don't know what "M-Bassy" means; probably the name of the person who started it: M. Bassy—Michel, Maude, Milo, something like that. The M-Bassy Ball is held every year in one of the oldest buildings, all the way in the heart of decadent Soho. They cordon the whole area off for days beforehand, and clean up the building and decorate it. And you can only get in if you're carrying a special invitation. People will do anything to get an invitation. But unlike most big parties and private clubs where you can use your power, money, or contacts to get in, the M-Bassy Ball is only for a select crew on a carefully picked guest list.

Invitations to the M-Bassy Ball can't be faked: they're hand-scribed and decorated by a different artist every year. If there's one thing Bordertown has, it's lot of artists looking for work. Whenever it's humans' turn to run the ball, Lena and Randal make a bit point of encouraging new talent. People (I use the term loosely) keep those invitations, have them framed and everything. I've got a terrific collection my parents gave me. But this is the first year I'm going to the ball myself.

I'm terrified.

I know I'm supposed to be this walking glamour: born and bred in exotic Bordertown, where every kid who hates his parents and can play three guitar chords runs away to be Artistic. I've known elves all my life, and every weird fashion that comes along I've worn. I heard Leaf and Winter's Sorrow play for one of my parents' dances when I was ten. Let me tell you something: it doesn't make a bit of difference. If you're born ordinary and clumsy and, let's face it, with a big nose and no cheekbones, you might as well come from East Succotash for all the good it does you.

Lena disagrees. She says every sixteen-year-old girl feels the same, that there's nothing wrong with my nose, and she wished she had legs like mine when she was my age. A lot she knows about it. She always had enormous eyes the color of poured chocolate. And she was brilliant. When my mother was nineteen, she was the go-between in a market fight between elves and humans. When she was twenty-one she was aide to Serif Boynton on the Bordertown High Council. The rest is history.

She even married a poet, when everybody told her

not to. This was Randal, a Worlder who'd come to the
Borderlands to learn enough magic to power the world's
fastest motorcycle. Not the sort of guy you'd expect a
rising young power to favor. But Lena says she's always
been mad for red hair. And in fact, Randal's not as
crazy as most poets. He spends most of his time now on
Council stuff and prettying up his cycle. It still doesn't
go very fast, but it looks real good.

So I know my mother means well, but I still want to
kill her when she starts going on about my Good Quali-
ties. It is a small, peevish comfort to me that, where her
only child is concerned, my mother's famous diplomacy
is a joke.

They want me to dye my hair. My very own silver
hair, which looks bleached but isn't, which looks elven
but isn't. The thing is, the M-Bassy Ball guest list is very
carefully made up to be half human, half elf. Just like
the High Council. All the Council folk come, along
with the seriously important ones they do business with.
It's supposed to be this big party where we all rub
shoulders and show how well we get along. In years
where the political situation in the city is tricky, the least
little thing can set off an Incident. Elves can be very
touchy when it suits them. Lena doesn't want any elf
getting the notion that her daughter is trying to look
Elvin.

It's not as though I couldn't dye it and get away with it.
Dark purple is a big thing this year, because of that
band, the Guttertramps. But I like my hair the way it is.
Everyone in the city knows I was born with it. I don't
see why, now that I'm sixteen and going to Council
functions, I have to pretend to turn into someone else.

My best friend Lise says she'd shave her head if it
meant getting a ball invite. But that doesn't mean much:
she shaved her head last year, and painted rainbows on

it. Lise is very artistic. I wish she could come with me, because I dance a lot better when I'm watching her, kind of following the steps. Two years ago we were going to run away together. Her father's wives were being a pain, and Lena and Randal were threatening to make me stay home at night unless my school papers got better. So we were going to get these grubby clothes and pretend to be boys and escape.

The dumb thing was, there wasn't anywhere to run away to. You can't get into Elfland (not that I'd want to!) and there are no other real towns in the Borderlands, just farming villages and stuff like that. Lise said if all the artists in the World really do come here, it meant there weren't any left down in the World, and if we went there, she could make a lot of money. But I said they all left because it was even more boring down there than here. Everyone knows the Worlders are totally without brains, music, or style. So in the end we stayed where we were. And Lise got picked to do the scenery for the Full Moon Festival at school. And my parents let me go with this boy to the Dancing Ferret in Soho. He kissed me after, but I didn't see the point, and I don't think he did, either. I think he only asked me out because his mother told him to: all the traders want to get in good with people on the Council.

I wonder sometimes if the elf kids have to put up with this kind of thing. Council elf kids and rich traders and such live on the Hill, too, but on the other side, nearer the river. They go to a different school, and they're always dressed really sharp. But you don't really hang out with them unless it's at one of those Soho clubs no one's parents really approve of. It used to be that only real Slummers went down there, trying to pretend they were some kind of gang; but things are different now. Slummers still slum, but the rest of us go for the music, when we get the chance. There are private clubs all over the Hill, but they're not too hot, and there's no mixing. A human could never get into an elf club on the Hill.

It would serve them right if I shaved my head.

II.

I'm scared now, really scared. Too much depends on this. And I have to do it alone. Which means that, no matter what happens, if I fail, there's no one else to blame. But there's no one else he can turn to. I'm his only hope.

Silvan. The man in green.

Two days before the Ball, the word went round the inner circles of Bordertown: important elvin personages would be attending, from the Lands Beyond the Border. (Of course it threw the balance of the guest list off. They had to suddenly invite more humans.) In Council the elves were especially touchy all week, trying to gain points, to show their power. Old disputes about fishing rights resurfaced, and Windreed proposed a tax on ground corn, of all things! Dinner at our house— when we got to eat in private—was nothing but griping from Lena and Randal, how impossible the situation was, how they'd trusted Riverrun to take a moderate stance on the fishing issue but she'd got a bug up her pants like all the rest, must be acting on higher orders and blah blah blah. At least they forgot to nag me about my hair.

So the night of the M-Bassy Ball I did myself up right: tight-laced boots up to the thigh, that flashed out between layers of elvin glitter cloth when I walked, moved, danced. Bare arms with silver cuffs. And black glitter in my hair. Conservative, but striking. If I wasn't going to turn heads, at least I didn't have to be embarrassed either.

We hauled out the carriage for the occasion. Because the night was warm, we got to ride with the top down, which I always love. It's such a heavy old piece of junk that it doesn't go too fast, even with both horses pulling it. And you have to take the widest streets. Once you get past the Old Wall, of course, that isn't a problem: they built streets for two or three carriages, back in those days. Finally we pulled up at the M-Bassy building. Behind the guards, Soho punks were hanging around watching to see who drove up next. We had to wait behind another carriage, a little number obviously made out of wood, with old machine parts tacked on to make it look more realistic. Then we passed our invitations by the gatemen and went on in.

I wasn't prepared to be so impressed. The M-Bassy Ball was like nothing I'd ever seen: more like the opening of Council than like going to a club or even a party. There was a giant staircase that curved, and you came down it with everyone watching from the bottom. Lena and Randal looked great, as always, but with all those eyes on them they seemed like stars. Like the best act in the hottest club in town. I had this stupid feeling like I was going to cry. Because there I was, their daughter, and even if I wasn't so great, like not brilliant or pretty or coordinated, we were all three of us a unit, we belonged together, and there was nothing anyone could do to change that.

At the bottom of the staircase was the crowd of people, the music, and the food. I mostly checked out what everyone was wearing. People were looking good. And everyone who'd been coming to my parents' house since I was a baby came up to me and told me how great I looked. Which was nice of them. I smiled until my face hurt.

This boy Johnsson who goes to my school and whose father is an important trader came up to me and rolled his eyes like, "Is this boring or what?" So I had to give the same look back like I agreed with him. He said, "You wanna dance later?" and I said, "Sure." *Later.* Maybe I'd better get drunk before then.

I wandered off in search of drinks. Then I realized nobody else was moving. The room went quiet. Everyone was looking up at the staircase.

Coming down it was the most beautiful woman I had ever seen. Elf or human. I mean it. Long silvery hair floated back from her face like a cloud or as if she were standing looking out to sea. She was slender and graceful. And her face was . . . well, it was perfect. I can't describe it any better without making it sound like I had a lech on her, which I definitely did not. It was just perfect.

Then something creepy happened. All the elves in the room got down on the knee. It made a rustling sound, like the wind on the hillside. Every human was left standing up, feeling awkward. We really showed, looming above their heads like that.

The band had stopped playing. In the perfect silence, there was the elf woman's glittery laughter.

Then everybody got up off their knees and began to move around again. It seemed that I was the only one still watching the stairs. Behind the woman came a man, elvin like her, all dressed in green, from boots to the tie that held back his long silver hair. There's a certain shade of green that only elves can look really good in. No B-town men were wearing long hair this year—everything about him said *Elfland*. The man in green was not perfect. He went beyond perfect to beautiful: nose not quite straight, eyes a little long. Not that anyone would find him ugly—certainly the gorgeous lady didn't. When he got to the bottom, she put her arm in his.

I'm not nuts about elves or anything. A lot of girls go through a phase when they get crushes on elves, especially musicians in bands, and they won't even look at human guys. The whole thing's pretty sick if you ask me. Nobody needs more halfies in the world.

So I turned away from the newcomers. I almost ran into Windreed. He bowed to me with that mocking half smile of his. "The daughter of the House of Flame looks splendid tonight."

"I thank you," I said correctly. There was a silence I was obviously supposed to fill. "Uh . . . that was some entrance, just now."

He looked pleased. Either I'd just made a fool of myself, or it was the right thing to say. "The new Lady and her Lord honor us."

"Yes," I replied, trying to keep from fidgeting under his pale gaze, "very much." Go away, I thought fiercely at him. Everyone knows you're the coldest, meanest, toughest elf in Council. Go pick on someone your own size!

As if in answer to my plea, Shoshana Mizmag appeared behind him. "Windreed!" she said. The woman knows no fear. I hope I'm like that when I'm forty. "I'll forgive you insulting me in Council yesterday if you'll come dance with me now!"

His formal face thawed a bit. Elves love to tease. "Formidable lady! At home we have a Dance Challenge. How I would love to test you in it!"

"How you would love to give me a heart attack!" She chuckled. "But not tonight, sir. I know about those elvin contests. Nice if we could settle all city disputes over possessions by dancing, but somehow I don't think the town would go for it. And this is a civilized party. Tonight we dance away our troubles, but nothing more substantial."

"Certainly not, to this music." The old elf almost sniffed.

"What a traditionalist! Elvin folk music by all means, but not at the ball; here we must be stylish or perish! Shall we hurl ourselves into the fray?"

"And let others profit by our example?" he said. "Look!"

We looked.

It was the Lady, the silver-haired lady, dancing with my father. Randal looked like an amiable, shaggy red bear beside her. He also looked like he was having fun.

"An example has been set," said Windreed smugly. He offered Shoshana his hand.

When the band really got going, there wasn't much for me to do but watch and listen. They were fantastic, and it was wild to see all the Councillors and powers, human and elvin, enjoying themselves like normal club-goers. I didn't see Johnsson, which was good: there's nothing worse than having to dance with the only free person in the room. It gives new meaning to the phrase, "I wouldn't do it with you if you were the last human in the World."

The silver Lady was everywhere. I'd sell my soul for a pair of enchanted shoes that could make me dance the way she did. It's a good thing that that magic stuff doesn't work reliably in Bordertown, or I'd be minus one soul now. As for her escort, he was hard to spot. I noticed him once, leaning against a wall peeling a piece of fruit with his fingers. But I quickly looked away. He was doing it so carefully, so smoothly, with delicate concentration; it was as though I had come on him undressing someone. *Someone.* All right—it was as though I'd come on him undressing a woman. I didn't stick around to watch him take a bite.

When the Lady left the room, everyone pretended not to notice. She paused in the doorway, and for a moment her eyes seemed to stare into mine. The dancers closed ranks over the silver trail she left. I followed.

I just did. It was the same impulse that led me once to the Elven Wheat Sheaf: wanting to get away with something I shouldn't. And a faint feeling that I could do it.

She didn't go far, just down a wide hallway, dimly lit and private. Her Lord was waiting there.

I didn't dare get close enough to hear what they were saying. I scrunched myself into the darkness of the window bay. Even just standing and talking they looked like they were dancing. It made my throat hurt, watching. Suddenly she turned sharply away from him, lovely as a swan wheeling over a lake. I heard myself make a small noise. He held out his arms to her. She pulled him to her, close, his green and her silver together. His mouth was against her ear, moving her hair. She stood back a pace, looking at him. Then she lifted her arm and slapped him, hard, across the face.

And he just stood there. He didn't even look angry. She took off a ring and gave it to him. And he put it on his finger.

I remember hearing the band playing a new hit, "Free Me," the music faint but followable if you already knew the words:

> Used to gaze with my heart,
> Follow my fingers home.
> Did you want me or my need?
> Then there was hope,
> Now there's none—

Free me!
Once I burned for your touch
Now even one look is too much—
Free me!

Rope me to the wind and set me free,
Cuts like a knife,
Power scream,
Ten thousand volts is not enough
To free me . . .

She left him then and went back down the hall to the dancing. I could have reached out and touched her drifting silver tunic. She was smiling to herself as she went by.

Of course it was none of my business. Some weird elvin ritual. Or maybe what I'd just seen was only your basic lovers' spat. Just because Randal and Lena never slug each other doesn't mean I'm ignorant.

I didn't even know who they were. Even in B-town, surrounded by elves, there's a lot about the customs of Elfland we don't know. You get the feeling that if the elves in B-town had been so in love with their home, they wouldn't have settled in the Borderlands. So it's no wonder they don't talk about Elfland much. "The new Lady and her Lord," Windreed had said. Some kind of rulers or powers, then, come down past the Border to check out the ball, pick up some good food for cheap, or maybe get a kick out of having a roomful of elves bow to them. . . .

She'd passed me, but I didn't know where he'd gone. So, cautiously, I stuck my head out to look.

He was standing where she'd left him, turning the ring on his finger. I don't know why he looked up then. But my hair was very bright in the gloom of the half-lit hall, and he saw me.

"Maiden," he said.

I just froze. I literally couldn't move. I didn't want to.

"Don't come out," he said. "Wait there for me."

What could I do, jump out the window? I watched him come down the hall to me, until we were both standing in the tiny space of the window bay together, looking out over Soho.

He reeked of magic. I felt dizzy. He might have been trying to cast a spell, but if he was, it wasn't working. I had the feeling, though, that magic just clung to him as grace and beauty did to the Lady.

He was much taller than me, so he sat on the windowsill. I could barely see his face. His words came out of darkness.

"The Summons," he said. "And so soon. Maiden, I am afraid."

"Oh," I said, because saying anything, no matter how dumb, was better than letting *that* lie there. "I'm sorry."

I mean, nobody had ever talked to me that way before. Beautiful strangers out of nowhere don't start suddenly telling you how afraid they are. Not in real life. Maybe in stories.

"Can I help?" I said.

I thought he'd say, like, "Oh, no, thanks a lot, it's just really got me down," (only Elfland-y). But he said, "Yes."

"I can help?" I repeated, to be sure.

"If you will. Because you've offered. I am not allowed to ask for help; but if you offer it, I can take it."

This was beginning to sound a lot like magic. I hated to disappoint him, but I'm not real good at that stuff. I can't even put a few extra RPMs on Randal's bike. "Are you under a spell?" I asked.

I could hear his smile in the dark. "No, maiden. Not really. The Lady chose me last year at Dancing Night. It is my pleasure to serve her"—here I'll swear he blushed—"in all things. I could ask for no greater honor." Suddenly he pulled off the ring. The twisted silver caught the light. "But this honor is too much!" he said angrily. "I had no idea she would Summon me."

"Summon you where?"

"Forever," he whispered, staring at the ring. "Not from one Dancing Night to the next, but to stay by her side for the rest of her life."

"You don't love her?" I asked softly.

"Love the Lady?" he said bitterly. "One doesn't love the Lady; one serves her. Maybe I'll learn to love her, over the years . . ."

"Is it someone else?" I couldn't believe I was daring to ask a question like that. But something about the way he was trusting me, putting himself in my hands, made me feel it was all right.

"No," he said. "There's no one else I've loved. And now there never will be. I'm young, you know; she was the first. And I was so pleased when she said she'd take me to Bordertown. I've always wanted to see it. I've heard stories about the music, the dancing . . . It's different here. You get the feeling that anything could happen."

Anything can, I thought.

"I would stay here, I think, if I could," he went on. "But we must be back to Kingsmound by the New Moon. And then we'll go back Under the Hill and that will be that. For our lifetime." He sounded so sad.

"I said I'd help. I will. Just tell me what to do."

"I'll tell you," he said, "but you must decide. If you are to save me, you must claim me before the Lady and all the company."

I gulped thinking of how much I hated speaking in public. "Sure," I said.

"But first, you must win the right to claim me. And that means Dancing the Challenge."

Then my heart froze. I'm just not a very good dancer. If it meant it was me against the Lady, there was no hope for him.

"Don't you dance?" he asked quickly.

"Oh, sure I dance, but . . ."

"I didn't see you dancing in the hall before."

"You . . . noticed me?" I couldn't believe it.

"I noticed you. You have beautiful hair."

I didn't know what to say. I've never, ever heard anyone tell me that before. Not anyone I wanted to hear it from.

"Let me tell you about the Challenge," he said. "It's not what you think. The Challenge is not a contest, it's a battle. A battle you win through your strength and your will. Style and grace don't mean anything there, you know. They never do, they're just the outer trappings of what's inside. In the Challenge Dance only one thing matters: that you outlast your opponent." He looked straight into my eyes. "You can do that, I think."

"I'll try," I managed to say. "Is my opponent you, or her?"

"Me, I hope. I have the right to Dance for myself. But if the Lady enters the Challenge, too, it will be hard. Hard but not impossible."

"I understand." I swallowed dryly. "Do I have to do it now?" In front of my parents? he wondered silently.

"No, not tonight. And not in this place. Three nights from tonight will mark the turn of one year from the night my Lady first chose me. While we are here, she wants to taste all the pleasures of Bordertown. So we are going to dance at a club called the Dancing Ferret

that she's heard about, to hear a band called the New
Blood Review. Can you be there then?"

"Oh, sure." I thought about ditching Scullion. And I
thought about bringing Scullion; he's a halfie, he can go
anywhere. If things get rough, he'll be good to have along.
I'm still thinking about it. I want to do this myself. It's
not through Scullion's strength and will that I can win
him free.

"Thank you," he said. "When you claim me, remember: my name is . . . you won't be able to pronounce the
elvin name. Here I would be called Silvan. Now listen."
To my surprise, he began to sing quietly:

Up she starts as white as the milk
Between the king and all his company.
His fifteen lords all cried aloud
For the bonny Lass of Engelsea.

She's taken him all by the hand,
Saying, "You'll rise up and dance with me,"
But ere the king has gone one step,
She's danced his gold and his lands away.

She's danced high and she's danced low,
She's danced as light as the leaf on the broken sea.
And ere the moon began to set
She has gained the victory.

Up then starts the fifteenth knight,
And O an angry man is he.
He says, "My feet will be my death
Ere she gain the victory!"

He says my feet will be my death
Ere this lass do gain the victory—
He's danced fast, but tired at last,
He gave it over shamefully.

She's danced off all their buckles and shoes,
She's danced off all their gold and their bright money.
Then back to the mountains she's away
The bonny Lass of Englesea!

His voice was soft and low, but I heard the song perfectly. It was a pretty tune, cheerful and eerie at the same time.

"You see?" Silvan said. "It's been done before by a white-skinned maiden. An old, old song among us. The Challenge is not new."

"How can you dance against me," I asked, "when you want me to win? Won't people think you'll throw the match?"

"Not when the Challenge starts. I will not be truly free unless you've won me fairly."

"I will."

He leaned forward, and I thought he was going to kiss me. And I would have let him. Maybe to have the mouth that the silver Lady owned be pressed against mine; and maybe because he was alone and I could help him and for once kissing felt like a prize I deserved, instead of a present some boy felt obliged to give me even though I was ugly.

It still scares me to think how much I wanted that kiss.

But I didn't get it. He leaned back with a sigh. "You are gracious," he said. "May the Stars always guide you Home."

It was too late to explain his mistake, if it was one. Because that's what the elves in Bordertown say only to each other. Did he really think I was an elf the whole time? A halfie? Doesn't he know? Doesn't he care? Can't they tell their own kind, even in the dark?

I can't help my hair.

I don't care, I don't care, I don't care. I'm going to do it. I said I would help him, and I will. He needs me, and there's nobody else to do it.

III.

I'm not going to die. I only think I am.

I went to the Dancing Ferret. That part wasn't hard. I even told Lena and Randal where I was going—just not who I was coming home with. Soho makes my parents nervous—too much weird stuff happens there—but they know you can't play it safe forever, and having a daughter who never went anywhere the other kids go would make the family look just as bad as having one who got into a Soho brawl.

Also, Scullion takes a lot of the risk out of it. Or so I thought. And I didn't see any way of giving him the slip. So I let him follow me to the Ferret.

I felt like I was going to war. I chose my clothing carefully, for wear and not for show: fitted tights that moved when I moved, soft boots, and a loose tunic without sleeves. Dancing for hours at the Ferret can really make you sweat, and tonight I meant to dance like I never had before. I tied my hair up off my neck with a twist of bright rag. My one really splashy accessory was a pair of earrings I'd just gotten the week before from one of the street people: miniature machine parts carved out of wood and painted silver to look like steel. I thought they were the greatest. I'm going to burn them.

Over the whole outfit went a giant wrap of elf cloth: black with silver spangles, like the night sky. My mother says it's too old for me, but I bought it with my own money, and Randal says it looks terrific.

Then I went out into the night. God, what a feeling!

Autumn chill in the air and darkness beckoning. I found myself whistling, but for a second I didn't recognize the tune. Then I realized what it was: Silvan's "Bonny Lass of Engelsea." Pleased with myself, I whistled it louder.

I crossed the Mad River on the arched bridge they call the Dragon's Claw. Usually I like to pause at the crest of the Claw to take in a really good view of the city below; but tonight it was rush-rush-rush, my heart beating in my ears like the river rushing under the bridge pilings. Behind me Scullion's steady footsteps echoed the beat. I heard a strain of music, and realized he'd picked up my tune: "Up she starts as white as the milk . . . She's danced light as the leaf on the broken sea . . ."

Under the Old Wall, then, with a nod at the punk guarding it. Ahead of me people were rushing, too, kids with a sense of the night, the glitter, and the dancing ahead.

It felt good to be in Soho, where anything could happen, where gangs who were as tough as I was going to have to be, and as desperate, held their rule. It felt good to be going alone, to meet someone I wanted to see.

Then I got to the club, and all my nervousness came rushing back with the business of getting in, paying my fee, adjusting my eyes to the gloom, and finding someplace to stand among all the people already crowding in to hear the Review.

I looked around for Silvan and the Lady. There'd been a lot of talk about them the last few days. More than one girl at the elf school around the corner from ours had been going around dressed in silver. And one from ours had abruptly gotten over her crush on Eadric Vole, lead singer for Magical Madness, and was trying to find out what clubs the Lord and Lady would be going to. It made me feel funny to hear other people talk about them. They didn't know. I think Lena must feel this way when she hears people in the market talking politics.

Politics had been rough lately, too. Ever since the ball, Lena and Randal had been complaining to anyone who would listen about how rotten things were in Council and out of it. The elves were making trouble, finding insults in everything from seating arrangements to old laws nobody's disputed for twenty years. The most annoying thing, Randal said, was how much they seemed to be enjoying it. On the streets elves are usually controlled and distant; there it's the hot-blooded humans who pick fights. There's even a saying, "Cold as elf blood." But when it comes to politics, elves seem to like it hot. It gives them a chance to be good and arrogant, I guess.

With Randal and Lena under pressure, and me almost jumping out of my skin with nerves over the upcoming Challenge, home had been tranquil as a pit of dragons. I could imagine what it would be like when I brought Silvan home.

It wasn't very exciting, but that was the best thing I could think of to do with him. My parents' house is very safe, and here he'd have time to think about what he wanted to do next. I know what I *hoped* he'd want . . . but being Lena's daughter *has* taught me *some* sense. You don't run off with an elvin Lord when you're sixteen and human. Rescuing him from the Lady was bad enough. I only hoped there wouldn't be an Incident. I knew Lena and Randal wouldn't exactly be pleased to find him on their doorstep, but I figured when I explained how much he needed help they'd understand.

If this doesn't sound like I'd thought it all out too clearly, it's true: I was really too worried about the Dance to put much thought into what would happen after. I wasn't even sure there'd *be* an after.

There certainly wouldn't be if Silvan and the lady didn't even show up at the Ferret. I looked around, hard. They were a hard couple to miss. And they were nowhere in sight.

I was early, I thought. They weren't there yet. They weren't even coming. I'd gotten the day wrong. They'd been already and left.

They came in the door.

This time no one went down on their knees, but everyone was looking, human and elf. Farell Din himself went over and said something to the Lady that made her laugh.

The New Blood Review got going with "Free Me." They were ten times better than the band at the ball had been, did things with the music I would never have dreamed of. They had no singer, but I remembered the words:

> Rope me to the wind and set me free,
> Ten thousand volts is not enough
> To free me . . .

The Lady and her Lord came onto the dance floor. In my stomach, someone was beating a cat to death. I kept thinking, Why did I wear these earrings, they look so dumb. . . .

Then I went up to Silvan and took his hands.

The Lady looked over her shoulder, amused. Then she must have realized what was happening. She shook her head at him, reached for his hand that wore her ring. But I held his hand safe in mine. I looked into his pale, still face. The music was too loud to hear anything, but I made my lips say, "I am not afraid."

Silvan's hands were impossibly cool, the bones almost weightless. Mine felt sweaty and grubby by contrast. Then I felt the tingle of wild magic in them, and the beat of the music got into my blood. . . .

I'll never dance like that again. But it was worth it, for the one night. Like my whole *body* was music, like the band couldn't play unless I was moving the beat. . . . I had my eyes closed a lot of the time, so as not to see the people watching me, and to better feel the bass in my bones, the shrill licks come off the top of my head. I didn't really care what I looked like, for the first time in my life. I got hot, the sweat ran down my chest. For once at the Ferret it felt like there was no one trying to dance in my space, and when I opened my eyes, I saw there wasn't. The whole floor around us was clear. Silvan was dancing elvin and liquid, putting little twists into the beat with his hands, his feet. It was great to watch, but I couldn't stop, and I didn't dare try to mirror him, for fear of losing what I had.

The band just kept going, riffing like crazy on that one tune, over and over, *free me, free me, free me* . . .

I smiled at him, and he smiled back. He didn't look that old. For a moment, we were just what we were supposed to be: two kids having fun, out free in the hottest spot in the World or out of it: the Dancing Ferret, Soho, Bordertown, Borderland, the Universe.

Then, with a flourish of silver, the Lady was there. She didn't touch him or me, just started dancing in the open space where we were. Her hair was braided all over her head, with silver bells woven in. You couldn't hear them, of course, but they trembled when she moved.

She looked better than both of us put together. I tried not to care. It wasn't *fun* she was having, just some old power probably my mother's age (*more*, if the stories about elves are true), trying to stay young by picking up some kid like Silvan, who'd probably never been to a decent club before in his life. . . .

As if she were pulling them in, the space around us started to close up with dancers. Everybody was on the floor, more people than I thought the Dancing Ferret could hold. They were crowding us out, so close it was hard to do anything but shuffle to the beat. And the beat was hard, now, all bass and drums, no lightness even of cymbals. Like there was no tune at all, just a steady thump like footsteps, a giant heart.

Now I wanted to stop. I couldn't even see Silvan. I couldn't see anything but some tall person's shoulder. For all I knew, he was gone, dropped out already, and I could stop. I was thirsty, and the bottoms of my feet ached. The beat was jerking me like a puppet, not *free me*, just *me—me—me—me—*

Then the treble, faint and faraway over the bass, sweet and clear . . . the jingle of silver bells, the Lady's laughter.

I stayed on my feet. I didn't lean on the other dancers. And when the music came back and the floor cleared down to normal, I was there and the Lady was there, and her Lord was gone. He was gone. He "gave it over" to me, and the Challenge was mine.

Still I didn't stop. I wanted to outlast her. The rules to the Challenge were strange to me, and he'd warned me something like this might happen. Since the Lady had entered the Dance, it might be that I had to go on to keep Silvan free from her. I wouldn't dance *with* her, but I'd dance against her. Nobody fresh from Elfland was going to outdance me. I was Bordertown, Dragon's Tooth Hill, and we bowed to no one.

It's pure charity to say I was really dancing. Moving to the music, maybe. My tunic was so wet it was sticking to me. But the Lady wasn't doing much better. More graceful, maybe, but not too exciting to watch anymore. The Glamour had gone out of it. It was going to end with two wet little heaps on the floor at this rate, I thought.

I'd reckoned without that good old elvin style.

She stopped.

Right at the end of a song, she simply threw back her head, brushed a few wisps of hair out of her eyes, and shrugged. Elegantly, of course.

I didn't know what to do. Had she thrown the contest? Or *was* there no contest? Maybe she just didn't think I was worth fighting with: no glory in beating some gawky little human girl.

Or maybe she'd been afraid to lose. Afraid to look sweaty and tired and as though she actually cared about anything. She didn't *care* about Silvan.

I saw him making his way to me through the press of people. His face was paler than even an elf's should be. Wordlessly, he took my hand. And he looked at me like there was something I should do. Something more.

I was scared to look at the lady, but I made myself do it. She was smiling, looking like she'd won. But she hadn't won. I'd won.

"I claim Silvan," I said to her.

She couldn't hear over the noise, but she knew what I'd said. The smile vanished from her face like the glue that had been holding it on had suddenly come unstuck.

"Take him," her lips moved. That was all. Then she turned away, back into the crowd that was already dancing to a new song.

We threaded our way out of the Dancing Ferret, out

into the cool darkness of Carnival Street, still holding hands. I could feel the ring on his finger, his Lady's ring, elvin-cold against my skin. I didn't look to see if Scullion was following me. I'd won Silvan, and that was all that mattered. Nothing could hurt me tonight. An entire gang of Bloods could jump me; I'd break their heads and play dice with their teeth.

I led my Lord through the streets of Soho, past graffiti-glittering walls. He finally pulled me to a halt to lean against one of them, still catching his breath. He looked so fragile. There was none of that elvin arrogance. Had I really outdanced him? And didn't he know yet what I was?

I guess not. He pulled me to him like he was terribly cold and needed me to warm him. And I lifted my head and got that kiss I'd wanted so much at the ball.

Even now, it feels better to remember the way it was then. Magic, it felt like magic all through me. I'd never been so happy. I'd almost stopped being me. I felt grateful and triumphant, both at once.

That was all there was. His mouth was still on mine when I felt a tremendous crash on the back of my head, and the world fell away from me.

I came to in a blurry room full of sunlight. I was home. My parents were sitting next to my bed, talking over my head, in the middle of a quiet argument.

". . . better that way," Randal was saying.

"Not this time, love," Lena said firmly. "She should know as soon as she—"

She stopped as soon as she saw my eyes were open.

"What?" I said hoarsely. "What's going on? Where's Silvan?"

"You're all right, honey, Scullion brought you home." Randal sounded real gentle, the way he did when I was truly young. It made me want to cry. "Here's something for you to drink. Let me help you sit up."

"My head hurts," I said, like a little girl. "What happened? Is Silvan all right?"

"He's fine," Lena said. "Drink your medicine."

I drank it, and then I went to sleep. Then the goodwife came and looked at my head, and made me tell her whether I could see things or not, and said I had a mild concussion and I'd be fine if I just rested. I was going to wait until they were all out of the room and then get up and find out what was going on, but instead I fell asleep again.

I woke up in the middle of the night. Lena was there, dressed up like she'd just come in from a party. She was wearing my favorite scent, the one that smells like the red flowers that come up from the south sometimes, the real expensive ones that won't grow in Borderland.

"Mumma," I said, "what's going on?"

She answered me in her most grown-up voice, the one I usually hear only when she's addressing the Council or I've really loused up my schoolwork. "I'm afraid there's been some political trouble, and you got caught in the middle of it. Nobody blames you. It's not your fault."

That got me mad. "If you think rescuing somebody from a place he doesn't want to go back to is—is just *political trouble*, then you've got the stone heart! Did it ever occur to you to wonder how people *feel*? Or is all you think about your precious politics?"

"That's enough," she said in a voice so controlled it scared me. "Or we're both going to start crying, and I'd rather not do that. Is that what he told you? That you were *rescuing* him?"

I didn't like the way she said that. As if she felt sorry for me. "Well, of course!" I almost shouted. "What did you *think* I was doing?"

"Scullion knocked you on the head and brought you home. *He* thought you were kissing the elf Lord."

"Scullion! Scullion did that to me? I thought he was supposed to protect me!"

"He is," said my mother dryly. "I hate to bring politics into this, but had you thought about what would happen to the peace of Bordertown if a human girl ran off with a Lord defecting from beyond the Border? It was bad enough you Challenging the Lady in a crowded club with half Soho watching . . . but we're all right there, because nobody at the Dancing Ferret is likely to know you by sight. For all they know, with that hair, you could have been some elf punk. You certainly weren't *dressed* like the hill!"

I felt like I was choking. "So you had Scullion bop me on the head to prevent scandal! Was that to protect my good name, or yours and Randal's?"

"It was Scullion's idea. He says he recognized the Challenge song you were singing. He's half-elvin, he knows these things."

"And have you considered"—I tried to sound as calm and cold as Lena—"what's going to happen to Silvan without my protection?"

"Nothing's going to happen to Silvan," she said bitterly. I was amazed at the anger in her voice. "God, maybe Randal was right about this. I'm not sure I can do it. Charis . . . It wasn't true, any of it."

"What do you mean, it wasn't true? Are you trying to make me believe it didn't happen, now?"

"Shush. Just listen to me. The Lady came down from Elfland to make trouble. She doesn't like the independence of the Bordertown elves. She and the elves in our Council have been feuding for years. She thinks they're too close to us humans—even Windreed, to *her*, is 'too friendly.' I hate to sound like some Ho Street bigot, but it was a masterly piece of elvin trickery: she looked around for some way to make trouble, to cut a rift between the two communities. They found it in you. I don't know . . . the elves have an unerring instinct for the vulnerable, for what and who will hurt the most. Sometimes I think life is just a giant story for them, an exciting game to win.

"The plan all along was for you to run off with Silvan. Then the lady would raise the hue and cry, claiming quite rightly that a Bordertown human had desecrated elvin rituals, that you had tricked Silvan into thinking you were elvin . . . they knew, you see, about your hair. They must have heard about you before the M-Bassy Ball, somehow, and decided to try it there. And they nearly brought it off, too. If Scullion hadn't brought you home before you were recognized with Silvan, it would all be out in the open now. Of course we would have stood up for you, but it would be your word against theirs. And that was what they wanted, a fight between the two communities."

I didn't say anything.

"It would have hurt you very much," my mother went on, "much more than finding out this way, my darling, believe me."

My jaw was clenched so tight it ached. "No," I said. "I don't believe you. You're lying. Somebody's lying. Silvan needed me. She was going to m-marry him and make him live under the ground for the rest of his life or something. Maybe *she* was going to do all that stuff you say—maybe she made him go along with it—but he wasn't going to hurt me, he needed my help! You don't understand *anything*. I danced the Challenge and I won, and everything was going to be all right until *you* came along and spoiled it! You think I didn't know what I was doing—you *never* think I know what I'm doing!"

I was shouting by now; I guess I was hysterical or something. Anyway, Lena's voice cut through it like ice. "Do you think *he* didn't know what he was doing? He has magic, and he has beauty, and you didn't stand a chance. She wasn't going to marry him, no matter what he told you. Silvan is the Lady's brother."

I felt like the bed was melting away under me, and I was falling without moving. "Her—brother?"

"Do you think *I* don't know what I'm doing?" Lena said. "Do you think I haven't checked all my sources thoroughly, just because I can't tell you where I got all the information? Scullion has a lot of friends, and there are some elves on the Council—"

"All right," I said tightly, just to shut her up, to stop her from being so right, right, right all the time. "I believe you."

"Thank you," my mother said softly. "Charis . . . if it helps at all . . . we heard about the Challenge, about what you did. You were very brave, and very strong. We want you to know we're very, very proud of you."

"No," I said, holding on to my pillow for dear life, because if she didn't get out of there soon I was going to throw it at her. "No, it doesn't help. Not one stinking little bit."

So then she left, and I cried until I was too sick to cry anymore.

So none of it was true. Maybe if I tell myself this over and over again I'll get used to it and it'll stop hurting.

Nobody needed me. I didn't help anybody. They made up a story they thought I'd fall for, and let me live in storyland for a while. That was real nice of them. And

HE WAS LAUGHING AT ME ALL THE TIME
HE WAS LAUGHING AT ME ALL THE TIME

Shit. I hate crying. I really do. Maybe I'll do some research on elvin customs and find out whether there really is a Lord and Lady, how he gets chosen and whether you can win somebody free of Elfland in a Dance Challenge, or is it all a crock of shit that sounds like what we think the elves are like and they're really up there smoking cigarettes and doing weird stuff with our cheese and light bulbs and laughing at us all the time . . .

Only now I hate elves so much I never want to see any again; I don't even want to think about them. I'd better get over this or I'm going to wind up like those assholes from the World who think elves are going to steal their babies. Maybe I'd better go live in the World after all, where I don't have to worry about elves, or the Council, or anything.

I also hate my parents—not who they are, but what they are. If I hadn't been their daughter, this wouldn't have happened to me. It wasn't just anybody's kid the elves wanted to make a fool of. I can't hate Scullion, because I haven't been out of the house, so I haven't seen him.

I certainly am going to be a busy girl, working so hard learning not to hate everybody. I won't have time for going dancing or stuff like that.

IV.

The Lord and Lady are gone, and no one's created a scandal. It looks as though the peace of Bordertown is secure. Yaay for our side.

Today a scruffy elvin punk came to the door with a parcel for me. It's a wooden box, carved in elf style with a pattern of leaves and waves. When you open it, there's a mirror set inside the lid. And in the box is a familiar silver ring on a green ribbon, and a lock of elvin silver hair.

About the Authors

Steven R. Boyett is the author of *Ariel*; short fiction appearing in the anthologies *Elsewhere* and *Faery*; and the forthcoming novel *The Architect of Sleep*. He hails from Florida and currently lives in Los Angeles, where he immerses himself in rock-and-roll and is at work on a sequel to *Architect* as well as a collaborative novel with housemate Jessie Horsting.

Bellamy Bach (who admits that is not his name, but says his real one is even more unlikely due to a mother who "over-indulged in the Sixties") was born on a commune in Indiana and currently has no home but his VW Van. He has published poetry in small press magazines, and has a novel, *Childe Roland*, forthcoming.

Charles de Lint is a folk musician with the Celtic band "Wickentree," a small press publisher, and the author of numerous short stories published here and in Europe as well as four fantasy novels: *The Riddle of the Wren*, *Moonheart*, *Mulengro*, and *Harp of the Grey Rose*. A new novel, *Yarrow*, is forthcoming. De Lint makes his home in Ottawa, Canada, with his wife Mary Ann, an artist.

Ellen Kushner is a folk musician, former fantasy/sf editor for Ace Books and Pocket Books, and the author of fantasy adventure books for young adults and an adult historical fantasy novel, SWORDSPOINT. She is currently at work on a horror series entitled *The Vampire Trilogy* for Armadillo Press.

New Worlds of Fantasy for You to Explore

**Buy them at your local
bookstore or use coupon
on last page for ordering.**